"How ... I'm ..."

Trystan couldn't help but chuckle. "Such indelicate talk for a lady." He gathered up the playing cards. "Perhaps I let you win. Regardless, I have lost and am prepared to pay my debt. When shall you collect?"

"I think now," she shocked him by replying.

"Now?" He slid one hand behind her back, and pulled her toward him. His other hand came up to cup the silken jut of her jaw. He caressed her flushed cheek with the pad of his thumb.

Her full lips parted on a sharp intake of breath that brought a smile to his face. At least she wasn't immune to him.

"You are very beautiful, Vienne," he murmured. "I find I don't mind losing to you—once."

She smiled at that, blue-green eyes brightening. "That sounds like a challenge, Lord Trystan."

"I suppose it is." He lowered his head. "I'm going to kiss you now, so I expect you to claim your prize with decorum."

When Tempting A
ROGUE

Kathryn Smith

AVON
An Imprint of HarperCollinsPublishers

This is a work of fiction. Names, characters, places, and incidents are products of the author's imagination or are used fictitiously and are not to be construed as real. Any resemblance to actual events, locales, organizations, or persons, living or dead, is entirely coincidental.

AVON BOOKS
An Imprint of HarperCollins*Publishers*
10 East 53rd Street
New York, New York 10022-5299

Copyright © 2011 by Kathryn Smith
ISBN 978-0-06-192301-2
www.avonromance.com

First Avon Books mass market printing: May 2011

Avon Trademark Reg. U.S. Pat. Off. and in Other Countries, Marca Registrada, Hecho en U.S.A.
HarperCollins® is a registered trademark of HarperCollins Publishers.

Printed in the U.S.A.

10 9 8 7 6 5 4 3 2 1

This one's just for Steve. Who loves you, baby?

When Tempting A

ROGUE

Chapter 1

Saint's Row, early August 1876

Trystan Kane wasn't entirely certain what he'd done to deserve it, but one thing was certain—falling in love with Vienne La Rieux had been God's way of punishing him for his sins.

This unfortunate, though significant, event had taken place almost seven years ago and he still had the scars on his heart—and pride—to prove it. It had been the kick in the arse that made him take the path that led him to the precipice he now teetered on.

Of course, he'd fallen out of love with the virago, the viper, the *vicious vixen* as quickly as a young man could shuck off the humiliation of pain and rejection. Now all he wanted was for her to recognize the man he had become. It was that simple. And to know for himself that when she looked at him, she saw a grown man and not a foolish, love-struck boy.

Certainly, as he watched her from across the

crowded floor of the gaming room at Saint's Row—
her club—he looked upon her in a manner much
different from any prior. She was on the arm of
some lord who looked vaguely familiar—a man old
enough to be his father, and perhaps Vienne's as well.
At one time Trystan would have viewed the man
with jealousy, and peevishness would be nipping at
his soul. Now he could see the scene for what it was:
Vienne La Rieux's damnable need to be in control of
every aspect of her life, especially her heart.

There was no doubt she liked the old lord well
enough. She smiled prettily when he spoke to her,
and laughed—he supposed—at all the appropriate
bons mots. But even though their arms were linked,
Vienne held herself away from the older man; and
when he wasn't looking at her, her cool green gaze
surveyed the room, taking note of who was winning
and who was losing. She did not, he noticed, glance
in *his* direction, which gave him some bizarre sense
of satisfaction. By pretending to be so blatantly unaware of him, Madame La Rieux proved just how
very much she was not.

Everything was in place. All he had to do was make
the decision, yea or nay, to pursue a plan that now,
when he thought about it, seemed a little dodgy. It had
taken so many covert transactions, so many carefully
planned strategic moves, to bring him to this place.

Did he strike now . . . or walk away?

Really, what was he trying to achieve? Success, or a petty triumph over a woman who probably didn't care if he lived or died.

She glanced at him—a discrete sweep of the room with her glittering gaze, which held just a half-second too long with his own. He didn't have a chance to react, not to raise his glass in a mocking salute nor to flash a sardonic smile before the connection was broken. It left him feeling like a dolt.

"You're going to stare a hole through her," came a voice at his elbow.

Trystan closed his eyes in silent prayer: *Dear God, why have you forsaken me?*

"You cannot wish me away, brat."

Sighing, Trystan opened his eyes and turned to face his elder brother, Archer—a master of the mocking smile. Archer would have given La Rieux a look to either freeze or melt her drawers. He wouldn't have just stood there like an idiot.

But then, Archer could be a pain in anyone's arse once he put his mind to it. "What do you want?" Trystan demanded churlishly.

Archer held out his hand. "Lend me five quid. I lost a wager and I'm tapped at the moment."

Trystan arched a brow. "You're tapped over five quid?"

"No, I'm tapped over the other ninety-five attached to it. Look, I'll pay you back tomorrow."

Shaking his head, Trystan pulled his billfold from inside his coat and peeled off a couple of notes. "Here's ten. Now, go bother someone else."

His brother took the money with a quirk of his lips. It was almost impossible to make Archer feel unwanted or bothersome—a trait Trystan rather admired even though at the moment it annoyed him.

"Don't get all hoity with me, my son. I'm not what's put an itch up your nethers."

Archer also had a gift for the strangest turns of phrase. "*What* the"—Trystan scowled—"devil are you talking about?"

"Her." His brother tilted his head in La Rieux's direction. "If you want her, go get her. If you want to be rid of her, don't come here. But don't stand there like a git and pine after her. It's unbecoming."

No. Archer couldn't possibly presume to lecture *him* on what was unbecoming behavior, could he? Even Arch couldn't be *that* barking mad. Then again, he was stupid enough to nod at Vienne with the subtlety of a stallion tossing its mane.

"I'm not pining, but if I were, I'd prefer my brand to yours." It was no secret that his brother was still mourning the loss of the Countess Monteforte, the lady having left the country to pursue dreams that did not include Archer.

"That was rather low," his brother remarked without a hint of injury as he wavered slightly.

"Indeed," Trystan agreed solemnly. "Apologies, old man."

"Accepted. My thanks for the blunt. Will I see you at Chez Cherie's later?"

Trystan thought about it. Normally he'd be up for a little female company, but not tonight. "No. But come by the Barrington for breakfast in the morning." He kept a set of rooms at the hotel he owned with his partner, Jack Friday, recently the Earl of Garret.

"Suit yourself. Make sure there's coffee." With that last edict, Archer sauntered off, notes in his fist. Absently, Trystan wondered just how much more gambling, whoring, and drinking his brother could take before he grew sick of all of it as well as himself. It was not going to be a pretty sight when it happened, of that he was certain. It disturbed him to see his brother acting this way—much like their eldest brother, Greyden, the Duke of Ryeton, used to. Grey had paid for his debauched ways and literally had the scar to prove it. "Ruined Ryeton" society used to call him. Trystan would hate to see Archer go down a similar path. Grey's attackers had meant to kill him but were frightened off. Archer might not be so fortunate.

But Archer had been right about one thing—he was paying far too much attention to Vienne. That had to stop. He didn't want her thinking he still cared about her, even though such a notion might, for the moment, distract her from his real intentions—which had more to do with the man who just appeared at Vienne's side, taking her away from her previous companion.

Lord Angelwood: tall, fit, a gentleman somewhere in his fifth decade, possessed of a strapping build attributed to his predecessors and a thick head of auburn hair only beginning to gray at the temples. He was handsome in a rugged manner, and had a confidence that could only come from having been born heir to a respected title.

Neither of these were traits to which Trystan could relate. He didn't fancy himself particularly attractive—though he'd been told by more than one lady that he had the most astounding eyes. (Grey's and Archer's were very similar, if not perhaps so dark a blue as his own.) His nose was too big to be pretty, and he was damnably tanned by peerage standards. He was a third son, not the spare—and certainly not the heir. Worse, he'd gone out and made his fortune—in trade. Something that was still looked down upon despite the growing debts of the aristocracy. In short, he was Lord Trystan Kane, with nothing to recommend him except his youth, which in this particular instance was not in his favor.

He took a glass of champagne from a passing tray and discreetly watched the couple over the top of it. Angelwood, to the best of his knowledge, was happily married, so his relationship with Vienne was purely platonic. Oddly enough, that needled him far more than if he *were* her lover, because she looked upon the man with such genuine emotion. She liked him. Trusted him. This man was more to her than a brief amusement. This man was her friend.

Which was why Trystan had something of a heavy feeling in his gut. His friend Jack would have tried to talk him out of his plan, calling it folly at best. But Jack wasn't here. He was still in Ireland working out the details of his inheritance, so there was no one to try to persuade him to a different course of action.

The next hour passed much like the two that preceded it. Trystan drank another glass of champagne as he waited, milling about the room making trite conversation with any and all who invited it. All the while, he never took his eye off the object of his current obsession.

Finally Lord Angelwood took his leave. Trystan set aside his half-empty glass and followed. He summoned his carriage, keeping a discreet distance between himself and the earl. Before settling back against the velvet padding he instructed his driver to follow Angelwood's vehicle. He had a fairly good notion of the man's destination.

The last earl had built the club Eden for his countess. At one time it had been mostly a social club for both men and women—segregated, of course; and it still had one of the best dining rooms in the city. But these days the club did more business in its gaming room, hosting high-stakes games, sporting events, and tournaments for charity.

Tonight was one of the rare occasions when his lordship joined in the play. It was also the night Trystan planned to sit in as well. It wasn't a tournament or for charity, it was simple high-stakes play. Fortunately, Trystan's business dealings had given him what some of his American chums referred to as a poker face—the ability to conceal all thought and emotion behind a blank expression and, even more importantly, behind empty eyes. He was also good at tallying odds—nothing like some of the gentlemen he'd encountered in San Francisco, but good enough.

Perhaps twenty minutes or a full half-hour later, his carriage rolled to a stop and the door was opened. He stepped out, instructed his driver to wait, and climbed the shallow steps leading to the door of the Palladian-styled building. He was greeted by a majordomo with posture so rigid he must have had a steel spine. The man took his name, hat, and greatcoat, and properly directed him. Trystan straightened his jacket lapels and cuffs and crossed the grand foyer of Eden toward a heavy door set into the walnut paneling. He knocked twice and the crystal knob turned a second later.

A footman opened the door, bowed stiffly and moved back so that he might enter. "Good evening, sir. Please come in."

"Kane!" He was greeted as soon as he crossed the threshold. Angelwood came forward with an easy grin and a handshake. "I thought that was you at Saint's Row. Good to see you. You know Vickery and Wolfram?"

Trystan smiled. "Of course. Good evening, gentlemen. I appreciate the invite."

Of course. Trystan had gone through a lot of trouble to assure an invitation to this particular evening's entertainment; he'd also gone out of his way to make certain Wolfram, Angelwood's boyhood friend and a notoriously cautious gambler, and Vickery, a notoriously bad one, were also on hand.

They made small talk until everyone was comfortable, and Trystan had the vague feeling that they were all "friends" now. Then they seated themselves at the table, he and Angelwood across from one another. A bottle of cognac was placed on the sideboard within easy reach, and each man was given an exquisite cigar. If not for his quest, Trystan would be quite content to simply play, smoke, and drink and say to hell with it, but he could not allow himself to be lulled. He had to make sure he won, so he would not imbibe much of the superb brandy.

His determination paid off. Three hours later, Wolfram decided he'd had enough. What the earl won was not much more than what he'd come in with. Apparently he was more about the camaraderie than the win. The three of them continued on, and almost exactly one and one half hours later, Vickery decided both Angelwood and Trystan had taken enough of his money and bowed out as well.

Trystan's heart skipped a beat. It was all going exactly as he'd hoped. When Angelwood asked if he would like to continue, he said yes. The earl was down a thousand pounds and eager to make it back. Trystan had no intention of letting that happen. After forty-five minutes of play, when the betting cycle was about to begin, he put everything he had on the table, along with the deed for a property he owned that Angelwood had tried to buy from him several times over the years. It wouldn't be a big loss to Trystan as he only purchased the property because he knew others would want it one day. He had a good sense about these things. Jack teased him that he could see into the future—funny, considering Jack's disbelief in the predetermination of fate.

Angelwood's eyes lit up at the deed. "Every instinct warns me to give up now," he said, "but damn my eyes, man, if you don't know how to tempt a fellow."

Trystan smiled, and play resumed. He focused on his cards, calculated his risks and his odds. Most of all, he watched his adversary. Angelwood was a consummate gambler, but everyone had their "tell"—and in the brief time he'd been back in London, Trystan had made it his mission to discover that one little gesture that gave the earl away.

And he found it.

So, he watched, and waited, and played—his mind whirling, chest tight. And when the cards fell, he was the victor to the tune of fifty thousand pounds. A staggering amount, but one both of them could lose with a minimum amount of pain. They both knew how to make it back again.

"I must say," Angelwood remarked, leaning back in his chair as he puffed on the cigar, "that this has been the most rousing game I've played in some time. Thank you, Kane."

Trystan nodded with a small grin. "My pleasure, sir."

"I shall give you my marker and bring your winnings 'round to you by Wednesday. How's that?"

Now was the tricky part. "I don't want your marker."

Angelwood frowned. "Surely you don't mean to demand immediate payment." He didn't have to say just how ungentlemanly that would be.

Trystan favored him with a small smile. "Of course not, my lord. What I meant to say is that it is not your money I want." He also sat back in his chair, crossing one ankle over his knee as he smoked. "You have something I hold in much higher value."

"And what would that be?" The older man was intrigued, and suspicious—with good reason.

Trystan tapped ash into a crystal bowl designed for such purpose. "I want the investment you made in Vienne La Rieux's emporium scheme."

The earl's dark brows rose. "I owe you more than the meager percentage I hold in that enterprise."

"Yes," Trystan agreed. "That is why I will also take the loan you so generously bestowed upon Madame La Rieux. Eight thousand, was it not?"

Scowling now, Angelwood leaned his forearms on the table, bringing himself that much closer to Trystan. "What the devil are you about, Kane? I warn you, if you mean Vienne La Rieux harm—"

"Save your breath—*and* your threats, my lord. I mean the lady no injury."

"Then what is the meaning of this?"

"I believe La Rieux's scheme to be the beginning

of a new era in commerce. I believe that she is on the brink of accomplishing something great." He meant every word, and made certain his sincerity showed in his countenance.

His companion waited, unimpressed and knowing there was more. Trystan grinned. "I also believe that with me as her partner, the two of us can accomplish something better than mere greatness."

The earl's lips twitched. "You have a lot of pride and hubris, young man."

"No, sir. I simply know what it is I am capable of—the lady does as well."

Angelwood's gray eyes narrowed. "Are you certain that's all there is to this?"

Trystan leaned forward, dropping his voice to little more than a whisper: "I'm certain, your lordship—and, if there is *anything else*, it is none of your business. Now, do we have a deal, or shall I remain here until the banks open and accompany you to collect my winnings?"

It was a low but effective threat on his part. Of course Angelwood wouldn't want such a humiliation as Trystan accompanying him to the bank. People would talk; speculate as to Angelwood's financial security. It would cost him business; and as a businessman, the earl knew just how much such talk was to be avoided.

"Damn, but if you're not a shark, Kane," the older man allowed, not without a little respect. "I'll give you what you want, but I want your word as a gentleman that you are not out to fleece my friend or bring her ruin in any way."

"And you have it, sir. The only plan I have regarding Madame La Rieux is to make both her, and myself, a lot of money."

The earl watched him for a moment before rising to his feet. He went to a painting on the wall behind his desk and took it down. Set into the wall behind it was a safe. Trystan averted his eyes as a courtesy. It wasn't as though he could make out the combination at this distance.

A few moments later he heard the painting being repositioned and the earl returned to the table. He set a packet of papers in front of Trystan. "My investment in the lady's emporium scheme, and her marker for eight thousand pounds."

It took all of Trystan's control not to crow with glee as he stared at Vienne's signature on the marker. *Finally*. Finally, he had her exactly where he wanted her.

"Thank you, my lord." Collecting the papers, he pushed back his chair and rose to his feet. "I will take my leave of you now."

"Indeed." The earl continued to watch him with

an assessing gaze. "She won't take this well, you know. This will not win you entry into her bed."

Trystan tucked the wonderful, treasured papers into his jacket. "Oh, that's the last place I want to be, my lord. The very last." As he made to leave, he turned and tapped the deed in the center of the table. "And you may have the property, my lord. Consider it a trade."

He left the astonished nobleman with a satisfied smile on his lips; and as Trystan collected his belongings from the majordomo and walked out into the wee hours, he reiterated to himself that he would never share Vienne La Rieux's bed. *Not again.*

But if she asked nicely enough, he *might* take her to his.

Dressed in a flimsy green silk peignoir, Vienne La Rieux stood on the balcony attached to her bedroom and stared down into the darkness below. There was no movement in the dense garden behind Saint's Row, but she'd wager at least one or two trysting couples remained in the private cottages she provided. She envied them for no other reason than the warmth of their sheets and the languid ease with which sleep would claim them. The rest of the melodrama she could do without.

I am glad for my life, she told herself as she sipped

a glass of whiskey, searching for a semblance of that warmth, of that melt in her bones. *No one to make me feel small, to wish I were somewhere else.*

Or worse—make her believe she was someone else.

Vienne was the kind of woman who harbored a general dislike for the company of others. Unfortunately, she loathed her own society almost as vehemently. But she was never quite as lonely by herself as she was in a room full of people with whom she had little or nothing in common. Even more unfortunate—or perhaps deserving—was the fact that lonely was exactly how she spent most of her life, except for when dear Sadie came to call, or when . . . *well*, that didn't matter.

Really, none of it mattered. She was only terribly, violently aware of being alone at this moment because the building was so quiet. The club had closed a few hours earlier and her employees had all gone home or retired for the remainder of the evening. The silence in the place—an old theater—was quite oppressive. The entire evening had been a trial. Not even her dear friend Angelwood, an investor in her newest endeavor, could cheer her.

And she knew upon whose broad shoulders she could lay the blame for that as well. Ever since his return to England, Trystan Kane had been a ghost in her establishment. Almost every night for more than a fortnight he had been there watching her or, worse, ignoring her. Not since that first night when she ran into him with that damned Jack Friday—Farrington, rather—had he deigned to speak to her.

Not that she had anything to say to *him*.

She refused to think about the look on his face when she told him it was over between them. He'd looked so young and lost—but now he didn't, and her first thought had been that he appeared more like a man on a mission. A man with a definite purpose— one that involved her. Vienne was not someone who suffered from an overly inflated sense of self-worth; she knew full well her own value and how, in the eyes of others, it varied from person to person.

Trystan Kane always made her feel as though that value was as precious as gold, a fact that had scared her enough that she couldn't stand to see the admiration in his spectacular eyes any longer.

If there was one thing she refused to countenance, it was fear. Only one man had ever scared her and gotten away with it. After that, Vienne vowed to never allow a man to have such power over her again.

Still, there had been a certain pleasure in seeing Trystan Kane and his pretty blue eyes again—a stutter in her heartbeat that flustered her and threw her world off kilter. For one brief and shining second, she had been happy to see him.

Just for one second. Perhaps two.

But here she was, doing the thing she had said she wouldn't do—thinking about him.

She took another sip of her whiskey and stepped into the warm and softly lit interior of her apartments. The French doors shut with a gentle click and she automatically locked them out of habit.

"You were out there a long time."

Vienne froze, heart hammering. She kept her expression composed as she turned to face the man—boy, actually—lounging on her bed. He was smiling, his handsome face all the more appealing for it. His shirt was open, revealing a tantalizing glimpse of curling golden hair. Long legs stretched downward, crossed at the ankles. At least he'd removed his boots before making himself at home on her quilt.

She arched a brow. "William. *Quelle surprise*. To what do I owe this pleasure?"

Green eyes sparkled. "Pleasure, exactly. You haven't invited me up for a while. I thought you might be in need of a little . . . relaxation."

Relaxation was exactly what she wanted, but not the kind he offered. It was her own fault; she should have ended their affair long before this. It was never a good idea to take lovers from the staff, but he was so pretty and accommodating. There was no excuse:

she had ignored reason and now she was going to pay for it.

"You are very sweet," she said, using a heavier accent, as she tended to do in such situations. "But I am *très fatigue* and wish to go to bed."

The grin stayed. "I'll join you."

Pretty, but not so bright. She set the whiskey on top of her delicately carved ebony vanity. "I wish to sleep alone."

William's smile turned to a frown. "Alone? Whatever for?"

She could say because she was tired, or because she was tired of him, or she could admit to not having much of a sexual appetite since Trystan Kane's return. Or, she could lie.

Instead, she smiled. "I do appreciate your . . . thoughtfulness, but I need you to leave. Now, please."

All affability evaporated from William's expression, turning his youthful face hard. It was an expression Vienne had seen before, and she knew what kind of trouble generally followed. She sent up a silent prayer that the young man wouldn't take it any further as she casually pulled open the vanity's top drawer.

William sat up, swinging his long legs over the side of the bed. He stood and began to move toward her with a slow, predatory stride. "I'll decide when it's time for me to leave."

Unflinching, though she very much wanted to flinch, Vienne raised her gaze to his. "This is my house, my club, and you are my employee. You don't make any decisions here that aren't mine." It was false bravado, but he didn't have to know that. A slight tremor quivered her right knee, but other than that she held no real fear. Unless William killed her, he couldn't do anything to her she hadn't already survived—only a new variant on it.

He sneered. So much for having any respect or degree of feeling for her. "I gave you what you wanted whenever you wanted it, you frog whore. Now you're going to deny me?"

Vienne lifted her chin with just a hint of a mocking smile that really couldn't be helped. "Yes, you did. And yes, I am. That is the way these things go when an employer makes the foolish choice of taking an employee to bed. You really should leave now."

"I'll leave when I've gotten what I came for." He smiled—a little sharper this time. "You, on your knees."

Vienne rolled her eyes. Why was it that so many men seemed to think it was their right to take a woman whether she wanted it or not, simply because she had given her body to them previously? Poor little *enfant*. William did not understand who had the power in their relationship. It really was unfortunate.

She had liked him before he chose to reveal his true nature. He had been most entertaining.

She withdrew her pearl-handled pistol from the drawer and pointed it at him. Her hand was steady, her aim true and fixed—right between his eyes.

"You are about to be very disappointed," she informed him coolly. "You're not going to get what you want, but you have succeeded in getting yourself dismissed. Now, I'm going to give you to the count of five to gather your belongings and get the hell out of my house."

The young man didn't come any closer, but he eyed the pistol with a cocky confidence that Vienne found terribly annoying. "You won't shoot me."

She arched a brow. How little he'd ascertained about her during their brief affair. If it were Trystan Kane standing in her sight, he would have had enough sense to back away by now. But William wasn't Trystan.

"My dear boy, I'll not only shoot you, but I know how to fix it so no one ever finds your body." She cocked the hammer. "*Une . . . deux . . .*"

He didn't move. He just stood there, smirking, so certain of his manly control of her. So certain she would cow before him.

" *. . . trois.*"

Vienne pulled the trigger.

Chapter 2

The following morning found Trystan enjoying a leisurely breakfast in the dining room of his hotel, the Barrington. He read the paper while sipping a cup of piping hot, strong Turkish coffee imported by one of his concerns in that area. On his plate was an assortment of tropical fruit, juicy and ripe, some crispy bacon, and toast.

"You eat like a woman," came his brother's voice above him.

Sighing, Trystan snapped his paper closed and set it beside his plate. He wiped his hands on his napkin and looked up just as Archer slid into the chair across from him.

"I eat like I want to eat," he replied calmly, waving a waiter over. "What will you have?"

"Steak and eggs—with fried potatoes and fried bread."

Trystan arched a brow. "Would you like your coffee fried as well?"

Archer brushed the remark aside, used to them as he was. "No, but I would like a shot of Irish in it."

The waiter nodded in acquiescence and walked away. Trystan waited until they were alone before commenting. "Do I even need to remind you how early in the day it is?"

Archer snatched a piece of toast from Trystan's plate. "Which is exactly why I need the Irish. Say, did you hear what happened at Saint's Row last night?"

"Obviously not, because I was there for several hours and nothing interesting occurred, unless you count Lady Gosling setting her sights on a new conquest. I hope Mason Blayne knows what he's getting into."

Archer leaned his elbow on the table, dangling toast from his long fingers. "He'll be getting into Lady Gosling, I do believe that's the point. But that's not what I meant. Apparently Madame La Rieux shot one of her footmen last night."

Trystan's spine snapped straight. "What?"

Archer nodded, pale eyes sparkling with mischief. "Caught the bloke *en dishabille* in her bed chamber. Seems he had *amour* on his mind—and other body parts. When he refused to leave, she put a hole in him. Winged him. He's fortunate she didn't aim lower."

"He's fortunate she didn't kill him," Trystan replied. She could have. Vienne is a crack shot. "Is she all right?"

"I was wondering when you'd inquire after the lady's health. By all reports, she's perfectly fine. The bloke will have a deuced hard time finding employment in London after this. Attempted rape of one's employer tends to diminish the number of available situations considerably."

"As it should." It occurred to Trystan—just for a moment—that he could find out the name of this footman with relative ease—and, with a mere word in the right ear and a few pounds in the right hand, make sure the man never bothered another woman ever again. He could do that. He *wanted* to do it . . . but wouldn't. He'd rather cut out his own tongue than let Vienne know he cared about what happened to her.

He glanced up to find his elder brother watching him with considerable concern—not a usual expression in Archer Kane's repertoire. For all his flippancy and rakish ways, Archer was a simple man who held family above all else. He never forgot a slight against a loved one, no matter how small. Archer knew that Vienne had broken Trystan's heart, and that alone was enough to make Tryst squirm under his brother's crystalline gaze, because he sensed he had forgiven the trespass far more readily than Archer had or ever would.

"What did you get up to last night?" Archer inquired, taking another bite of toast. "Given the footman scandal, I know you didn't take another run at La Rieux."

There it was, out in the open, although it wasn't as if this was the first time Archer had brought up his past entanglement. "I played a little cards with Lord Angelwood."

His brother's sharp brows rose. "Did he clean you out?"

Trystan allowed himself a self-satisfied smile. "No. Unlike you, my dear brother, I know how to gamble and win."

Archer scowled. "No one knows how to gamble and win, that's why they call it gambling."

Trystan shrugged, watching his sibling carefully as the waiter returned and set Archer's breakfast in front of him. He waited until the man had left before asking, "How in debt are you?"

Archer's head snapped up. "I'm not. And it's none of your damn business." With that, he slapped a wrinkled fiver on the table between them. "Here. Thanks for the loan."

"Arch—"

The older man pointed a fork at him. "*Not* a word. Just because you've off and made something of yourself doesn't give you the right to judge me. You think I spend all my time whoring and drinking, throwing money and my self-respect to the wind?"

"Don't you?" Trystan inquired before he could silence his tongue.

Archer's mouth twisted and his eyes went as hard and cold as ice. At that moment, for what was probably the second time in his entire life, Trystan recognized his brother as a dangerous man. If he told anyone that, no one would believe him. No one in all of London thought Archer Kane anything but a charming, self-centered rake. Five minutes ago Trystan would have agreed with them.

Then, as quick it had come, the danger was gone, replaced by a devil-may-care twinkle. "Of course!"— Archer sliced into his steak with a smirk—"What else is a second son to do? Someday, no doubt, a lady will take a shot at me as well."

Trystan remained silent as his brother added a bit of egg to his fork and lifted it and the meat to his mouth. If anyone shot Archer it probably wouldn't be a woman, he thought—and doubted the person would live long enough to claim credit. It unsettled him, seeing his sibling that way. Chilled him to the bone.

"So," Archer asked after a few moment's silence, "how much did you win off Angelwood?"

"It's not how much, but rather *what* I won from his lordship."

Archer took a sip of his coffee and smiled. "God

bless the Irish. Allow me to rephrase, then, Mr. Subterfuge. *What* did you win from the earl?"

One thing that hadn't changed was the fact that Trystan had always trusted Archer with even his deepest secrets. Oh, he might rub his little brother's face in a mess, but he never, ever revealed what Trystan told him. "Vienne La Rieux's I.O.U."

Fork and knife in hand, Archer put both of them to rest against the sides of his plate and stared at Trystan. The younger man grinned at his brother's surprise.

"What exactly does this I.O.U. entail?"

"Let's just say that madam now has a partner in her emporium scheme."

"Good lord, boy. Some day someone's going to *shoot* you."

Trystan's smile faded. "Don't call me *boy*. You know I hate that."

There were six years between the two of them. Comparing the closeness in age of Grey and Archer, Trystan would often keenly feel the gap. It didn't matter that Bronte, their sister, was eight years his junior and the youngest of the family. Being the baby of the sons made him all too aware of how his brothers and society viewed him. He was the youngest Kane boy, forever compared to his notorious older siblings, the eldest of whom just happened to be a bloody duke.

Cutting another piece of steak, Archer eyed him with undecipherable scrutiny. "Fair enough. My apologies."

Of course, this instantaneous contrition made Trystan feel every inch a stupid arse—exactly the effect his brother no doubt hoped to achieve.

"Though, given how indubitably in shock the lady must be over the events of last evening, perhaps I will refrain from sharing the news with her just yet."

That got a chuckle. Archer raised his cup in salute. "Sound judgment, brother."

Trystan smiled and returned the gesture with his own cup, connecting the porcelain rims with a solid but gentle *clink*.

"Lord Archer, Lord Trystan. Good morning."

Both men glanced up at the familiar voice and then promptly stood as gentlemen ought when in the presence of the fairer sex. Before them stood Sadie Moon, who was the wife of Trystan's business partner, Jack—only there seemed to be some dispute as to whether the two of them were actually married. But the eager look, often seen in the lady's large, unusual eyes while in Jack's midst, showed her true feelings.

Trystan bowed over her bright purple glove. The lithe woman, in her colorful clothing, stood out like an orchid amid daisies. "Madame Moon. How good to see you again. Have you word from our mutual friend?" It was the most tactful way he could think to ask.

She inclined her head, the huge hat she wore tipping dangerously, plumes trembling. "I have. He hopes to be back in London within the fortnight."

Trystan had tried to do as much as he could for Jack after the unfortunate death of his grandfather, but it had been Sadie who had done the most. And now she waited while Jack tied up loose ends at the family estate in Ireland. "If that is what he says, then that is how it will be."

Sadie smiled softly at that. Her shoulders heaved ever so slightly, as though she silently sighed in relief. "Where are my manners? May I present one of my dearest friends, Miss Indara Ferrars?" She gestured to the exotic beauty standing next to her, dressed in a spicy-colored costume of English design that only served to highlight her Indian heritage. Her eyes were like bright jewels, indicating English blood even more strongly than her surname.

Trystan bowed to the lady. "A pleasure, Miss Ferrars." Archer, he noticed, was a little slower; couldn't quite seem to take his gaze off the young woman. But his interest didn't appear to be totally physical—for the slightest bit from his earlier danger had crept back into Archer's expression. *What the devil?*

"Would you ladies care to join us?" Trystan inquired. It was propriety that made him ask. As Jack's partner, he felt somewhat responsible for his woman, in his absence, especially since Jack had indeed asked him to watch out for her.

The women exchanged a silent glance, communicating in that strange telepathic way only women seemed to master.

"We would love to," Sadie replied. "Thank you very much."

Trystan snapped his fingers and two more chairs instantly appeared, each held by an obliging member of his staff who also assisted the ladies in sitting at the table. Waiting until they were settled, Trystan and Archer then flipped the tails of their morning coats in almost perfect unison, and sat themselves.

The waiter appeared immediately with cups and more coffee. Miss Ferrars enthusiastically accepted the offered beverage in an English accent touched with a hint of India. It made her voice as intriguing and exotic as her face. Sadie asked for tea.

And additionally requested toast brought with her tea, while Miss Ferrars, taking one look at Archer's half-finished meal, said, "I would like the same, please."

Archer smiled. "I must admit, Miss Ferrars, to having an appreciation for ladies with a healthy appetite."

Trystan almost choked on his coffee at the innuendo in his brother's voice.

Miss Ferrars, however, seemed unbothered. She returned Archer's smile. "So I have heard, Lord Archer."

Turning to Sadie for something of an explanation, Trystan found her looking as surprised as he was. She shrugged at him.

"I heard there was some excitement at Saint's Row last night, Madame Moon," he said, hoping to distract both his brother and Miss Ferrars from wherever their strange flirtation/provocation might lead. "I do hope your friend Madame La Rieux is quite all right." Even though he'd gotten the news from Archer, Sadie would be a much more reliable source.

"Indeed," she replied, casting him a hesitant glance. "She is quite well. Thank you, Lord Trystan." *Wonderful*. She knew about his past with Vienne, it was obvious from the way she tried *not* to avoid his gaze. Was there anyone in London who didn't know that that he'd gotten his heart broken? Would any of them believe he was over it?

"I believe my friend was going to visit the site of her emporium this morning." She didn't look at him as she spoke, but it was as broad a hint as he had ever experienced.

"She has raised enough blunt for the scheme?"

Pretending ignorance was something he'd learned to excel at. "As an investor I must admit I'm pleased."

"As is she," Sadie replied, turning those strangely colored eyes of hers on him. He couldn't tell if they were blue or green or even brown. "Perhaps you would like to see the site as well? I planned to visit after breakfast."

What is she up to? Trying to push him and La Rieux together, was she? Playing matchmaker? He wished her luck.

"Capital idea," Archer joined in. "Why don't we all go?"

Trystan tried very hard not to let his surprise show. He fixed his brother with a questioning gaze but said, "Yes, why don't we?"

Archer turned to the beauty sitting to his left. "Miss Ferrars, I trust you will accompany us?"

She smiled sweetly. "I would be delighted, Lord Archer."

Stifling a groan, Trystan hid his annoyance behind his coffee cup. So much for his speaking to Vienne privately. He wanted to tell her in private what he had contrived. He didn't want anyone else to see her reaction when he informed her they were now partners. She would school her expression for an audience, but not for him. Now he would have to wait and hope she didn't hear the news elsewhere. He didn't think

Angelwood would gossip, but he might tell his wife, who might tell a friend; or a servant might over hear a conversation and repeat it to another; or . . . Eventually, Vienne was going to find out what he'd done, and he'd much rather be that messenger.

Oh well, he thought as he drained his cup. At least with an audience Vienne wouldn't shoot him for stepping onto her precious site.

At least, he didn't think she would.

La Rieux's was going to be the most incredible shopping experience British women ever enjoyed, Vienne promised herself as she moved through one of the buildings that would be altered, or demolished, to make way for her dream. Her location was situated just west of where Mr. Harrod had recently begun expanding his own enterprise, but east of where Mr. Whiteley opened his—on the cusp of the Bayswater and Knightsridge neighborhoods, just south of Hyde Park. It was the *perfect* location for aristocratic ladies to come and spend their husbands' money. There would be dressmakers of the finest caliber, glove makers and milliners too. She would offer perfumes and soaps, the finest cosmetics and powders. And shoes! Oh, the beautiful linens and housewares that would be available as well! Everything a lady could ever want, all under one roof. It made her giddy just thinking about it.

Of course, there were others before her, but her emporium was going to be the finest and the best. The most exclusive. The place little girls aspired to visit when they were grown and had money of their own. And she would be the woman that little girls who could never marry rich husbands would want to emulate. This wasn't just about taking as much aristocratic money as she could; this was also about showing the world what a determined woman could do.

She stopped on the first-floor landing and looked out the window at the busy street below. Thank God for Angelwood and his loan. It wasn't much in the grand scheme of such business, but it was an extra amount she would never have been able to come up with on her own. She was a wealthy woman, but she already had most of what she owned invested in Saint's Row. She refused to think about what might happen if it all fell apart. She would be ruined. Back to relying on nothing but her own wits.

It would be easy to find a man all too willing to "take care" of her. *Too* easy. She would be a trophy for many, some of whom would like nothing better than to see her powerless. *No.* She'd crawl on her belly to Trystan Kane before she let that happen. Trystan would save her.

For that reason alone she vowed she would drown

herself in the Serpentine before she would allow this venture to fail—because the last person she wanted coming to her rescue was Trystan Kane. The boy would take the job far too seriously for either of their safety.

As though the devil himself knew the direction of her thoughts, she caught sight of Trystan Kane exiting a carriage just below the window. He was with his brother Lord Archer, a man with secrets behind his eyes. Vienne knew his type well because she was that type herself. Sadie and Indara were with them; no doubt that was how Trystan had managed to find his way to this particular part of the city. She couldn't refuse to see him. After all, he was one of her investors. If he decided to pull out because of her rudeness, she would have to find someone else to invest his portion. She had waited long enough for this, and wasn't about to wait any longer.

Her gaze settled on the younger man. There was a few years difference in their ages? But when they'd had their affair it had felt more like full decades between them. He'd been so fresh and young and she'd . . . well, she'd already seen more of life by four and twenty than most women ever experienced, or ever should for that matter.

Funny how a few years could alter a person. She didn't notice much of a difference in her own face, but she sensed that, when Trystan looked at her since his return, he'd noticed a few new lines around her eyes. Did he wonder now what he had ever seen in a body as lived-in as hers? Or, did he suffer the same pangs of regretful attraction and annoying happiness whenever their paths met as she did?

He had aged well, her boy. *No.* No longer a boy; he looked like a man now—a fact that made her all the more anxious to stay as far away from him as she could. He had stubble on his jaw and lines around his eyes; even a few on his brow and around his mouth. Did he not have a birthday this month? He had to be close to thirty now.

He glanced up. Until that moment, she hadn't realized her fingers were pressed to the window, as though reaching for him through the glass. Their gazes met. She jerked her hand away and stepped back from the window, out of his line of sight.

Her heart was pounding. She brought her hand up against the soft dark green merino of her jacket, feeling the coolness of the brass buttons beneath her palm. Why such a fearful reaction to a lover who had never been anything but respectful and generous to her?

Perhaps that was an answer in itself, but Vienne had no time for such useless contemplation. Instead, she straightened her clothes, adjusted the set of her

jaunty hat, and went down the stairs to confront . . .
er, welcome her guests.

Sadie and Indara were all apologetic smiles when
she greeted them, each with a kiss on either of their
cheeks. She did not blame them for this not entirely
unwelcome intrusion, knowing how persuasive
Trystan could be.

"Gentlemen," she said, her gaze flitting over both
of them, "how lovely of the two of you to stop by.
There isn't much to see just yet, I'm afraid."

"Just seeing you is pleasure enough, Madame La
Rieux," Lord Archer replied with his trademark lopsided grin. He was one of the few men who had never
taken advantage of the grottos and private rooms at
Saint's Row, despite his reputation as a lothario. She
found that odd and yet somehow endearing, and returned a smile to his before allowing her attention to
drift to his brother, the younger Kane—who wasn't
looking at her at all, but rather surveying the inside
of the empty building.

"You'll be tearing this down?" he asked as he
moved deeper into the room.

"Actually, this building will remain, save for the
side walls. The two flanking structures will be demolished and rebuilt to match the exterior of this
one. They will be connected, but I want to create the
feeling of crossing thresholds into new shopping

departments. Each space will occupy a unique yet easily accessible area."

He nodded, as though giving his approval—something she found a little strange, but nothing she hadn't experience before where men were concerned. They seemed so surprised when a woman had a sound plan or thought.

"Household goods in its own building?"

"Yes, with a tearoom on the bottom floor so ladies might refresh themselves."

"Brilliant. I assume you'll have a powder room as well?"

How polite the English were when asking about toilets. One would think they never defecated. "Of course. Also a delivery service so maids and footmen don't have to carry all the purchases. Plus, I plan to offer credit for regular customers—at a fair rate of interest, of course."

He turned his head just enough to smile at her, as though they shared a private joke. "Of course."

In response, Vienne's heart gave a traitorous thump in her chest. He had the *most* wicked of grins—which *always* made her a little weak in the knees. It was as though all the world existed only for his enjoyment and he wanted only to share it with her.

"How about a tour, Vienne?" Sadie suggested.

"You can talk to us about how it will look and allow us to imagine it."

Trystan turned to her. "Will you be running the tearoom, Madame Moon?"

Sadie looked at her and Vienne gave a small nod. She didn't mind if Sadie told him. He was Sadie's landlord, after all. "It will be another very much like the one I'm opening in your building on Bond Street, yes."

He nodded. "Having your name attached will definitely be a boon."

Sadie lit up under the praise. Vienne might have rolled her eyes were it anyone else, but her friend deserved every kind thing anyone had to say about her.

"If the four of you would care to follow me, I would be happy to give you a tour of the premises such as they are," she offered. Of course they all readily agreed, not that they would dream of being rude enough to refuse, not even if their feet had fallen off. It was a delightful little quirk she'd learned to love about this country, even though it had driven her to distraction when she'd first arrived in London.

Vienne led them through the ground floor first, pointing out where the wall would be knocked out to provide entry into the neighboring building, and described the store section that would reside there.

Then she led them up the stairs and repeated the process, showing them where the lift would be so ladies and, in particular, their help wouldn't have to carry packages up and down flights of stairs. It would also be easier for elderly or infirm ladies to do their shopping.

"You truly have thought of everything," Lord Archer remarked as they walked. "I'm impressed, Madame La Rieux. If I weren't a dedicated bachelor, I might have to marry you."

Vienne took the remark in the spirit it was meant. "Then let us be happy for such dedication, Lord Archer, for I would make a terrible wife." They shared a chuckle even though Vienne noticed Trystan didn't seem to join in the mirth. He merely smiled absently and peered out a window at the street below.

After she had taken them through the entire building, they returned to the ground floor, where Sadie and Indara announced it was time for them to depart.

"Madame La Rieux, if you have a moment, there is something I would like to discuss with you," Trystan remarked as the ladies made ready to depart.

Vienne blinked. She hadn't expected him to make such a request. Still, it wasn't an odd one. He was an investor, so perhaps he had questions he didn't want to bore the others by asking in front of them.

"Of course, Lord Trystan. I have a little time before I must return to Saint's Row."

"I will accompany the ladies home," Archer said, offering each an arm. Vienne thought Indara hesitated a moment before accepting.

"You are too kind, Lord Archer," Sadie demurred.

"Nonsense," the nobleman replied. "I simply cannot resist surrounding myself with beautiful women."

He said it so smoothly even Vienne almost believed it. Yes, she had known many men like Lord Archer. Why couldn't his younger brother be more like him?

When the trio had departed, she was left entirely alone with Trystan. She wasn't concerned that he sought to renew their prior acquaintance, for she saw no amount of caring or emotion in his remarkable blue eyes. In fact, he was almost totally devoid of expression.

"What did you wish to speak about with me?" There were times, when she was nervous that English still felt awkward on her tongue, and she wondered if she had spoken correctly. This was one of those times when the words seemed wrong.

If she had spoken incorrectly, Trystan either didn't notice or chose to ignore it. "This," he replied, handing her a slip of paper.

Vienne didn't frown. Frowning gave a woman wrinkles, her mother used to say. Yet, more times than naught, she ended up with her brow furrowed, but she didn't want to look any older than she was in front of him. The urge to frown grew as she realized the paper was from her own desk.

It was the marker she gave Angelwood.

"*How* did you get this?" she demanded.

"I won it," he replied coolly. "Last night at cards. Don't even think of tearing it up; it's a binding contract."

She knew that, damn him to hell. "What do you intend to do with it?"

"I had thought to collect."

"I don't have that kind of money readily available—" *Didn't have it at all!*

"I don't want money."

Vienne stiffened. So this is what it came to. Had the wonderful young man she had shared her bed with truly sunk so low? She thrust the paper at him. "What *do* you want?"

He took it and refolded it, forcing her to wait as he slipped it into his inside breast pocket. "I want an additional two percent share in the emporium scheme."

She could have laughed, her initial relief was so great. "Is that all?"

He nodded. "That is all."

"Fine. Come by the club later today. I'll have the paperwork drawn up."

Trystan offered his hand. "Shall we shake on it, then?"

She stared at his hand. It looked bigger than she remembered, but perhaps it was the gloves he wore. "Do you not trust my word, Lord Trystan?"

"Just treating this as I would any other transaction, Madame La Rieux." Meaning, she realized, that he was treating her just as he would any man. The thought pleased her—*almost* as much as it irritated her.

She slipped her hand into his, gasping slightly as the strength of his long fingers closed around hers. "We have an accord," she said. "Two percent in exchange for the marker." Why hadn't she thought to make Angelwood the same offer? Losing two percent still gave her the controlling share in the venture. She'd been very careful not to allow any one investor to buy in too deeply as to upset her control of the project. Even with the two percent gone, she still had a full fifty percent of her own.

"Very good," Trystan replied, releasing her hand. "I will come by at three. I have many ideas I would like to discuss with you for the venture. I would like to see your architect's designs as well."

Vienne smiled at him, rather like she would smile

at anyone who made such a request. "Of course you do, and I look forward to hearing them, but I cannot take the suggestions of one investor over all others, Lord Trystan. It wouldn't be good business."

He met her gaze calmly, so calmly that it immediately set off warning bells in Vienne's head. "But I'm not simply one investor, Vienne."

It was the first time he'd called her by her Christian name since his return to London. "Perhaps you should explain to me just what you believe your role to be," she suggested. Surely he wasn't about to throw their past in her face? "I don't believe a what—twenty-two-percent share—guarantees you a say in design."

A ghost of a smile curved his lips, forming a cold knot between Vienne's shoulder blades. "I have *more* than twenty-two percent interest in this scheme."

Vienne quickly redid the math in her head. She knew how much of an investment he'd bought. She'd seen the papers. "How much do you believe you own?"

"With the two percent you just gave me? Half."

She laughed around the lump in her stomach. "Impossible! No one investor was sold such a large sum."

"No, they weren't. You were very careful about that. I had to buy Jack Friday—Farrington's—shares from him, and I had to buy the rest through various other concerns I own. The last bit came from Angelwood, and now you yourself. I have all the papers to back up my claim. Believe me when I tell you that I do indeed own a fifty-percent share in this scheme."

No. The blood rushed from Vienne's head in one hot surge that left her dizzy and swaying on her feet. "Why?" Such a helpless lament, but she couldn't seem to stop it from falling from her lips. *Was it revenge?* Why would he go to such lengths, through such deceit?

All traces of humor vanished from his handsome face—a face she could cheerfully claw the eyes out of. "Your scheme is a brilliant one, which I have no doubt will be a huge success. Why wouldn't I want a chunk of it?"

She shook her head, holding on to her control by some small thread of determination. "I will not let you destroy what I've worked so hard to accomplish."

"Destroy? Why the devil would I want to destroy it?" He looked as though he thought her daft to even suggest it. "No, I want to help you make it the greatest thing London has ever seen."

"I don't want or need your help."

His expression was far from contrite; his brilliant eyes bright. "Then that's unfortunate, because we're partners, Vienne. Whether you like it or not."

Chapter 3

Obviously she had shot the wrong man.

Immediately after discovering Trystan's machinations, Vienne climbed into her carriage and instructed her driver to take her to Lord Angelwood's home. She had time to stew during her journey, and her earlier outrage strengthened. So, on the heels of Angelwood's wary butler, she stormed into the earl's study.

His Lordship, at his desk and teacup in hand, looked up with a resigned expression on his handsome face. "I thought I might have a visit from you today."

"What the devil were you thinking?" she demanded as soon as the door closed behind the departing butler. "You gave Trystan Kane my marker!"

"I didn't *give* it to the man. He asked for it as payment. I had to consent; it was a matter of honor."

Vienne snorted. "*Your* honor—at the expense of mine." She dropped into a chair, slumping as much as her corset would allow. "What were you thinking, *mon ami*? You know the boy and I have history."

Angelwood rose from behind the desk, crossing the Axminster carpet to pour a generous measure of bourbon into two glasses. He gave one of the glasses to Vienne when he returned. "He assured me he meant you no harm. Are you here to tell me he lied to me?"

"I don't know." She took a slow sip, and the liquor burned all the way down. "He claims to want to make the venture a success, but I cannot believe that—not completely. He has the look of a man with something to prove, and my business will suffer for it."

"Perhaps he wants to prove himself to you," the older man suggested, leaning against the edge of his desk rather than sitting behind it once again. "Perhaps he wants the venture to be every bit as successful as you wish it to be. Perhaps having his input will prove a good thing."

She shot him a disbelieving glance. "Of course, you would be on his side. You are both men."

"Yes. Trystan Kane is a man, my dear friend. That is a fact you would do well to remember when next you have dealings with him."

She shrugged off the suggestion, though his words burrowed into her brain like a worm in an apple. Years had passed since she and Trystan had their affair. He wasn't that boy anymore, but a man. He was older, as was she. And the progression of time was not nearly as kind to a woman as to a man. He increased in social value with age—like fine wine. But a woman began to lose worth after twenty, socially souring like vinegar.

She was on her way to bitterness while Trystan Kane had yet to reach his full potency, and there wasn't even five years difference in their ages—but those years might as well have been fifteen for all the differences between them.

Yet she would always remember that he was the only male to ever say he loved her. No women forgot such a gift, no matter how old or bitter she was. Foolish romanticism remained despite a woman's experience and knowledge, no matter how clear was her vision of the world. Concerning her time with Trystan, there was still a tint of rosiness. But that fondness had been directly related to his youth. Now that he was older and better acquainted with the world, he had, no doubt, lost that sweetness.

Yes, Trystan was a man, and therefore she would treat him as one when next she saw him. After all, Vienne knew how to "handle" men.

"I don't have any recourse, do I?" she asked after another sip.

Angelwood shook his head. "I don't believe so.

Kane didn't break any laws or oaths by buying up interest in your scheme. His behavior might not have been completely honest, but he's done nothing criminal. You have all the capital you need, Vienne, and a partner who has made a reputation and a fortune in commerce. I understand being upset over losing complete control, but the situation could have been far worse."

He was right, of course. Angelwood usually was, but that didn't make hearing it any easier. Vienne was unused to depending on anyone else. She was not good at sharing and trusted in her own instincts above all others.

And her instincts told her to get as far away from her new partner as possible. There was nothing for it. She was going to have to show Trystan Kane who was in charge.

When a note from Vienne, saying that she wanted to get together to discuss their collective "vision" of the emporium, arrived later that day, Trystan was not surprised. Vienne had time to think about the situation, and now she would have come up with a strategy to either get rid of him or manipulate him.

Obviously she was intelligent enough to know getting rid of him was not an option—especially not with the amount of money he'd already invested in the scheme—so this meant that she was going to sally forth with manipulation. She wanted to meet him for drinks at Saint's Row later that evening. Was he available?

Smiling, Trystan set the note aside and leaned back in his padded leather chair, propping his feet on the polished walnut top of his desk. He would make himself available—*of course!*—if for no other reason than to discover exactly what she had in mind.

He pulled his watch from his waistcoat pocket and checked the time. He had an appointment he needed to get to.

He swung his feet to the floor, stood, and swept his jacket from the brass rack in the corner, slipping his arms into the sleeves as he left the room. He almost forgot his hat, whirling abruptly to snatch it up. He neatly tucked the key to his apartments into his pocket after he locked the door. His rooms took up half of this floor; Jack Friday's took the rest. If Jack and Sadie renewed their relationship when Jack returned to London, they could offer up his rooms as a luxury suite for wealthy visitors.

Trystan paused on the threshold of the lift, his hand braced against the gate. *Luxury suites!* Why hadn't he thought of that sooner? So much of Grosvenor Square and Mayfair land was tied up in leases. He might be able to acquire a large house or a parcel with smaller buildings nearby, or he could build a series of opulent accommodations—all for those who traveled to the city not in need of an entire house, such as bachelors or ladies without husbands or children. A home, albeit smaller, for when you're away from home. *Brilliant!*

The boy who operated the lift looked at him. "Are you all right, sir?"

Trystan's head jerked up and he grinned at the boy. His embarrassment at being caught dreaming paled in comparison to his enthusiasm for the new idea. "I'm more than all right, Jones. In fact, I think I might be something of a genius."

A wide smile claimed Jones's young face. "Won't argue with you there, Mr. Kane. Down, sir?"

With an enthusiastic yes, Trystan stepped into the cagelike box and rode it down to the foyer. The marble floor gleamed, the windows shone, and everything smelled clean and fresh. He took a moment to stand there and glance around. Perfectly groomed and uniformed employees smiled and waited on guests from Britain and the Continent, all of whom were there because the Barrington was not only the finest London had to offer, but one of the best in all of Europe.

And it was his. Most men would be pleased with this accomplishment—satisfied even—but not him. He was proud of everything he had achieved since setting out on his own, but none of it was enough. He still felt like the Duke of Ryeton's youngest brother—constantly held up against the flaws and virtues of Grey and Archer. He still felt like that boy who foolishly fell in love with the wrong woman only to be rejected just when his heart was fully engaged.

Trystan knew himself enough to have long ago realized that proving himself to Vienne would ease that need inside him. Why else go through so much trouble to force her to work with him? He could have built his own emporium and made himself her competition if all he wanted to do was make her squirm. He didn't want to be her enemy— Actually, he didn't know *what* he wanted to be where she was concerned. But what he did know was that he wanted to go more than a handful of days without thoughts of her taunting him.

Obsession wasn't a trait he found attractive in himself.

His carriage was waiting for him on the street outside.

"Chelsea," he instructed, giving the man the direction as he stepped into the vehicle. He set his hat on the seat beside him and raked a hand through his hair. A copy of the *Times* lay on the cushions across from him, put there by his thoughtful driver, Havers, who knew he hated being stuck in a carriage with nothing but his own company.

He read, having long ago trained himself to not get nauseous during a drive. There was another article on the shooting at Saint's Row, and mention of an inquiry. Trystan snorted. He wisely hadn't mentioned the incident to Vienne when they spoke—mostly because she would have taken it as an affront. Also because it would drive her to distraction if he pretended ignorance. Vienne was not a woman accustomed to indifference.

Though, if she found out what he was up to right now, she would realize just how far from indifferent he was.

Sometime later, the carriage rolled to a stop and Trystan opened the door. The metal steps were flipped down and he stepped onto the sidewalk in front of a pretty stucco house with a flower garden in front.

He offered the paper to Havers, perched atop the box. "I won't be any longer than an hour."

The craggy-faced driver tipped his hat. "No worries, sir. A lovely day to sit and read the rag."

Trystan left him and took the pretty flagstone walk up to the whitewashed front door. He rapped the knocker and stood back, waiting. It hadn't been difficult to find this place; a few succinct, discreet questions and here he was.

The door opened, revealing a thin middle-aged woman in a housekeeper's uniform. "Yes?" Her tone was cautious, almost wary as she took in his fine dress and posture.

He removed his hat and smiled at her. "Trystan Kane to see Mr. William Jones."

A ginger brow rose—the only discernable reaction to his request. Of course, it wasn't well known that this was where the man had come to convalesce. The housekeeper stepped back to let Trystan cross the threshold. "Come in, sir."

Once inside the doorway, Trystan surveyed his surroundings. It was a lovely, tidy little home—one which the lady who lived there had no doubt earned. Camilla Lake had been a successful actress in her day, and an even more successful mistress. In her prime she never took a lover who was below the rank of viscount or had an income less than thirty thousand. He admired her shrewd business sense, if not her choice in lovers.

The housekeeper led him down a corridor carpeted in a Morris print of black, peach, and green; the walls were painted a warm ivory. They stopped at the last door on the right. The woman announced him to her mistress, and Trystan was allowed inside.

Camilla Lake rose from her chair to greet him. If she was surprised to see him, she didn't show it. "Mr. Kane, what an unexpected pleasure."

She was still a beautiful woman, with thick sable

hair and eyes as gray as a thundercloud. She was fashionably dressed, but not overly so. Neither was she heavily made up. Clearly she was a woman who understood the art of subtlety. When she offered her hand, Trystan bowed over it.

"Mrs. Lake, I beg your pardon for barging in on you like this." He glanced at the man who reclined on the sofa. The arse hadn't so much as sat up at the arrival of company. Trystan wasn't terribly offended. No doubt the bullet Vienne had put into Mr. Jones afforded him quite a bit of discomfort.

"No apology is necessary, I assure you," his hostess replied. "Will you sit?"

He held up a hand. "Thank you, but I won't stay long. I wanted to inquire after Mr. Jones's health."

The lady looked surprised, as did her patient. "That's very kind of you, sir."

"Kindness has nothing to do with it," he replied with a smile, which faded as he turned his attention to Jones. "Winged you, did she?"

Jones scowled, but his gaze didn't quite focus as it met Trystan's. Laudanum, *no* doubt. "Bitch wanted to kill me."

"William," Mrs. Lake admonished. "Language."

Jones swore—a foul, harsh word that brought a dark stain of humiliation to his lover's fair skin.

Trystan's ire rose. "That's no way to speak to a lady."

Jones snarled at him. "I'll speak how I goddamn well please, and I hope that slut La Rieux gets the pox."

Trystan turned to Mrs. Lake. "My dear madam, you have my sincere condolences. I believe your generous nature has been abused in the most grievous manner."

The lady's blush deepened. It was obvious that she kept Jones, just as it was obvious that she could do much better.

"Perhaps you are right, Mr. Kane," she replied in a low tone. "I will leave the two of you to your discussion. Good day."

He bowed to her, and watched as she escaped from the room with as much dignity as she could muster. Her spine was so rigid, he thought she might never bend again.

The moment the door clicked shut behind her, he approached the sofa on which Jones had himself propped up on several cushions. His right arm was in a sling. He was young—younger than Trystan by about five years at least. Vienne seemed to have a penchant for men in their early twenties.

"There's talk of an inquiry into your shooting." He kept his tone light. Conversational.

Jones shifted on the cushions, wincing when his shoulder moved the wrong way. "Good. The bitch tried to kill me."

Trystan chuckled. "*Son*, if Vienne La Rieux wanted

to kill you, you'd be dead. She was trying to teach you a lesson."

"I'll teach her a lesson, the bitch. Thinks she can command me to her bed whenever she wants, then say no?"

A strange bitter feeling rose in Trystan's chest—a foul taste in his mouth. "Yes," he said, "that's exactly what she can do. You obviously don't lack in feminine companionship."

Jones glanced up at him, a sloppy smirk curving his lips. How could anyone think this piece of shite was attractive? What did women see in him other than his youth? He had to be extremely well endowed, because he certainly wasn't charming. "You've had her too, haven't you? Then you know just how sweet that honey pot between her white thighs is. A man could die happy buried to the hilt in Vienne La Rieux."

"She should have aimed lower," Trystan muttered, then loudly said, "Look, Jones. You're not going to take any action against Vienne La Rieux, lawful or otherwise."

The younger man scowled, looking like a petulant, drunken cherub. "Now, see here. That bitch— *Ow!*"

Trystan had gripped Jones by the shoulder, digging his thumb into the spot where he estimated the bullet tore into his flesh. Then he bent down so no one but the now-fully alert bastard could hear him. "You see here, you little prick. You deserve what you got. You deserve worse than that for trying to force yourself on a woman, your lover or not. If you so much as breathe in Vienne La Rieux's direction, I'll finish you. Understood?—*FINISH* you. And no one—*no one*—will ever find your useless corpse."

Jones stared up at him as Trystan straightened. Shock and pain brightened his green eyes. He swallowed and nodded, but didn't speak.

Trystan smiled. "Excellent. I suggest you find yourself another place to sleep tonight as well. I don't think Mrs. Lake is too terribly impressed with you at the moment."

Then he left the room and made his way back the way he'd come, tipping his hat to the housekeeper as he passed. "I'll show myself out, missus. Good day."

Outside, it seemed a little brighter, a little sharper, yet the day was just as it had been when he first arrived. He certainly had no business doing what he had just done—threatening a man over Vienne's honor—but he had done it all the same. He couldn't afford to have her distracted by thoughts of persecution or further scandal. He needed her sharp, alert, and able to make sound decisions where their joint venture was concerned.

He needed her attention fully focused—on *him*.

* * *

Later that day, as Vienne sorted through her gowns, searching for the correct one to wear to her meeting with Trystan, she received word that a workman had suffered an accident at the emporium site and would be unable to return to work for several weeks. The man was a master craftsman; and she had hoped that his delicately carved woodwork would be a focal point, uniting all the different shops and floors into one cohesive space.

While she would never belittle a man's personal injury by making it a slight against herself, she did take a brief moment to ask God why this had happened to her—at a time when Trystan Kane was looking over her shoulder.

There was, though, a bright side to the unfortunate incident: the workman would recover, and he had several apprentices who could continue the work he had started. It might not be as perfect, but it would be close. She would have to be happy with that.

Also, she'd just heard from her solicitor that William Jones planned to go to Scotland Yard and tell them that the "altercation" between them had been nothing but a huge misunderstanding—an accident.

Vienne had been tempted to go to the authorities herself and tell them it was not an accident at all, that the weasel had tried to force himself upon her—

but it wasn't worth the scandal; her name was in the papers often enough. Yet not for anything quite so ... colorful. She wanted to keep what tenuous good standing she had in this city, but hadn't thought of that when she pulled the trigger. She'd been so outraged by William's behavior, so indignant, that she could only at that moment make her point.

Hopefully it had been a lesson young Monsieur Jones would not soon forget.

Now she was dressed in an exquisite new gown designed by Mr. Worth—a shimmering gold fabric, embellished with tiny copper crystals that sparkled under lights and hugged her snugly from shoulder to hip. Its swaths of fabric were gathered in the back and tumbled down to the floor in a short train. A simple design that allowed the fabulous confection to stand out but not overpower. After all, it should be the lady in the gown that received the attention, not the gown itself. Her sister had told her that ... a long time ago when they still spoke to one another.

But she would not think of her sister. Not tonight.

Vienne stood in the door of the club dining room, her gaze drifting over the early supper crowd. There would be a steady flow in and out of this hall for at least the next three hours. By that time the gaming rooms would be filled as well. There was no entertainment this evening, but later in the week a famous opera singer would regale guests with her amazing voice.

Personally, Vienne couldn't stand opera.

She glanced at the ornate clock in the corner. Trystan would arrive soon. The realization caused her heart to give a sharp thump—as though in protest of the meeting? Or perhaps in anticipation of it? She hadn't yet decided how she felt about the youngest Kane brother's reappearance in her life, or how he had gone about it. Still, she saw the situation as a challenge and did *so* enjoy a challenge, even when it gave her butterflies.

Her solicitor had also told her that, based on the wording of the contracts she'd given investors to sign, Trystan hadn't done anything illegal. As Angelwood had suggested, the methods might not have been entirely morally aboveboard, but they were binding.

And Trystan claimed he did not want to ruin her. He insinuated that his hopes for the emporium were as high as her own. That she doubted, but not his enthusiasm—at least not right now. Trystan Kane had become something of a legend in the business world; and while she didn't trust him on a personal level, she was impressed enough with his accomplishments to give him the benefit of the doubt.

That didn't mean she was going to give him control. He could have half the venture, but he would not change her vision—and he'd better not assume she'd just stand back and allow him to take over.

"Mason Blayne and his escort have finished their wine," she told one of the waiters, stopping him with a hand on his arm. "See that they have another bottle."

The young man nodded. "Of course, Madame La Rieux."

The corner of Vienne's mouth lifted. The boy couldn't seem to decide where to look—her face or her breasts. He was a charming young thing, handsome as well, and undoubtedly hers for the taking. But she had no desire for him. It was Trystan Kane that made her heart trip all over itself tonight.

She released the waiter and sent him back to his duties before leaving the dining room. Time to return to her office. She'd arranged for a light repast for herself and Trystan—mostly fruit and some cold meats and cheese. He once commented to her that he enjoyed eating with his hands. Yes, he did so enjoy food. . .

Then she remembered just how very sensual was his nature.

And as she did, a surprising flush flooded her skin. He had worshiped her body as though it was his own personal conduit to God. No one before, or since, had ever made love to her with such . . . *en-*

thusiasm, and wonder. He had known just where to touch, to kiss . . . and he had found new places for his lips and hands to play as well. Spoiled her, he had. She would never admit it, not even under torture—Trystan Kane had been the best lover she'd ever had.

Could anyone blame her, then, for severing their connection? Prolonging it would have surely led to heartache.

Her footsteps were muffled by the plush crimson carpet. Very few people—none of them patrons—knew about the narrow, secret corridors that ran throughout the club. They were used only by entertainers, employees, and Vienne herself. The secret passages and false panels harkened back to the club's former days as a theater, and now made it easy for Vienne to avoid being delayed by guests who wanted her attention.

She entered her office through a side door. The food had been delivered and a pretty little table set. A bottle of wine chilled in a nearby bucket. One thing she and Trystan shared was a preference for white wine—German and slightly sweet. Perhaps his tastes had changed since they spent time together, but hers had not.

Which would explain why her breath caught in her throat when he stepped across the threshold at exactly the appointed time. She had seen him in evening clothes many times, and certainly on a few occasions since his return, but it never failed to impress her. Men always looked best in stark black and white.

Impossibly bright blue eyes seemed to take in the entire scene, lingering for a moment on the table and the wine before meeting her gaze. Hopefully she appeared less shaken than she actually was.

She rose from the sofa where she had sat down barely moments earlier. "Mr. Kane. Punctual as always, I am pleased to see."

He arched a brow at her convivial tone. "I recall how much you despise tardiness, Madame La Rieux."

How formal they were being! How stilted and awkward. One would think them strangers. Or perhaps one would instantly see them for what they were— former lovers who did not part on the best of terms. She regretted *how* she ended their affair, but she did not regret the action itself. The fact that her heart was pounding at three times its normal rate supported the decision.

Obviously, even after several years, Trystan still affected her—while he looked calm and serene and not in the least bothered by being alone in a room with her. Perhaps she could change that.

"Come," she invited. "Sit and eat with me." She moved toward the table, watching him out of the corner of her eye.

Trystan hesitated, but only for a moment. Vienne had to hide a pleased smile as he did as she bid, joining her across the snowy tablecloth. She didn't have to ask him to attend to the wine; he did so immediately, in the manner he had years before—pouring generous amounts in both their glasses before raising his.

"A toast," he said, "to a successful partnership."

Vienne raised her wine as well, flashing a bright smile. *"Salute!"*

He watched her over the crystal rim as they both drank. What was he thinking? She could discern nothing from his posture or expression, nor even his eyes—those beautiful eyes . . . from which he'd broadcast every happiness *and* every tragedy.

When had he gotten those lines around his eyes and mouth? When had he changed from a bright-faced youth to the man before her? He looked good, even more handsome than he had been. How did she look to him? Unchanged? Or was she older too—perhaps faded and past her prime?

"Why did you invite me here, Vienne?" he asked before he plucked a strawberry from the platter and popped it into his mouth.

She shrugged in that laconic manner her people were known for. "We are partners now. I thought it would be pleasant if we sat down together."

"Pleasant?" He wiped his fingers on a napkin. "Is that what you thought?"

Oddly, something seemed to sink in the vicinity of her stomach. Had some part of her actually hoped he would have forgotten her dismissal?

"Yes," she admitted. "Or rather, I had hoped we might be civil."

He seemed to consider that. "What prompted this sudden change of heart? Earlier you were angry enough to want my head on a pike."

Such a lovely and descriptive attempt to capture how she had felt. "My solicitor tells me there is nothing that can be done. If I am going to be forced to work with you, then I must make the best of it. I will not risk all I've worked for because we are no longer friends." Now there was a pinch beneath her breast. Perhaps she should see her doctor. Hopefully he would prescribe something for indigestion, because that was the only explanation she would accept for this queer reaction.

He smiled, but the gesture never made it to his eyes. "Were we ever friends? It hardly matters now. The past is best left in the past. I'm much more interested in the future."

How did he make that sound both insulting and seductive at the same time? "As am I." She toyed with the stem of her wineglass, watching tiny droplets of condensation bead on the crystal. "You said you had ideas for the site. Why don't you share some of them with me now?"

Suddenly, Trystan's cool composure began to melt. As soon as she made the suggestion he sat up straighter, his eyes brightening. "We want this to be the kind of place in which ladies love to spend their money—will *want* to spend their money."

Vienne appreciated that he did not naturally assume the money would belong to husbands. In this modern world, the number of women inheriting and making their own fortunes was constantly increasing. "Of course."

"I'd like men to spend their money there as well. A gentleman's boutique with a tailor on staff, and perhaps a small salon where they might smoke and have a drink."

She opened her mouth to protest, but stopped herself. Yes, women did most of the household shopping, but men and their valets still had to purchase clothing and toiletries. Why narrow her market by catering only to women? "Perhaps if we make ourselves available to gentlemen, society won't be so quick to denounce us as corruptors of women."

Trystan nodded. "We should carry shaving and other grooming supplies as well. What do you think of a chemist of sorts on site to custom blend aftershaves and soaps? We could make creams and perfumes for the ladies as well."

It was a brilliant notion. "I like it. We could keep all the formulations on file for when shoppers run out and require more."

"For that matter, we could keep a tally of each customer's purchases and use that information to let them know when something new they might like arrives at a particular shop."

Vienne drained what little wine was left in her glass and refilled it. She topped Trystan's off as well. "So, if your sister-in-law the duchess purchased a pair of brown leather boots, we could alert her if matching gloves become available."

"*Exactly!* Or, if a gentleman buys his wife a necklace, he could be sent a notice if the matching earrings are reduced in price."

"We could notify all our customers when items are reduced to make room for more stock. If there's one thing rich people love, it's getting more for less money."

He laughed, and Vienne's heart leapt at the sound. That was the Trystan she remembered.

The Trystan she had fallen in love with.

She sent for more wine. They finished the first bottle and began the second as they talked, each tossing out ideas that were either met with delight or rejected outright. And they didn't argue about it. It seemed that on most points the two of them were in perfect alignment. They talked as though their affair had never happened or, worse, had never ended. Vienne didn't care if it was dangerous. He had some incredible ideas for their business and that was more important, especially when she knew better than to let her heart rule her again.

Her libido, on the other hand, was humming inside her. She was very much aware of a slight, delicious tightening between her legs—a sweet ache that wanted to be rubbed. Her blood was like warm honey in her veins—and when she licked the juice from gorgeously ripe strawberry at the corner of her mouth, she saw Trystan watching with brazen appreciation.

She had brought him here with seduction in mind, hoping to play on whatever attraction he might still feel for her. But before the second bottle of wine, she had already realized what a bad idea that would be. Sex always complicated relationships; it was never as simple as shared pleasure should be.

But now, staring into those amazing eyes, remembering just how easily he used to bring her to climax—and the various ways he did so—made seducing him seem like it wouldn't be such a mistake after all. She wanted him, and he obviously wanted her as well, so what was the harm in giving in to temptation? If it made him easier to manage afterward, so much the better. And if it did not . . . well, she would have assuaged the ache and they would perhaps enjoy each other for a little while. Until he left London again.

Vienne rose to her feet, swaying ever so slightly. Trystan, gentleman that he was, stood as well, which was exactly what she had wanted him to do—*such* an agreeable boy.

She closed the short distance between them, moving nearer so that they were mere inches apart. She looked up—not far, given her above-average height—and found herself staring at his shapely mouth.

She remembered that mouth. Her hands reached out suddenly and clumsy fingers gripped the lapels of his jacket.

"Vienne, what are you doing?"

"What we both want," she replied brazenly, and then up on her toes she went—and pressed her eager mouth to his.

Chapter 4

For a moment, Trystan allowed himself to enjoy the sweet pressure of Vienne's lips against his—and when her wine-flavored tongue eased inside, he met it with his own, bringing a hint of strawberry to the kiss.

She felt exactly as he remembered, perhaps even better. Soft and pliable in his arms; slender but curved in all the right places. He thought he would never have the opportunity to hold her again. His hands itched to explore her; his mouth grew more thirsty. Arousal surged, heavy and tight. His desire for her was as much emotional as it was physical—he didn't want to let her go.

But he did just that. And when she gazed at him with heavy-lidded eyes—filled with confusion more than desire or any other feeling—he knew he'd made the right choice, as difficult as it had been.

"What's wrong?" she asked.

Mouth twisting, still tasting of her, Trystan pushed

her away with more force than he intended. In her slightly inebriated state, Vienne stumbled but did not fall.

"What did you hope to accomplish with tonight?" he demanded somewhat bitterly. "Sweeten me up, pretend to like my ideas; feed me, pour wine down my throat, and then insure that I was good and under your thumb with a little well-timed seduction?"

The expression on her face supported his suspicions. "I do like your suggestions."

He let loose a bark of harsh laughter. She didn't even try to deny the rest. "You and I already had that dance, Vienne. I'm not one of your boys who will do whatever you want for the pleasure of warming your bed; and I will not allow you to railroad me into being your subordinate. We're business associates—and I do not make a habit of screwing the people I do business with."

She put on a seductive, placating smile. "Trystan—"

"No! . . . Do whatever it is you need to do to accept that I am your partner and will not be manipulated or controlled by you—but *do not* make the mistake of thinking I'm still that boy who worshiped the ground upon which you trod. Good *night.*"

He strode from the room with a stiff back and clenched jaw. She didn't follow him—Vienne would never lower herself and chase after a man—which saved him the humiliation of being caught. His fingers curled into fists as the maelstrom of emotions inside him warred for dominance. He was embarrassed and angry and disappointed and . . . still aroused. *Damn her to hell.*

He was pissed at her for trying to maneuver him and even more pissed at himself for falling for it. He wanted Vienne to offer herself to him because she wanted him, not in some kind of power struggle or bid for dominance.

Damn it. He wanted to be the one in charge. That didn't make him any better than she, did it? At least he had the excuse of a broken heart. No man would refute his lowly desire for a little revenge, the satisfaction of having the choice to take Vienne or refuse her.

And he had refused her just now. Yet, there was little pleasure in it. Was he the first man to say no to her? Probably. That didn't offer the satisfaction it should have either.

He was disappointed, though Vienne had acted exactly as he expected her to. That didn't make any sense, but then again Trystan was beginning to think perhaps he wasn't a good judge of what made sense and what didn't. He had drunk more wine than he should have . . . Vienne had been so animated and seemed so engrossed in the sharing of ideas. . .

For a moment it had felt like they were actually

partners. Why did she have to go and ruin it?

Enough. She had made her play and he rebuffed it. Nothing more needed to be thought or picked apart. Vienne would not do it again; she was too smart for that. She would, however, change tactics.

As would he. Instead of leaving as he had intended, he went to one of the gaming rooms. Within moments of entering the brightly lit room that practically reverberated with the sounds of roulette wheels, chatter, laughter, and the occasional cry of defeat, he found the person he sought.

Archer was talking to a young widow who had something of a reputation for appreciating both male and female companionship. Trystan had imbibed *just* enough liquid courage and was irritated *just* enough that he had no compunction about striding right up to his brother.

"Let's go," he said.

Archer turned to him with an expression that was as much disbelieving as it was annoyed. "Beg pardon?"

Trystan bowed to the lady. "Apologies for my rudeness, but would you mind if I spoke to my brother privately?"

"Of course not," she replied easily. "Lord Archer and I can continue our *conversation* at his earliest convenience." There was no mistaking the promise of pleasure in her voice, but then both of his brothers had inherited a charm with the fairer sex that seemed to elude him.

"What the devil is wrong with you?" Archer demanded in a low voice as soon as the pretty blonde left them. "Have you been drinking?"

The scowl on his sibling's face brought a grin to Trystan's own. He was still enough of a brat that he enjoyed discombobulating his brothers. "I have. I'm on my way to Chez Cherie's. Care to join?"

Archer's jaw sagged as his pale eyes widened ever so slightly—it was quite the coup to illicit such a reaction from a man as schooled at hiding his true feelings as Archer was. "Chez Cherie's?"

"Am I not enunciating clearly?" He was being deliberately glib. "Yes, that is exactly what I said and where I am bound. Will you join me or not?"

"Not," his brother replied. "I promised Grey I'd meet him for a game of snooker in ten minutes, and I hope to catch up with Lady Mitchell afterward—if you didn't succeed in scaring her into another man's arms."

"Or woman's," Trystan offered brightly.

Archer raised a sharp brow. "I am a gentleman and more than willing to share with a lady, but my generosity does not apply to a bloke. Why don't you stay here? I'm sure you can find someone more than willing to have you for free, even though you are the ugliest of our lot."

Trystan wasn't offended, though it was true. Their oldest brother, Grey, Duke of Ryeton, had rugged features while Archer's were sharp; neither had any trouble attracting lovers. But Trystan's features were more a combination of the two of them, making his nose perhaps a little too big and his mouth a little too wide. Still, his mother always claimed he had the prettiest eyes. And he had learned not to underestimate the power of such a gaze where women were concerned.

"Tonight I think I would prefer to pay," he confided. "One knows exactly where one stands with a professional. Little room for disappointment or humiliation."

Archer frowned, his countenance all concern. "Perhaps I should take you home."

He clapped his elder sibling on the shoulder. "Don't be ridiculous. I'm the most reliable, steady, and least reckless male in our family."

"Yes," Archer agreed, looking not the least bit comforted by the reminder. "That is what concerns me. Let me tell Grey we're leaving and I'll take you back to the Barrington."

Trystan's fingers gripped his brother's shoulder and squeezed forcefully—not hard enough to hurt but with enough pressure to get his attention. "I'm not going home and I don't need you acting like my frigging governess. Come with me or don't, but I'm going."

Archer stared at him, long and hard. It was deuce impossible to decipher what the look meant, or guess at what he saw, but eventually he nodded. "As you wish. Breakfast tomorrow, then?"

Trystan smiled. "On me." He lifted his hand from his brother's shoulder. "Have fun with Lady Mitchum."

"Mitchell."

"Of course." But Trystan was already walking away and really didn't care what the woman's name was. He snagged a glass of champagne from a passing footman's tray and downed it in one gulp in time to deposit it on another.

He ran into Vienne on his way out, just as she was coming in, still wearing that gorgeous gown that molded to her like a layer of brilliant skin. "Trystan," she said a little breathlessly—a tone that brought back so many arousing and heartbreaking memories. "I want to talk to you."

"Tomorrow," he told her, barely stopping. "Let's meet at the site around two and we'll discuss how to best incorporate the new plans. Now, please excuse me, I have another engagement."

He left her there, staring after him. *That* gave him some measure of satisfaction. Let her try to explain herself tomorrow, in the harsh light of day when both of them were sober and completely aware—and undoubtedly mortified—about this night. He looked forward to it.

But for now, he was going to go to a high-class brothel to find a woman who was the exact opposite of Vienne La Rieux.

And he was going to shag her senseless.

She should know better than to drink wine. She always woke up with a headache that lingered throughout the day.

Vienne sat at her desk with a pile of papers in front of her and, to her right, a cup of tea with a headache powder dissolved in it. The tea masked most of the bitter taste, but occasionally she took a sip that made her shudder as soon as the medicine hit her tongue.

"Madame La Rieux?"

She glanced up. Her secretary stood in the doorway. "Yes, Victor? What is it?"

The effeminate young man looked a little nervous. "The Duke of Ryeton is here to see you, ma'am."

Ryeton, at this hour? Why, it was just passed eleven. Most aristocrats were still abed. "Show him in."

She rose to her feet, wishing she'd had time to

consult a mirror. She absolutely abhorred looking anything less than her best when important people came to call—not for their benefit, oh no. Her appearance was her armor, and she despised showing any chinks in it.

The duke swept in like the force of nature that he was. He was one of those noblemen who lived life exactly as he wanted and had paid the price on several occasions—the wicked scar marring the left side of his rugged face was one such consequence. There was a family resemblance between Greyden Kane and his youngest brother, more so now that Trystan had returned, but the duke was larger and more rugged. Truth be told, Vienne found him somewhat intimidating and at the same time a kindred spirit—for both he and she would do whatever they had to in order to achieve their goals.

And judging from the look on His Grace's face, Vienne was an obstacle in his path.

"Your Grace." Somehow she managed to keep her voice normal. "To what do I owe this unexpected pleasure?"

Cold gray-blue eyes locked with hers. "Last night my brother Trystan stormed out of here as if the hounds of Hades were snapping at his heels."

"Did he?" She was all surprise and apologetic ignorance. "I am sorry to hear that."

The duke shrugged. "I understand a single man's enthusiasm where a trip to Chez Cherie's is concerned, but I think there was more to it than that."

Vienne swallowed, trying to force her heart out of her throat and back into her chest, where it belonged. Trystan had gone to a *brothel*? He wouldn't take what she freely offered, but he would pay a whore? Oh, that stung. Did he know he was the first man to ever refuse her?—to make her doubt her appeal as a woman? The first to see through her machinations.

Oh, how she loathed the thought of him taking solace in the body of another. She had gone to bed tipsy, regretful . . . and unsatisfied, while he—

"I don't see what this has to do with me," she quickly remarked, lifting her chin.

His Grace tilted his head to one side in contemplation. It was as though he could see right into the soul of her. "Let us not play games, Madame La Rieux. It's an insult to us both. I know this happened immediately after meeting with you. Whatever happened in this room last night made Trystan behave like Archer—or worse, like me. Seeing as how my youngest sibling is the best my family's had to offer in three generations, I'd like to know just what you did to him."

"I did nothing." *Only offered myself on a platter!* And what did she get for it? Stripped bare, seen for the manipulative woman she was.

The duke didn't look convinced, but then she didn't sound very convincing. "I understand you and Trystan had something of a relationship in the past."

"That's really none of your business."

His gaze was hard. "My brother is. You and I are very similar, Madame La Rieux. We both have made a habit out of doing whatever necessary to get what we want, but I'm warning you . . ."

She braced her palms on the surface of her desk. "*You're* warning me?"

Then his broad hands planted themselves not far from hers, and suddenly she and the duke were nose to nose. "You listen to me, Vienne Moreau . . ."

Vienne felt the blood drain from her face when he called her by her correct last name. She had changed it years ago in an attempt to put that life behind her. She had told no one in England about that name.

The Duke of Ryeton rose a notch in her estimation—higher on her list of men to stay as far away from as possible.

Obviously the duke noticed the change in her because he continued: "I don't care if you sleep with him. But if you make a fool of, or hurt, my brother in any way, I will *ruin* you."

Mon Dieu. How fortunate Trystan was to be so loved, so protected. Why had her siblings not protected her in this way? Why had they sided against her instead of standing up for her?

Her gaze locked with the duke's. She lifted her chin, then dipped it again in agreement. "I understand you perfectly, Your Grace."

"Good." He straightened. "I don't know why Trystan is hell-bent on impressing you, but God knows there are worse notions for him to get into his head. Hopefully, he'll disabuse himself of it soon enough."

"Yes," she murmured. "Was there anything else, Your Grace? I do have a business to see to."

The duke smiled then—a little twist of his lips that she supposed was supposed to be humorous. "Then, I shall leave you to it. I do admire your backbone, madam."

"A girl's got to have something to recommend her," she quipped, with much more disinterestedness than she felt.

Still smiling in that unnerving fashion, Ryeton bowed and took his leave of her as though he had taken tea rather than threatened her. Once he was gone Vienne slowly sat down. Her knees trembled slightly, and not only because the duke had gotten to her.

Trystan wanted to impress her? It seemed preposterous. She would think herself the last person on earth from whom he would seek approval. Surely his brother was mistaken. If Trystan wanted her approval, it was because he wanted to rub her face in his own achievements or make a fool of her in the process. After the way she ended their affair, she couldn't blame him for that—it was what she would do were the tables turned. She'd learned long ago that making oneself vulnerable to a person, trusting in them—especially a man—was just asking for trouble.

Trystan had made her feel so vulnerable. She'd had no choice but to end things. It was either hurt him or risk having her heart broken—and she had too much self-preservation to allow that.

She forced her attention back to the papers in front of her, but her mind refused to process the information on them. She kept thinking about Trystan and the kiss they'd shared the night before. He had enjoyed it, if only for a moment or so. She had enjoyed it as well, and that in itself was reason to never do it again.

Seducing Trystan to assert herself was not the right choice; it was far too risky to her own safety and there was too much to lose concerning the emporium. They were partners now, whether she liked it or not. Even she had to admit that he had some very good ideas—ones she never would have thought of.

If making the venture wildly successful meant working with Trystan and putting aside their differences, then she could do that. There were other ways she would insure the realization of her dream without sacrificing her vision.

She picked up the invitation that had been sitting on her desk for almost a week. Trystan's birthday was tomorrow. She'd been invited to the party at Ryeton House and intended to go, even though the duke would no doubt monitor her behavior the entire evening. It would be the perfect time and place for her to offer Trystan an apology for the kiss. Knowing him, the pleasure of seeing her admit to being wrong would be the best gift anyone had ever given him.

It hadn't been his idea to have a party celebrating his thirtieth birthday, and Trystan had little choice but to go along with the plan—just as he had no choice but to meet Archer for breakfast that morning. His brother hadn't been content to dine alone and instead had breakfast brought to Trystan, banging on the door of his rooms at the ungodly hour of ten o'clock.

Normally Trystan was up, dressed, and fed long before that time, but he hadn't staggered home until almost six and was very much asleep in his bed and—blessedly—still dressed when his brother came barging in with three of the hotel staff carrying trays of food and a large pot of strong coffee.

Fortunately Archer waited until the staff left them and he was sopping up egg yolk with his toast before asking for details of his evening after leaving Saint's Row. Trystan, however, refused to share the embarrassing details and, in the end, managed to keep most of them to himself. There were some things a man didn't want to share—not even with his brother. Oddly enough, Archer chose that morning to be tactful and didn't push, so Trystan escaped relatively unscathed.

It was probably too much to ask that the same apply to that evening.

He thought by thirty he would feel like a man. He *should* feel like a man, and for the last five years or so he had. But that was time spent mostly abroad—away from family and old friends who had known him his entire life. New people treated him like a man of business, but people who had known him all his life treated him as they always did—like Grey's and Archer's younger brother.

It was his party, but he stood off to one side, nursing a glass of scotch. No overindulging for him to-night; he had yet to recover from the night before. And should have known better—about everything.

A movement at the entrance of the ballroom caught his eye and he turned his head for a better look. Standing just over the threshold was a vision in chartreuse silk, and wisps of copper hair curling around her face. The world seemed to slow and stop when he looked at her. His chest felt tight, as though his lungs were compressed as well. The music faded away, all the inane chattering and laughter drifted into nothingness. There was no one but her—and him—in this moment.

And just as quickly it was gone and the world came rushing back in a cacophony of music and voices. His field of vision cleared and he could see that Vienne was just another beautifully dressed woman in a ballroom full of other glittering, beautifully dressed women.

But perhaps she shone a little brighter than the others.

She was late—fashionably so—but it didn't appear that she wished to create a stir, or even be noticed, for that matter. Trystan watched as she surveyed the bustling gathering—a party he hadn't felt part of until her arrival. She found who she was looking for, and it wasn't him. It was Grey. The two of them exchanged a look that Trystan could only describe as one of intense understanding. It was almost as though each of them dared the other to do something he couldn't quite fathom.

It wasn't a look between former lovers, or even current ones for that matter. He knew Grey was totally devoted to Rose—now a *former* lothario, of the worst kind, brought to heel by a woman just as determined to have what she wanted. But he did see some kind of tension between his brother and Vienne.

When Vienne looked away, his heart quickly gave a queer pulse. *What* had Grey done? As the thought flickered through his mind, an answer came just as quickly: Archer had told Grey about him taking off for Chez Cherie's half pissed—and his big brother had decided to confront the person he automatically blamed for Trystan's lack of sense.

The thought of Grey visiting Vienne—challenging her—on his behalf was mortifying. More so than Vienne's rejection of him years earlier. More so than the fool he had made of himself trying to win her back.

Thirty years old and his brothers were still trying to fight his battles for him.

Perhaps he'd have another drink after all.

He made his way through the crowd of well-wishers—smiling mamas who had daughters for him to meet, men who had schemes they wanted him to support, and the odd old friend who sincerely wanted to reconnect, perhaps over a meal or a drink at a club. Those were the ones he agreed to immediately. They eased the anger bubbling inside him, the humiliation. His friends didn't want anything but his company, and they weren't going to hold him up against some foolish measuring stick only they could see.

By the time he reached the bar where one of Grey's liveried footmen doled out scotch, bourbon, brandy, wine, and several lighter spirits, Vienne was already there, accepting a double scotch with a thankful smile.

"I'll have one of those as well," he told the footman. When Vienne turned, he watched as color that had nothing to do with the drink in her hand filled her cheeks. God love her, she was embarrassed. That took a bit of the sting out.

"Happy Birthday, Lord Trystan," she murmured in that throaty voice of her, all the more sultry for the French that clung her words.

"Thank you, Madame La Rieux. I'm happy you could share it with me."

She started but quickly recovered. "Of course. I wouldn't have missed it for all the world." But he knew just from looking at her she'd rather be anywhere else, with anyone else.

So much for taking the sting out. She just shoved it right back in again, deepening the wound.

Trystan wasn't about to go down this path, not tonight. He hadn't the fortitude or the appetite. The footman gave him his drink and he raised it to her. "Well, enjoy your evening." He turned to leave.

"Wait."

A small smile curved his lips in response to the jolt of pleasure shooting through him at the sound of that word on her lips. He hesitated—purposefully—before slowing turning once again. "Yes?"

High color stood out on her ivory cheeks. Her skin was almost pure white, touched by the tiniest bit of golden warmth—like the sun creeping over fresh snow. Such beauty would be cold in an English woman, but no one would ever call Vienne cold. She burned like a flame, the brightness coming out in her vivid hair and sparkling blue-green eyes, the natural crimson of her lips.

"I wonder if I might have a moment?" Her chin came up. "In private."

This was interesting. Was it another ploy on her behalf? Did she have some new trick up her sleeve? Whatever her motive, Trystan's foolish curiosity got the better of him, as did his gentlemanly honor. It would be rude to deny her an audience, he told himself.

"Of course, madam." He gestured to the French doors leading to the large stone balcony that over-looked the garden. "Shall we?"

He put one hand at the small of her back, just above the gather of material that cascaded down her skirts. The boning of her corset, molded to her body like a lover's hand, was unyielding at the pressure of his fingers.

She had a particular liking for pretty corsets, if memory served . . . and *of course* it did. There was nothing he didn't remember about her, from the tiny flowers embroidered on her undergarments to how to she liked her tea, to the sounds she made in bed—and not just those made during lovemaking.

The scent of her perfume teased him, bringing back memories best left in some dusty, distant corner of his mind. Did she remember him with such painful clarity? At night did she ever lie alone in the dark and imagine she could hear him breathing beside her?

Of course she didn't. She hadn't been stupid enough to fall in love.

Something made him turn his head as they walked, and his gaze met his brother's. Grey's stormy eyes narrowed slightly, but he raised his glass. Trystan raised his in response and then looked away before his brother could peer into his soul. Archer used to laugh when Trystan claimed Grey could see inside them, to their darkest secrets. Of course Archer would laugh, because he had the annoying tendency to view what lay beneath the surface as well. Only Trystan seemed to have missed out on that trait, at least where family was concerned. In business, he rather fancied he was a fair judge of character.

When they reached the balcony doors, he turned the handle and opened the etched glass door, then followed her into the night.

Light from flickering torches greeted them, casting a warm glow over the stones and creating seductive shadows. Beyond the City, there was a faint glow over the trees—London, a candle burning through the earth's star-dappled darkness.

Trystan drew a deep breath, his lungs and senses filling with roses and jasmine and all the other flowers of Ryeton House's garden. The smells were the same since he was a boy. His mother had overseen all the planting then, and it was nice that Grey and Rose hadn't altered it. Perhaps later that evening, he'd mention to his mother how much he had missed being in her garden. She and his newly married sister, Bronte, had arrived together, along with Bronte's husband. It did seem odd that his mother no longer lived in this house, but then it was equally odd without his father there. Yet they all had grown accustomed to his absence since his death.

Vienne had crossed to the balustrade and propped her forearms on it. He watched for a moment as she took a sip from her glass and raised her face to the warm breeze. If she took the pins from her hair, she could be a pagan goddess worshiping the night.

"What is it you wished to discuss with me?" he asked, going to her. He braced one elbow on the smooth railing, leaning his side into it. The sooner she said her piece, the sooner he could return inside and stop waxing romantic about how perfect she looked in the moonlight.

She closed her eyes—*gathering her courage?*—then turned her head toward him, eyelashes parting with grim determination. "Last night, it was wrong of me to kiss you. You were correct when you accused me of trying to manipulate you. I thought I could seduce you into doing what I wanted."

Her honesty astonished him, as did the utterly open and shameless way she confessed.

"Just what is it you want? How do you know I don't want the same?"

She smiled—an impish expression that seemed so out of place on her face and took him back to a place he didn't want to visit. "Because I want to be the one in charge."

He chuckled. "I'm not surprised. Has it occurred to you that I don't want to challenge you? I want to

work with you; we both want this endeavor to succeed. Butting heads will only hamper that."

She took another sip and shrugged. "It was my
idea. My baby. I suppose I'm overly protective of it."

"As am I. If you don't agree with my ideas, all
you have to do is tell me. I'm sure we can reach a
compromise."

" 'Compromise.' " She repeated the word as though
she had never heard it before. She probably hadn't.
"I want to trust you, Trystan."

"I hope you can."

"What do you want?"

For a moment the word *you* hovered on his lips,
but he bit it back. "I want to make us both very rich."

Vienne lifted her glass with a grin. "Then here's to
both of us getting exactly what we want."

"Yes," Trystan replied, something strange unfurling inside him. He couldn't put a name on the emotion, but it felt vaguely like determination and . . .
hope. "Exactly what we want."

Chapter 5

For the following week, relations between Trystan and Vienne were civil and relaxed, bordering on friendly without actually crossing that bridge. They were often together at the construction site, often staying as long or longer than the workmen. Unfortunately both of them had other business concerns to think of, so there were days spent apart. Even so, it was a rare evening that Trystan didn't make an appearance at Saint's Row, either to meet another business associate or to meet with Vienne. Once, they shared a supper at the club, this time with no kissing.

On the eighth day, Trystan received what could only be described as a summons to attend dinner at Ryeton House. Apparently his mother wanted the family together for a meal and Rose gave in and offered to play hostess.

More than likely his sister-in-law hoped that by having him under her roof she might be as nosey as she wished. He had known Rose for most of her life, their fathers having been close friends. If someone had told him ten years ago that her spoiled little self would have ended up married to Grey—happily so— he would have advised them to give up drinking.

Dinner, however, would provide him with the perfect opportunity to mention to his brothers that he would prefer the two of them keep their considerable noses out of his business.

He had spent most of the day catching up on business and personal matters with his partner, Jack Friday—or Jack Farrington as he was known now. Jack had recently inherited an earldom from his grandfather, and was having a little bit of trouble acclimatizing to the role. Something about worrying about having so many people depending on him for their livelihood. Trystan reminded him that they'd had plenty of people dependent upon them over the years.

"Yes," Jack agreed, "but this time I don't have you to help me shoulder it."

That might very well be one of the nicest things anyone had ever said to him.

Trystan wore a dark gray suit with a matching cravat and port-colored waistcoat to his family home that evening. He wasn't as fastidious as Archer with his clothing, but he liked to be well turned out whenever he might be seen. People judged a man by how he presented himself; and with brothers as socially notorious as Grey and Archer, he needed to present all the positive impressions possible.

As usual, Havers already had the carriage waiting for him in front of the Barrington. Trystan considered having his own vehicle and driver to be his crowning achievement—next to the hotel, of course. The Barrington was magnificent, but there was something about having the freedom to come and go as he pleased, without having to hail a hackney and risk a stinking, poorly springed trip.

There was something about having his own driver and coach that said a man had means, that he was important. It was just another way to present himself to prospective business associates and instill confidence. He couldn't very well show up to a meeting on a bicycle.

"Ryeton House, my lord?" Havers asked as one of the bellmen opened the carriage door.

"Indeed," Trystan replied, removing his hat as he stepped up. "Make certain my brother's cook sends you home with supper and sweets for Margaret and the children."

"Aye, I will. Thank you, sir."

The lamp in the carriage was lit, bathing the interior in a golden light bright enough for Trystan to read by. Tonight he read not the paper but a ladies' fashion periodical. Not his usual preference, but the emporium would cater predominantly to the fairer sex and he would be remiss if he didn't educate himself on what they wanted to buy and thought important.

He was reading an oddly interesting article on the proper use and care of hairpieces when the carriage turned up the lane to his brother's house.

The entire family was waiting for him in the rose drawing room, including Bronte's husband, Alexander Graves, who would be a baronet or viscount, or something like that, one day. Trystan didn't care about the sandy-haired man's lineage—all he cared about was that Graves seemed completely in love with his sister.

Bronte had the same bright eyes as Archer, but hair as dark brown as his own. Though separated by a decade, he'd always enjoyed a special relationship with her, and he took pleasure in knowing that he was her favorite. She had always looked up to him and followed him around. At times that had been annoying, but after years of chasing after Grey and Archer, it was nice to have someone chase after him.

His sister rushed into his arms. Laughing, he hugged her, picked her up, and gave her a little twirl before putting her down. "I wished everyone was as happy to see me as you are, Bee."

"If you'll pick *me* up and whirl me around, I'll pretend," Archer offered drily, lifting a glass of wine to his lips.

"Too much work," Trystan replied, accepting the glass Rose offered him. "I might overexert myself."

The family laughed, and then drifted into the usual conversation about his work, society, upcoming social events, and added a touch of gossip. Through all this, Trystan said nothing about Vienne. His former relationship with her, and his annoyance at his brothers, was not something he wanted to share with his mother and sister—or sister-in-law. He waited until after dinner, when the ladies retired to the drawing room and left the men to their port and cigars.

He got right to the point. "What did you say to Vienne?" He directed the question at Grey.

His eldest brother rolled ash from the tip of his cigar into a crystal receptacle. "On which occasion?"

It was an old tactic the three of them had used since childhood: don't confess to anything until you are certain of what you are being accused. "After Archer opened his big mouth and told you I went to Chez Cherie's." Archer protested, saying his mouth was not big.

Trystan ignored him. "You paid Vienne a visit, did you not?"

"I may have," came the noncommittal reply.

Trystan slammed his glass of port on the table, causing both brothers to jump. "Do I interfere with your lives?" he demanded.

Archer and Grey exchanged bewildered glances. "No," they replied in unison.

"Right. Because you are grown men capable of getting yourselves out of whatever mess you've stepped in. What in the name of hell made either of you think you had any right to discuss not only my private life, but to then confront someone with whom I do business?"

"It was for your own good," Grey told him. "I don't want to see that woman hurt you again."

"That's my decision," he retorted. "Do you have any idea how humiliating it is, knowing that you confronted her—like I'm an idiot, or child incapable of taking care of myself?"

"See here," Archer straightened in his chair. "It was completely out of character for you to race off to a brothel so deep in your cups."

"You do it all the time."

Archer frowned. "But that's me."

Trystan practically growled at the pair of them.

It was Grey's turn: "Tryst, I'm not sure what she told you—"

"She told me nothing. Good lord, do you think I

don't pay attention? I'm not stupid, Grey. I saw how you looked at her at the party, and how she reacted. You bullied her, didn't you? Threatened her in some way?"

His brother squirmed ever so slightly—he was a duke, after all. It didn't do to show weakness. "I merely suggested that she be careful how she treats you."

Trystan closed his eyes. *Sweet lord.* What had he done to deserve this? "From here on out, both of you will stay away from Vienne. If you have to speak to her, you will leave me out of the conversation; and if you have any concerns about my behavior, you will take them up with me so that I might tell you both to bugger off and mind your own business before you go off and do something that not only *humiliates me*, but pisses me off as well!"

Grey and Archer stared at him. Their expressions would have been comical were he not so very, very angry. He hadn't known he was this angry until the words started pouring out, his emotions rising with every syllable.

Archer opened his mouth, "We—"

Grey stopped him with a hand on his shoulder. "Understood, little brother. Your life is your own."

Trystan nodded, trying to hide his surprise.

"Thank you. I also expect you to apologize to Vienne. A nice bouquet of lilies ought to do the trick—along with a heartfelt note."

Grey's face darkened. "Now see here—"

"*No.*" Trystan leaned forward, steadily holding his brother's steely gaze. "You stepped out of line, Grey. You used your title to threaten my business partner, and jeopardized a scheme in which I have invested a large chunk of my personal fortune. *Now* . . . be a big boy and fix it."

His brother looked positively murderous, but Trystan refused to turn away. He'd stared down men scarier than Grey, though he would never tell *His Grace* that. If he backed down now, Grey would think he'd acted rightly and would continue to believe he could interfere in Trystan's life as he saw fit.

"Might as well give in, Grey," Archer commented, pouring himself another glass of port. "He's got your stubbornness. Really, a bouquet of flowers and a nice card is a small price to pay. You've lowered yourself more than that in the past."

Grey's mouth twitched. "I suppose I have." He didn't immediately break his gaze away from Trystan. "Lillies, you say?"

It was all he could do not to sag in relief. Trystan grinned. "Yes, the brighter the better."

"I will take care of it tomorrow. Pour the boy another glass, Archer. Perhaps he'll tell us when he developed those huge bollocks."

Trystan chuckled. "They showed up shortly after I no longer had the two of you standing in front of me, trying to protect me from the big bad world."

Archer topped off Trystan and Grey's glasses and raised his own. "To the Kane family bollocks. May they be forever monstrous."

Trystan drank to that.

The wood step gave way as soon as Vienne brought her full weight down upon it. Only Trystan's quick reflexes prevented her entire leg from going through and being torn open by jagged splinters. He caught her about the waist, pulled her back . . . and she felt the hard press of his chest against her shoulder blades.

Heart hammering and gasping for breath, Vienne sagged against him—but only until her pride overrode the adrenaline surging through her veins. She was not a simpering, weak-kneed female who needed a man to protect her.

"Are you all right?" Trystan inquired, instantly releasing her when she made the slightest hint at pulling away. "Are you injured?"

"I feel a fool," she replied with a weak breath of

laughter, "but I am unhurt—thanks to you." Prideful she might be, but let it be known that she was not rude. Not usually.

Trystan crouched, brushing her skirts out of the way as he examined the broken step. They had both been there the day before, when the staircase was completed. Made from sturdy English oak, it was designed to bear the weight of a person almost a full five to six stone heavier than she.

"Someone tampered with this step," he said softly—for her ears alone.

"What? *No*. It is impossible." Her accent always became more pronounced in times of stress, and at this moment she sounded as though she should be sitting in a café in Paris. Still, she maneuvered her skirts to squat beside him, holding on to the railing so she would not fall. "Show me."

He gestured to the splintered wood. "Look how thin it is. A child would have broken it."

Vienne looked where he pointed and saw that it was indeed very thin—almost paperlike. On closer inspection, she could see that the wood had been stained to look like oak, but the color varied ever so slightly from the rest of the staircase.

"Why would someone do this?" she demanded.

Trystan raised his head and regarded her with eyes that—at this moment—were the color of brilliant sapphires, and deadly serious. "Either someone engineered a stupid prank, or it was done to deliberately hurt someone."

The way he looked at her made her uneasy. "Me?"

He shrugged. "Or me. Perhaps one of the workmen. Regardless, someone went through a hell of a lot of effort."

"You do not think the carpenter did this, do you?" What an awful thought. There might be God knows how many other hidden traps scattered throughout the site.

He shook his head. "No. He and his men take far too much pride in their work. This was done by someone skilled, but with mischief in mind."

"Why?" It didn't make sense to her.

Trystan stood and offered her his hand, which she took, allowing him to help her to her feet. "In case you haven't noticed, there are a lot of people out there who think emporiums are akin to the devil's work—designed to lead righteous women down a long path to ruination and corruption."

Vienne remembered that another proprietor of a emporium had been terrorized and an effigy was burned in the street by protestors. She had received several letters condemning her own project—both delivered to her personally and printed in the papers. But going so far as to actively promote injury was beyond her understanding. It made her wonder if any other incidents—such as the injured woodworker—were truly accidents at all.

"I think perhaps we might want to consider hiring more watchmen," she suggested.

Trystan nodded in agreement. "Firing the ones we have and hiring anew might be the best option. Our vandal might have paid one of them to turn a blind eye."

Indignation stiffened Vienne's spine. "Then we should question them. Immediately!"

Still holding her hand, Trystan led her down the stairs. They would tour the upper floor once the step had been repaired—a feat which she hoped could be accomplished sooner rather than later. "No one's going admit to taking a bribe, Vienne. You are as aware of that as I am. No, we will fire them and hire new security. I have several men on retainer who I trust impeccably. Would you care to meet them?"

She shook her head. "No. If you approve of them, I am certain they are above reproach."

He stopped suddenly and turned. She was on the bottom step, but the movement threw her off balance and she only barely managed to avoid falling into his arms again.

"Why, Madame La Rieux," he began, all affected

surprise and humility, "I do believe that was a compliment."

Vienne rolled her eyes at him as she stepped down, though should have stayed where she was and taken advantage of the extra height. Now she had to look up to meet his gaze. "You are a good judge of character, Trystan. We may have our . . . disagreements, but that will never be one of them."

He folded his arms over his chest—*when had it gotten so broad?*—and leaned one shoulder against the pale peach wall. "I suppose I'm such an excellent judge of character because I had the good taste to fall into your bed when you issued the invitation?"

The remark was so unexpected, Vienne felt heat rush to her cheeks—and, at that moment, despised him for it even as she gave him a certain respect for the well-placed barb. "Of course," she replied, covering her embarrassment . . . and hurt, which lay under a veneer of brazen flippancy. It was an affectation that had served her well in the past, especially in regard to Trystan.

But instead of retreating like a slapped little boy— as he had years before—he grinned. "There's the Vienne I know. For a moment I thought the matter with the stairs had you completely flummoxed."

The nerve! Vienne opened her mouth to tell him just what she thought of his assumption when one of the large double doors not far from them opened, revealing a man in the Barrington Hotel uniform. He carried a large picnic basket, and his face lit up when he saw Trystan. "Mr. Kane, sir. I have the luncheon you requested." He tipped his hat to Vienne. "Ma'am."

Vienne managed a tight smile in response. Trystan, however, greeted the young man as though they were old friends. "Thank you, James." He took the basket and slipped what appeared to be several pound notes into the servant's gloved hand. "Tell Havers to take you back to the hotel and then return for me here at five."

James grinned. "Yes, sir. Thank you, sir." He tipped his hat again at Vienne and then exited, leaving the two of them alone again—or as alone as two people could be in a building full of workers and craftsmen, all of whom were making noise while conveniently remaining out of sight.

"Care to join me?" Trystan asked, gesturing to the basket.

From where she stood, Vienne could smell the scents of warm, yeasty fresh bread mixed with sharp cheese and fresh fruit. Her stomach growled at a most unladylike volume—enough to take all the spite out of a woman. She smiled when he chuckled and said, "I'll take that as a yes."

They left the front foyer for a quieter locale—a mostly finished boutique, one they couldn't decide whether to sell ladies' hats and gloves or personal toiletries.

Trystan took a blanket from the top of the basket and opened it, spreading it on the gleaming floor with great flourish. Once again, he offered her his hand, this time to help her sit.

Vienne arranged herself as comfortably as she could in a corset and confining skirts, peeled off her gloves, and removed her hat. The feathers on the brim bobbed as she set it aside.

From the basket came an array of delicious fruits, cheeses, bread, and meat—enough to feed six people at least. The English were *such* gluttons. There was a bottle of wine as well.

She looked up to find Trystan watching her, eyes sparkling as a naughty grin curved his lips. "If I open this, you're not going to kiss me again, are you?"

Vienne arched a brow. "You should be so fortunate. No, I do believe I can control myself this time, monsieur."

He wasn't the least bit fazed. "Oh, there's the French." He popped the cork. "I must have struck a nerve."

"I'm dangerously close to striking you with my boot."

Trystan laughed then—a sound that cleaved right through to her heart. She had heard him laugh many times before, but she couldn't remember any of it sounding this lovely.

He poured rich red wine into two etched crystal glasses. "I did miss you on occasion, Vienne."

Only on *occasion*? "I will admit I have thought of you over the years." More than she was willing to admit.

He looked as though he hoped she might say more, but she had no idea what it was he wanted to hear. "Of course, I read about your successes in the papers. You must be very proud of yourself."

"Not really," he replied, setting the bottle aside. Much of the humor seemed to have drained out of him. "I'm proud of what I have accomplished, but I consider myself a work in progress, as the artists say."

"I suppose we all are," Vienne said before taking a sip of wine. It was divine. "A work in progress, that is. Each human, desperately trying to make something of him- or herself before meeting the maker. *As if* God cares how much money we have or how many buildings have our names on them."

"But we don't do it for God. Our achievements are for ourselves, aren't they? And to impress others?"

His words grabbed her heart and shoved it into

her throat. Did he suspect that proving herself—her worth—was what drove her? That some mornings it was pride and spite and little else that got her out of bed? Lord knew, there were plenty of things she'd done that she wasn't proud of, so she needed that spite, that anger, to push her forward, even though the people she wanted to prove herself to would never know what she had achieved.

Unless the Duke of Ryeton revealed her last name to the world. She didn't think that was a viable concern, however, not if the beautiful bouquet that had arrived from him that morning was any indication. Wondering what prompted Grey's apology, her gaze turned to Trystan. He was still unpacking the basket, seemingly unaware of the fact that in his presence, she was as uncertain as a mere girl. She wanted to impress *him*, and knew herself well enough to know that could only lead to trouble. He would be the last person to look at her and find anything extraordinary. Once, he had looked upon her as though she was a goddess, but she had taken good care of that.

"You're quiet all of a sudden," Trystan remarked, offering her a plate loaded with various offerings. "Something on your mind?"

Vienne accepted the food with murmured thanks. "Simply woolgathering, as you English put it. Nothing of importance."

He glanced at her as he filled a plate for himself, peering at her through the lock of hair that had fallen over his brow. "Everything you think is important, Vienne. You are the least capable person I know of being frivolous."

He said it with a generous amount of teasing in his tone, but it stung just a little—more than it ought. "I can be frivolous. I once bought six pairs of the same shoe in different colors just because I adored the look of them, yet I can't bring myself to wear half of them. I keep saving them for a special occasion."

Trystan grinned. "A frivolous person would wear them to clean out the stables, not treasure them."

"I've cleaned out a stable before, so I can honestly tell you I would never treat those shoes with such wanton disrespect."

He popped a grape into his mouth and said around it, "I can't imagine you shoveling horse manure."

Vienne smiled. "When I was a girl we had horses. Oh, how I loved to care for them! Such beautiful animals." Just the thought of them made her feel so warm inside. Why didn't she own horses now? Other than the ones that pulled her carriage, she didn't have any—not even one to ride. She missed riding.

When she looked at Trystan, she found him regarding her strangely—almost as if he fancied her a goddess again. Her traitorous heart spasmed in pleasure. No, she was not a good person at all to want his adoration. She would only crush him again. Trystan wasn't as hard as she was—wasn't as damaged. He was good and pure. There had been an innocence to him that attracted her; a sweetness that made her want to take everything he offered and give everything she had to him in return.

That was why she ended the affair. She had given everything once and paid a horrible price.

"What?" she demanded when the silence ran on too long and her thoughts began to stray to things best left alone.

He shook his head and plucked up a piece of cheese. "I suppose I have a hard time picturing you as a young girl."

"Why? Because I'm so old?" She certainly sounded like a crone; was behaving like one.

Trystan snorted. "Positively ancient. It's a wonder you haven't crumbled to dust on this very blanket. Don't be so foolishly reactionary, Vienne. It doesn't suit you."

"As if you know what suits me." That had a little more bite than she intended, but the damned man didn't seem to notice.

He simply took a bite of cheese. "I know you better than you think."

How many times had she heard that before? Every

man that ever shared her bed had made a similar declaration, so she shouldn't be surprised that Trystan felt the same. Truth be told, this somewhat disappointed her.

"Enlighten me," she invited. Hopefully he would fail miserably and she could go back to thinking that leaving him had been the right thing to do. She could stop wondering what would happen if she kissed him again. Would he reject her, or would he give in?

It irked her that he refused her last time. She was unaccustomed to being turned down.

Trystan stretched out on the blanket, leaning on his elbow as he reclined on his side. He picked up a piece of chicken from his plate and took a bite, chewed, and swallowed. He followed it with a drink of wine.

Vienne smiled. "Nothing to say?" Disappointment eased a little under the pleasure of being right.

His gaze locked with hers and the smile fell from her lips. "You are the youngest in your family. Most of your siblings are much older than you and spoiled you. You were taught to believe that everything you did was perfect, and then something happened, something that made you not so charming and wonderful anymore. That's why you keep reaching for a bigger and better goal. You're trying to show the world that you are still perfect."

Ice pooled at the base of Vienne's skull, freezing

her very blood. She couldn't find words to make him stop, couldn't make herself move or run away. She was helpless, pinned there by his unnerving gaze.

"I'm not certain how you came to believe that men were for little more than entertainment and to be used as stepping stones to get where you want to go, but my guess is that someone abused your trust very badly and taught you that very valuable lesson. Now you prefer lovers who are older and only want you for how you make them feel, or younger ones who want you as a sexual trophy. That's all right because you have your uses for them as well— How am I doing thus far?"

Vienne looked away, her appetite suddenly gone. "You paint a very unflattering portrait, Mr. Kane."

"You weren't a trophy to me, Vienne. I would have laid down my life for you."

If anyone else had said it, she would have laughed at the melodramatic pronouncement, but when the words were on his lips, they only served to fill her with a deep sense of guilt and regret. "I would not have appreciated the sacrifice, surely you know me to be that selfish at least."

"Yes, I do. I also know that my turning you down that night in your office has been like a thorn in your paw ever since it happened. You don't have no said to you very often, do you?"

Anger made it easy to look him in the eye. "That is why you did it, is it not? To teach me a lesson? So you could be the man who turned down Vienne La Rieux?"

His smile was grim, to say the least. "I turned you down because if anything romantic does happen between us, you will be sober and it will be my decision."

Vienne snorted in disgust. "Trust me, Trystan, nothing *romantic* will ever happen between us."

Her mockery brought a dark stain to his cheeks—one that both pleased her and made her want to take the words back. "It was simply a figure of speech, Vienne. I know you treat everyone in your life like a business transaction. That's why you're so good at screwing people in bed, and out. I paid for it last time we slept together; I have no illusions about getting it for free this time."

How had their pleasant lunch, their weeklong truce, disintegrated into *this*? "I beg your pardon, Trystan. Obviously, you continue to harbor much resentment toward me. If you will excuse me, I will return to work rather than take this unfortunate conversation any further." She managed to get to her feet, though the effort was far from graceful. She couldn't stop herself from informing him, "I am not the same woman I was back then, and I apologize for hurting you, but I cannot apologize for ending our relationship. It was best for both of us."

"It was best for you," he shot back as she turned to walk away. "You've always been top-notch at placing the blame on someone else, but I'm not the same boy I was back then either, Vienne."

She hesitated on the threshold—chest tight. Slowly, she turned her head to glance at him one last time over her shoulder. The harshness of his features and the coldness in his eyes tore at her insides like sharpened claws.

"No," she replied, not bothering to hide her disappointment. "You certainly are not."

Chapter 6

It seemed Trystan was the Kane male who now owed Vienne an apology, only a bouquet of lilies wasn't going to do the job. Quite frankly, he wasn't quite certain what to do to tell her how sorry he was.

The purpose of becoming her partner was to make her look at him as a man, but he had acted poorly—as had she!—and now she looked at him as though she didn't like the man he had become. Of course, she would prefer the more malleable boy, but he had behaved like a dolt, and for that he was truly repentant.

Vienne was the kind of woman accustomed to receiving gifts from men of her acquaintance, which made it even more difficult for him. He had to get her something she would like, that would prove his contrition. But it had be something she could enjoy for years ahead. Jewelry was too cold—any man could buy jewelry.

And then inspiration struck.

It took a couple of days to organize. Vienne was

avoiding him like the plague, and had given herself the task of letting their current guards go while he hired new ones, so it wasn't difficult to make arrangements without her catching wind of his plans. He had to admit to being fairly impressed with himself when everything fell into place, but a queer sense of anxiety claimed him as well. Would she like it? Was it too much?

He knocked on the front door of Saint's Row early Friday morning, and was immediately shown to Vienne's office. He might have known she'd be up already. Quite frankly, he wasn't certain when the woman actually slept.

She sat behind her desk dressed in a rust-colored silk day-gown that brought out the creaminess of her skin and the fire in her hair. She looked up as he walked in; her expression neutral, eyes guarded. "Trystan. Good morning. I did not expect to see you until this afternoon at the construction site."

Trystan turned the brim of his beaver hat around in his hands. "Yes, well . . . I have something for you."

She arched a brow—and for a moment he was one and twenty, dry-mouthed and uncertain in her cool, sophisticated presence. "A gift? That isn't necessary."

She wasn't impressed, just as he had thought. Gifts were little more than currency to her, and she clearly suspected him of trying to buy her forgiveness and good favor once again.

"I know it wasn't necessary," he replied. "But I thought when combined with my apology for the way I spoke to you the other day, you might see your way to forgiving a thoughtless dolt."

She eyed him warily—suspiciously even. "You seem somewhat agitated. Have you discovered who sabotaged the steps?"

"No. No one seems to have seen anything. The carpenter, as you can imagine, was horrified . . . I'm a tad bit nervous as to whether or not you'll like my gift."

Vienne leaned back in her chair, still watching him. "Because you think it may not be enough to secure my forgiveness? You needn't have bought me anything for that, Trystan. You only had to ask."

"I'm asking." He held out his hand. "But that's not why I'm agitated. I sincerely want you to have this."

She opened her arms in an expansive gesture. "So, give it to me."

He wiggled the fingers of the hand extended to her. "You have to come with me. It's outside."

Ginger brows jumped. "*Mon Dieu*, it's not a carriage is it?"

Trystan smiled at the horror in her tone. "No, it's

not a carriage." Although now she really had him anxious. "Will you please just come with me?"

Hesitantly, she took his hand and rose to her feet. She dropped his fingers as though there were hot. "Lead on."

They made the short journey to the entryway in silence. Trystan thought for certain she could hear the pounding of his heart, it was so loud in his own ears. "Close your eyes," he commanded as he closed his hand around the doorknob.

An exasperated sigh slipped from between her peach-hued lips. "Trystan . . ."

"Please."

Another sigh, but she did as he asked and closed her eyes. He kept his gaze on her as he opened the door, and tried not to notice the dark circles beneath her eyes in the bright daylight. She was working too hard.

"Keep them closed and give me your hands."

She did, letting him steer her out onto the shallow stone steps. His gift was right before them in the drive. "All right. Open them."

He actually held his breath as her lashes fluttered open, and watched as her carefully guarded expression fell away, revealing a shocked wonder. "Oh." Her voice was a squeak. "Oh, *mon Dieu. Quelle surprise.*"

Trystan grinned. "She's yours. A year old, from Irish racing stock."

Hand to her mouth, Vienne slowly descended the low steps to the paved drive, where her surprise stood.

Watching her, Trystan knew he'd made the right decision in purchasing the beautiful chestnut mare whose shiny coat was an almost perfect match for Vienne's dress. Never in their brief affair, or in all the time he'd known her, had he ever seen Vienne look so unguardedly happy. The horse had been worth every penny.

"Pretty isn't she?" he asked dumbly, just so he could get some sort of response from her. She just stood there in front of the animal, petting it like she could not believe it was real. The young groom holding the reins stood smiling, Vienne's joy so infectious.

"She's *beautiful*." The word came out as a sigh. Finally, she glanced over her shoulder at him. "Wherever did you get her?"

"Jack knows the breeder. He found her for me and I had her brought over." He watched as Vienne moved around the young horse, examining her from tooth to tail. She couldn't seem to keep from touching the animal, nor did she seem the least bit aware of anyone else around her.

Back at the horse's head once more, Vienne seemed to have proven to herself that the mare was real, and fully turned to face him. "How did you know?"

He didn't pretend to not understand, just so he could hear her say how much this meant to her. He could see that in her bright, wide eyes.

"The other day, your face lit up when you talked about having horses." He descended the steps to come stand beside her. "I could tell that you missed it."

Vienne ran a long hand down the mare's velvety neck. "I do, but I haven't the time to care for her."

That was just foolishness. "Make time. Vienne, life is more than business and commerce and making money. You must make time for the things you enjoy or life becomes rather pointless."

She glanced at him from the corner of her eye. "Perhaps I enjoy making money."

Trystan smiled. "Riding this beautiful girl won't cost you a cent. Just think of how many potential customers and business associates you might meet while out for a ride."

Vienne turned her head, but not before he caught a glimpse of the smile that curved her lips. "She is a beauty."

"You like her?"

"I love her." She sighed. "But Trystan, I cannot accept . . ."

"You have to. I refuse to return her. She is yours, end of argument. In fact, we're going to go riding tomorrow morning. I'll meet you here at nine."

Laughing, Vienne turned her head, stopping Trystan's heart dead in his chest. "You are the most stubborn, overbearing man."

He grinned and shrugged. "Part of my charm, I'm told. So, am I forgiven for being such a bore?"

She nodded, once again stroking the pretty mare. This time he saw her blink back moisture from her lashes. "Yes, Lord Trystan, I dare say you are."

The following morning, Vienne was up and ready to go when Trystan arrived atop a beautiful gray gelding. Her horse was saddled and waited for her out front of the large Palladian building that was both club and home to her.

Trystan was dressed in a dark gray coat and dove trousers with matching top hat. He looked very dapper. Very masculine. A smile curved her mouth at the sight of him, and damned if she could do anything to prevent it.

The sly dog had wormed his way into her good graces with his wonderful, thoughtful—and expensive—gift. And when he had left without expecting anything in return . . . well, her regard for him grew. He hadn't asked for a thing, not even a kiss. Only demanded that she take time to ride the mare she'd yet to name.

Once upon a time she might have suspected him of trying to coerce her into ignoring her business, so that he might take over. But he didn't seem interested in running things; he seemed to legitimately want to be her partner. Why? After how she had treated him and tossed him aside, why would he want anything to do with her? It boggled the mind.

"Good morning, Madame La Rieux. Might I say that you are looking splendid this fine morning."

Vienne blushed like an innocent schoolgirl— something she was fairly certain she had never been, at least not for a very long time. "Thank you, Lord Trystan. You look very well yourself." Though, she'd wager he took considerably less time getting ready than she had. Good Lord, she'd gone through three outfits before finally deciding on the moss green riding costume she now wore. Thankfully she had listened to her modiste when the woman told her she had to have at least four choices for riding, even though she had no horse.

One of the grooms from her stables—where many of her patrons often left their carriages—was there to help her mount. It had been a long time, but her body remembered how to get into the saddle and arrange itself once there, hooking her knee around the horn so she wouldn't fall. With the reins in her gloved hands, she felt as though only days had passed since she last rode.

Saint's Row was located closer to Covent Garden than Hyde Park, so it was that neighborhood to which they kept. No one paid them much mind, despite their fine dress. Most people in the neighborhood knew Vienne by sight; and if they thought seeing her on horseback was strange, none of them let on.

"Lovely morning, isn't it?" Trystan remarked.

Vienne smiled. The English and their bizarre small talk. Always with the weather. "Yes. It is quite fine, though I suppose we shall have rain later."

"Wouldn't be England if we didn't," he replied with a quick grin. He really had become a truly striking man. He'd always had a certain charm, but now he seemed positively roguish.

She'd always had a soft spot for rogues. And puppies.

But Trystan was not for her. She had known this years ago when the sight of him set her heart pounding. No, he was a danger to her—and if she was smart, she would keep him at arm's length and not do anything to jeopardize their friendship. Now that Sadie was with Jack, Vienne didn't see her friend as often; and other than Indara, she had no other friends. It was nice to count Jack among the pitifully small number.

And it was nice to be out of the club, doing something that wasn't business related, though she would never admit that aloud.

It didn't mean that she couldn't discuss business, not when it was the glue that bound them.

"I have given some thought to these incidents at the construction site," she announced.

His horse was in step with hers, his leg close enough that she could reach out and touch it if she were so inclined. "What have you deduced?"

"Based on my memory, they seem to have started right around the time you arrived back in London."

She literally saw him stiffen. His back snapped rigid, his jaw tightened. "Are you accusing me of being behind the mischief?"

"Do not be so ridiculous," she reprimanded with a scowl. "Why would I do such a thing?"

He glanced at her, eyes as cold as ice. "When I first approached you as a partner, you accused me of wanting to ruin you. Perhaps you believe that still."

She snorted. "Honestly, Trystan. How can you know me so well and not at all? If I truly distrusted you, do you believe we would be here right now?"

The man actually had the nerve to think about it. "I suppose not."

"Of course not." Truly, she was frowning so deeply she feared the furrows might mar her brow forever. "Idiot man."

He made a choking noise. "What did you expect me to think when you say something like that?"

Perhaps he was right. If he had said the same to her she might have acted a little prematurely as well. "I did not mean to offend you. Do you want to hear my theory or not?"

"Oh, there's more? Does it involve me creeping around behind your back, trying to destroy your reputation? Perhaps I might despoil a few virgins."

For some reason the notion made her chuckle. "I believe despoiling virgins is my job." She shot him a meaningful look, reminding him of how she had done that very thing to him in the privacy of her bedchamber many years ago.

To her surprise he flushed a deep, dark red. "Done a lot of that, have you?"

Vienne's smile faded. She had wounded him, embarrassed him. "No," she confessed. "Only once."

Trystan kept his gaze focused on the street ahead, his color still very high, his shoulders stiff. "It must have been very tedious for you."

"*Au contraire,*" she murmured, just loud enough to be heard over the morning bustle. "It was very much the opposite. I have a great deal of pride in knowing

I was the first woman to bed you, Trystan. Though I would never humiliate you by advertising the fact."

His head turned toward her. "Why?"

She knew exactly which part of her statement he questioned. "Because you have become so very successful. I hear ladies talk of you all the time—how you would be such a good husband, or lover. I rather like knowing I have some responsibility for it."

He swore and looked away. It occurred to her that she might tell him how she sometimes thought of their first night together and how sweet he'd been, how gentle. No man had ever touched her as though she were made of glass or gold. No one but young Trystan Kane who had cared more about pleasing her than his own pleasure, who apologized for climaxing before her and did all that his youthful body could to make it up to her.

But then he would know that every man she'd been with since had been compared in some way to him, and she wasn't about to make herself that vulnerable, not when she knew he didn't want her anymore. Her feminine pride could only take so much; and knowing he wasn't attracted to her, when she found him even more captivating than she had years ago, was a slap she no doubt deserved but regretted all the same.

She could control her desire for him, however. Her

attraction would not interfere with their business relationship. Men were not so skilled at such things, so perhaps it was for the best that he no longer saw her in a romantic light. He would want someone younger, someone from a better family who preferably still had her hymen intact. Primogeniture was so very important to his class, unlike her own.

Of course, in any social sphere, a man could make love to whomever he wanted without any ramifications, but if a woman did she could find herself tossed out with no friends and no family. That was a lesson she had learned in a very, very painful way when she gave her heart and body to the wrong man.

She would not think of it. Nothing good ever came out of living in the past.

"Anyway," she said, clearing her throat, "I meant to imply that perhaps the mischief at the construction site is directly aimed at you. Do you have any enemies who would like to see this venture fail?"

Trystan pinched the bridge of his nose between his thumb and forefinger. "Not that I know of. I haven't exactly built a career out of being ruthless, you know. Taking chances, yes; but never advantage of others."

"Are you certain? No one upon whom you skimmed the fringes of good faith? Or bent the rules, such as with me?"

She thought she heard him laugh as he shook his head. "No, Vienne. You are my first and only dupe."

She smiled sweetly. "I'm honored."

His lips quirked, and when she let her smile stretch into a full grin and laughter followed, the air filled with his laughter as well. People turned to look in their direction, smiling in response to their unfettered mirth.

He was right, it was a lovely morning.

There hadn't been anymore "mishaps" at the construction site since the hiring of new guards, a fact that made Trystan's nightly sleep better. He didn't believe Vienne's theory that the accidents might have more to do with him than the emporium. It just didn't make sense.

He also slept better knowing that things were good between them. Oh, he still felt as though he had something to prove to Vienne; wouldn't be content until he knew that in her eyes he was her equal, not just a man. But they *had* reached a truce. In fact, it seemed as though they might actually stand a chance at becoming friends—something he had never been with a female who wasn't family. It was refreshing, talking to a woman who knew as much, if not more, about certain aspects of commerce. At times he educated her as well, bringing a balance to their relationship that he was certain only he felt.

Anything else was impossible, and he daren't let himself entertain the possibility. As tempting as Vienne was, he didn't think she was capable of love. Oh, she could feel it if she let herself, but that was just it—she wouldn't allow it. She had spent too many years using her wiles and body to manipulate men to get her way that he doubted she knew how not to. He didn't know what had happened to make her distrust and despise his sex so very much, but he'd like to slap the mouth of the man responsible.

Still, he and Vienne shared an energy that was contagious. Once one of them hit upon an idea for the emporium, the other surely followed with a dozen more suggestions built off that one. The various boutiques, especially those on the ground floor, were beginning to come together nicely; several of them were already painted and only needed trim and plasterwork on the ceiling. Vienne's detailed sketches of the space were slowly coming to life, and it was amazing to see—especially when she incorporated his suggestions as well.

He was growing accustomed to spending much of his days in her company, and they often took at least one meal together—most of which was spent discussing business. It appeared Vienne was enjoying his company as much as he was enjoying hers.

They went riding together as well: he on his horse, Domino, and she atop Versailles, the name she'd chosen for the pretty red mare he'd given her.

But spending so much time with her meant he had to witness how other men were with her—and how she behaved with them. He knew he had no right to feel any sort of irritation, but he did. It bothered him when other men watched her, nudged each other when she wasn't looking. It bothered him even more when she flirted with them, because she talked and joked with them in a manner far different from the one she affected with him.

Most of all it bothered him that there were no women about for him to flirt with so she could see. When he had first arrived back in London, he'd flirted a little with Sadie, Jack's wife—nothing disrespectful, but just enough that he knew it had bothered Vienne. That's what he wanted to do right now. He could only hope that she would be half as peeved.

It wasn't that he still had feelings for her, or had developed any new ones. It wasn't. He just despised being made to feel so left out while she basked in attention and rubbed his face in it. As though they were having some sort of popularity competition! He *hated* seeing those men act as though they had a chance with her. Most of them didn't, but they talked as though they did. Vienne only heard what insipid wit they used on her, while he had to hear what they truly thought—and there was little eloquence involved.

He almost clocked one of the bastards when he heard the man say what a good "ride" he thought Vienne would be. But it wasn't his business, and Vienne would not appreciate him defending her honor at the cost of good workmen. She was odd that way.

Though, what was fine behavior for her was not for him, it seemed. Earlier that day, Jack and Sadie had stopped by the site with Sadie's friend Eve Elliot in tow. Lady Eve was to be married the following week to Bramford Gregory, a man everyone expected to become prime minister one day.

"Lady Eve, you grow more and more lovely every time I see you," Trystan said as he bowed over her gloved hand. It was a sincere compliment, because the pretty blonde did seem much altered lately. There was a confidence in her that hadn't been there before.

Eve smiled prettily, taking his remark for what it was, but not quite so seriously. "How very kind of you, Lord Trystan."

He had looked up to see Vienne arch a brow at him. "What?" he demanded as their guests drifted away to inspect some of the more recent construction.

"She is an engaged woman."

"I'm aware of that."

"Then do you not think you should be respectful of that and not flirt so brazenly with her?"

Trystan gawked at her. "What I said was a compliment, not flirtation."

Vienne had the nerve to roll her eyes at him. "Please. Men never say such things without the hope of it leading elsewhere. Or women for that matter."

He folded his arms across his chest. "Vienne, if that were true, I would accuse you of trying to bed every man on our staff."

"I never flirt with the married ones," she shot back. What kind of answer was that? So he thought she was trying to bed every man she flirted with?

"Lady Eve is not yet married and I was *not* flirting. I have no desire for her in that way."

"Hmm," was her only reply before she walked away to join the others. Trystan could only stare after her in a kind of shock. The woman was mad; that was the only explanation. How dare she accuse him of flirting when that was *all* she *ever* did!

Later, after Jack, Sadie, and Lady Eve had left, he happened to turn his head and see Vienne talking to a young workman of perhaps two and twenty. The handsome youth hung on her every word, trapped in her seductive web as she leaned toward him and placed her hand on his chest as she spoke. The lad looked positively forlorn when she removed her fingers a few seconds later.

Mad, yes. And she had balls the size of an omnibus. *Damnation.* She was far more of a flirt than he was. And he was sick and tired of having to watch it.

Trystan waited until Vienne flitted off to attend another matter before approaching the workman. He helped the boy with a strip of baseboard, and held the length of gleaming oak while the boy hammered it in place.

Afterward, when he caught the young man watching Vienne, who was in another boutique across the way, Trystan said, "That Madame La Rieux is an incredible woman, isn't she?"

"Yes, sir." The boy was positively enthusiastic with his response. Foolish git.

"Smart, driven, beautiful. Hellion too." He leaned in conspiratorially: "Did you know she *shot* her last lover?"

The young man's face turned pale. "No, sir. I did not."

"Really?" His surprise was real. Where did this boy live, under a rock? "It was in all the papers."

"I don't often read the papers, sir."

"Ah. Apparently the young man displeased her by not doing what she told him to do, so she popped him one in shoulder. He might never regain full use of his arm."

To a man as dependant on physical labor as this one, that was a sobering thought.

"You're a braver man than I to flirt with her," Trystan went on. "Have a care, though, Giles. I'd hate to see you plugged full of lead as well."

"You may depend on me, sir."

The shaken young man turned his back on Vienne and returned to his work. Trystan walked away with a satisfied smile.

Chapter 7

"Now that you are back in England, it is time you began looking for a wife."

Trystan set down his knife and fork, wiped his mouth with his napkin, and turned his attention to his luncheon companion—his mother. They were sitting at his private table in the Barrington dining room. Thankfully there weren't any other diners sitting close enough to hear their conversation.

"Mama, I'm very busy right now. There was another mishap at the construction site last night. One of our guards was badly injured."

Trystan and Vienne had to offer higher wages to keep workmen from quitting because now they were afraid to be on site. The building was close to completion and they couldn't afford to have everything come to a grinding halt.

Besides, it's obviously what the culprit wanted. In fact, Trystan had been a little late to luncheon because he'd been in a meeting with a private-inquiry agent. They needed to find the person or persons responsible for these "accidents" and put an end to this mischief before someone was killed. Vienne had been beside herself when she heard about the workman—she was known for taking good care of her employees, and felt as though she had personally allowed the man to be hurt.

Trystan hadn't the heart to tease her about the "good care" she'd given the footman she shot.

"Ridiculous," his mother told him. "Honestly, darling, you spend far too much time working. You need to find a nice girl who will divert you from all of that. It's not as though you need the money."

He didn't remind her that one of the reasons his family was so bloody rich was because he had made smart investments on their behalf. "Why don't you pester Archer about this? He's older than I, and still very much a bachelor."

His mother smiled slightly as she cut a small piece of duck. "Archer is more of a project than I care to take on at this moment. Nevertheless, he has no shortage of female attention. You, on the other hand, rarely attend important social functions."

"I'd hardly call a piano recital by Lady Willoughby's talentless daughters an *important* social function."

She gave him that frown that had always meant

that he was trying her patience. "Any event that puts you in the path of eligible young ladies is important. Goodness, Trystan. You are thirty years old now. A man. It is time you set up your own household."

Trystan was so astounded that she had called him a man, for a moment he could only sit and stare at her as she ate. "I'm not for sale, mother."

She smiled—determinedly. "Think of it as searching for a business partner with whom you can spend the rest of your days."

Why did a vision of Vienne fill his mind at those words? Surely he didn't still have feelings for her? Attraction, yes. That had never gone away, but romantic feelings? *No.* He respected her, liked her even, but as for romance. . .

Dear God! He had feelings for Vienne La Rieux. Had he no bloody sense? When had he gone from wanting her respect—wanting to make her see him as an equal—to wanting her to see him as an attractive man? This would not do. It must be as his mother suggested. Had he been in the company of other females on a regular basis, he would not feel this way about Vienne. It was only because they spent so much time together.

"Fine," he said, hoping he sounded resigned rather than desperate. "I'll start accepting more invitations. Does that please you?"

Judging from his mother's smug expression, it did indeed. Her blue eyes sparkled. "Excellent. I took the liberty of accepting an invitation to Lord Angelwood's annual End of Season Ball on your behalf. I will attend with Bronte and Alexander, but expect to see you there no later than eleven."

At least Angelwood was an intelligent man, and his wife was no less impressive. They were certain to have filled their guest list with decently entertaining people. Perhaps he might talk up the emporium, which Vienne wanted to call La Maison de Monde. Trystan thought the name and the French pronunciation might not work in their favor. After all, this wasn't just a clothing boutique; and they needed a name that screamed opulence without being so pretentious they scared potential customers away.

Potential customers one might meet at a ball.

"I'll be there, but I will choose my own dance partners. *Understood?*"

Still smiling like a fat tom that had just landed a plump mouse, his mother nodded. "Of course. I know of several young ladies whom I would love for you to meet."

Internally, Trystan shuddered and berated himself for not wording their "contract" more carefully. Of course his mother would allow him to pick his own partners—from the eligible ladies she shoved in front of him.

It was going to be a damn long night.

From time to time, because of her own wealth and somewhat eccentric lifestyle—there were those who called it scandalous—Vienne found herself invited to certain societal functions that might normally be closed to an unmarried woman of dubious virtue. But Vienne was a careful woman—she never slept with married men or young men still clinging to their mamas. She was discreet, and her freedom made her the envy of many women. Hence, there would always be those dying to be in her company and those who would rather die than be in the same room with her.

Her business relationship with Lord Angelwood, and her respectful relationship with Lady Angelwood, had gotten her an invitation to their annual ball signifying the closing of the season. It was August and society had already thinned. It wouldn't be long before those with homes in the country abandoned the city altogether, and the rest would wait for invitations to house parties and hunting parties that could sometimes last until late into the fall.

Normally she enjoyed Lord and Lady Angelwood's hospitality, but tonight she was in decidedly poor temperament. And it didn't take much to ascertain why.

Trystan Kane was there, looking gorgeous and dancing with every predatory young miss who hadn't yet managed to land a husband this Season.

"Time is running out little birdies," she muttered into her champagne glass. Would they resort to gouging each other's eyes out to win his attention? Perhaps . . . If plumage didn't do the trick. Every one of them was dressed at the height of fashion—and mostly in the delicate pastels favored by virgins.

Was it low of her to want to swoop in and parade her own bronze-swathed self around them like a true bird of prey? It was certainly foolish. She would look like a vulture picking at scraps. She'd never had to fight for a man's attention, and she wasn't about to now.

Though, why it should bother her so much she didn't quite fathom. Of course, Trystan would want to start looking for a wife. Of course, he would pick some pretty young thing from his own class. She would be able to tease him about it tomorrow when they met for breakfast.

"You look like you swallowed something foul," came a voice from behind her. She turned and found Sadie standing there, as usual dressed like a peacock in a stunning gown of purple and orange. Her thick dark hair was swept up, set atop her head, and little bits framed her pale face. Large multicolored eyes sparkled.

Vienne shrugged. "It annoys me, watching these young women vie for the attention of one man."

Her friend stepped closer. "Is that a generalization or specifically because the man in question is Trystan Kane?"

She made a face—and threw an eye roll in for good measure. "Of course not. You know I despise the whole marriage-mart ritual in which you English engage."

"I'm not English," was her friend's cool reply. "No more than you."

Vienne deflated a little, though she made certain not to show it. Sadie was her dearest friend and now she'd gone and insulted her. "Forgive me, *mon amie*. I am a proper bitch this evening."

Sadie stepped closer. "Which takes us back to my earlier question. Is it because of Trystan Kane?"

She could lie. She should lie. "Look at him. He is in his prime, is he not?" As she spoke, she watched as he went through the steps of a quadrille with a particularly pretty partner. "I am past mine, Sadie."

"Don't be such an idiot. You are beautiful and could pass for a women ten years younger."

Vienne tried to smile, and realized too late how

sad and pathetic it must appear. "It hardly matters. He should find someone to marry. He should find love if he can."

"My friend, you deserve to find love as well."

She shook her head. "I do not believe so. To find love you must first be willing to give it. I am too distrustful to offer anyone my poor wizened heart. Besides, men do not want experienced women. They want sweet virgins who will do their bidding. I would not suit as an English wife." Then she pushed some real feeling into her smile. "Perhaps you know of an Irishman who might not mind a free-thinking woman?"

Sadie linked her arm through hers. Vienne patted her friend's hand. "I'm not sure there's even an Irishman alive who could handle the likes of you," her friend remarked in her familiar teasing tone.

Vienne tore her eyes away from the dancers and took a sip of champagne. "Enough about my maudlin thoughts. How are you, dearest? You must be very happy to have his lordship back from Ireland."

Sadie made a face. "It will take a while for me to get used to his being an earl . . . but yes, I am glad to have him with me."

"How long before you allow yourself to be a countess?" Though Jack and Sadie had married years ago, it had been a pagan ceremony, so there was some dispute as to whether they were married or not.

"He's asked me to marry him, and I will, but I want to take things slowly this time. We rushed into it last time, and I want to be certain this is what we both want."

Vienne chuckled. "Coward."

To her credit Sadie laughed. "Fine words coming from you, missus. If you're so brave, why don't you saunter on over to Lord Trystan and ask him to dance. Show those insipid little girls how a real woman behaves with a man she wants."

"Oh no. I'll never be invited anywhere ever again if I make such a spectacle of myself."

Sadie scowled. "What spectacle? Lady Gosling's husband is expected to die before morning and she's here."

That was true. The lady's husband took a nasty fall the day before and hadn't recovered. "Yes, but everyone knows she despises the man—he is a monster. People expect her to be outrageous."

"People expect you to do whatever you want. Seriously, Vienne. You and Trystan are business partners; it would not be odd for the two of you to dance. You must dance with someone. I will not stand by and watch you play the wallflower another moment."

Sadie was right, of course. She usually was when it came to giving advice to others. "I should have you read my tea leaves," Vienne remarked. "Perhaps then I will know what the future holds."

"Your future holds a wee dance with a handsome man. Now go."

Vienne laughed as her friend practically pushed her toward the dance floor. Trystan wasn't dancing at the moment. She could walk right up to him and ask him for the next waltz. It would be scandalous, of course, but fun.

Yes! Why shouldn't she have a little fun? She gave her empty glass to an obliging footman and made her way toward Trystan with a determined stride. He turned to grin at her as she approached, breaking off his conversation with a lovely young girl. Vienne smiled back.

"Madame La Rieux," he said when she reached him—the debutante had been smart enough to take her leave prior to this. "I was just about to come looking for you."

"Were you, Lord Trystan? Whatever for?"

"To ask you to dance, of course. Will you do me the honor?"

So much for behaving outrageously by asking him. "I would be delighted."

They only had to stand there a moment or two, awkwardly looking at one another and not talking, before the orchestra began to play the scheduled waltz. Trystan smiled and offered his arm, which she happily took.

She didn't remember ever dancing with him before, something she regretted the moment he took her into his arms and began to move. He was a wonderful dancer—one of those rare people with a natural grace. It was confidence. He knew exactly where to step, instinctively knowing he would not trod upon her toes nor she upon his. His gloved palm was warm, but not humidly so, against her back. And even with their gloves on, Vienne fancied she could feel the flesh of his fingers entwined with her own. Her heart began to beat a little faster.

"You dance well," she admitted.

He inclined his head. "As do you. A pity we never tried this before."

"I was just thinking the same."

"Of course, we had more intimate pursuits on our minds at the time." He flashed a charming grin.

"Trystan!" She had to keep her voice low so no one would hear. Still, she looked around to make certain no one had. "You should not say such things in public."

"You know, for a modern woman you can be quite the prude," he informed her, eyes sparkling with humor. "Everything we've ever done together we've done well, Vienne. Dancing should be no different."

With that he whirled her around so fast she laughed in joy—which *did* gather a few glances.

"You are right, sir. But then, you usually are. I should expect no less."

"I was wrong to let you leave me."

Her heart came to a sharp halt before quickly coming to life once more. "You couldn't have stopped me."

"No?" He eyed her intently. It seemed he could strip the layers of fear and artifice from her with frightening ease. "I think I might have, had I not been too wounded to try."

"I never meant to hurt you."

"Yes. You did." This was said without malice. "How else could you make certain you were rid of me?"

She opened her mouth to protest, but nothing came out.

"It's all right," he informed her. "I understand it so much better now."

"You do?"

He twirled her again. "I do. I've enjoyed working with you, Vienne. Perhaps we can do it again sometime."

Why did she feel as though he was talking about more than the emporium? "We're not done yet, sir."

He smiled—lips in a slow, seductive curve that

unfurled a sweet ache deep inside her. "No, we are not. Not at all."

The only thing Trystan despised more than having to dance with every debutante his mother tossed at him was watching Vienne dance with other men.

After his waltz with Vienne, Trystan wanted her for his partner the rest of the evening—an impossibility in many ways. It would bring scandalous whispers down upon both of them, make him look rude to other ladies, and make her appear loose. Still, he wished for it.

Every time he saw her with another man, or his partner trod on his toes, Trystan's ill temper increased. When supper was announced it was a welcome reprieve—except that he saw Vienne being led into the supper room by a widowed viscount who was said to be trolling for a new mistress. Trystan himself was stuck escorting a lovely young woman whose name he could not remember. She was a sweet girl, but had so little experience with the world that conversation was torture.

After supper he danced with two more similar girls before finally breaking and informing his mother he was done. She was to introduce no one else to him.

She merely smiled. "There is no one else, darling. Now, who are you going to ask for a second dance?"

He might have snarled at her then, before turning his back on her and walking away. He made it to one of the small retiring rooms—a comfortable space where partygoers might take a break from the festivities—and fell into one of the overstuffed leather armchairs.

"You look completely done in," came a familiar, French-kissed voice.

Trystan smiled, but he did not open his eyes. "Madame La Rieux, are you following me?"

"But of course," came the sarcasm-laden reply. "I used my powers of mind reading to determine where you would go, and conspired to be here before you."

He opened his eyes and saw her sitting in a chair similar to his near the window. He hadn't heard her walk by, so it made sense that she had already been sitting there, in the shadows, when he came in.

"Which means I essentially am following you."

She smiled, teeth flashing white in the dim light. "I would have it no other way, *n'est-ce pas*?"

He had to grin. "No, I don't imagine you would. Tell me, why are you in here? You seem to have been very popular this evening."

"Ugh," she replied in a most unladylike and endearing fashion. "Do you know I have been propositioned three times this evening? *Three!* Two were by married men. Degenerates."

"Who were they?" he asked with false breeziness. He would like to have a private word with each of them.

"Bah, they are of no importance. I told them I was not looking for a new association, and one of them accused me—"

She didn't continue, and he turned toward her, lifting his head from the back of the chair, saying, "*Of what?*"

She looked away. He couldn't see if she was flushed or not. "Of being involved with you. Romantically."

Romantically had not been the word used by said gentlemen, Trystan would bet on it. "Let them think what they want, if it means they will leave you alone."

She smiled faintly. "Too bad we cannot do the same with your debutantes, no? We could hide behind each other for a little while."

"You shouldn't have to hide, Vienne. Stars are so much more brilliant when they are allowed to shine. Just like gemstones."

He thought he heard her breath catch, but the orchestra started up a lively tune at the same moment in the ballroom and he couldn't be certain.

Silence fell. There was nothing but muted music and chatter and the sound of their breathing.

"Since we're here, shall we play a game of something?" he asked. "I'm not ready to return to the party just yet. There should be a pack of cards in the drawer in front of you." He rose from his chair and approached her, bringing the lamp with him rather than bothering to ignite any of the wall sconces.

It was strangely intimate, sitting with her at this little table amid so little lamplight. It was as though they were in their own little corner of the world, far away from civilization.

"I meant to tell you how lovely you look this evening," he commented lightly as he shuffled the cards.

"Thank you," she murmured. "I'm certain you already know how very dashing you are."

Trystan chuckled. "Of course, but I thank you all the same. Piquet?"

It was a game for two players with the winner being the first to get to a hundred points. When Vienne nodded in agreement, he set out removing the unnecessary cards from the deck until they were left with the required thirty-two.

"Should we make a wager?" he inquired.

"What sort?" she asked warily. "The last person to gamble with you ended up getting me a new partner."

He grinned. "Aren't you glad for it?" Her reply was a lopsided smile that made his chest feel tight.

"Nothing too dear," Trystan replied. "If I win, you will let me name our venture."

She considered it. "All right. And if I win . . . I want a kiss."

Trystan started, dropping the cards and scrambling to collect them. "Vienne . . ."

"I'm not attempting to seduce you, Trystan. I made a fool of myself by kissing you. The only way I will feel as though we are on an equal footing is if you kiss me."

He wasn't quite certain what she was playing at. Part of him suspected this might be another ploy to give her dominance over him, but to be honest he didn't really care. He was an excellent card player and intended to win, but losing would not be so awful if kissing Vienne was his punishment.

In fact, staring at her in this light, seeing that determined yet uncertain expression on her pale face, in her bright eyes, he very much wanted to kiss.

"Agreed." He dealt the cards.

They played mostly in silence, breaking it occasionally to taunt one another. He had forgotten what an aggressive player she was—and skilled. But he was skilled as well; and kiss or no, he didn't relish losing.

"Consider this your Waterloo, La Rieux," he taunted as his tally approached a hundred points.

"Are you comparing me to Napoleon?"

"Of course not. You're not quite as pretty as he was." Thankfully she laughed at that. But Trystan's bravado was short-lived.

"I am afraid you will not be Wellington tonight, my dear sir," she crowed when she beat him to the hundred-point mark. "How does defeat taste anyway? I'm told it's bitter."

Trystan couldn't help but chuckle. "Such indelicate talk for a lady." He gathered up the cards. "Perhaps I let you win."

She snorted. "I could have offered you fellatio and you would not have *let* me win."

Warmth filled his cheeks and he laughed a little harder. "No. I just might have considered it for that." When he looked up, she was watching him with a warm smile. "What?"

"You don't find me shocking at all, do you?"

He shrugged. "Not really. I like that you say whatever is on your mind. I think you try to shock people to keep them from getting too close."

She tilted her head to one side. "Perhaps. Or perhaps I am simply terribly shy and try to overcompensate with outrageous behavior."

"Mm. Yes, you are terribly shy. Regardless, I have lost and I am prepared to pay my debt. When shall you collect?"

"I think now," she shocked him by replying.

"Now?" He glanced toward the door. "We might be seen."

She shrugged one shoulder. "So the gossips will think we're lovers—they already do."

Suddenly anxious, Trystan rose to his feet. "All right. Stand up."

She arched a brow. "No wonder you turn all the ladies' heads."

He grimaced. "My apologies." He offered her his hand, still eager but able to be a bit more polite about it. He wanted this over with.

Vienne placed her hand in his and rose to her feet. She was so tall. He wouldn't have to bend his neck much at all to kiss her, wouldn't get a crick from simply looking at her.

He lowered his head. She stopped him with a hand on his chest. "Is this how you kiss ladies now, Trystan? I remember you being a bit more . . . affectionate."

He gritted his teeth. Wanted affection did she? She had to be playing games with his mind, trying to throw him off kilter. Why? Just because she had to be the one in control? Disappointment dissolved bitterly on his tongue. He had hoped they were beyond this, that she might actually be seeing him as her equal.

That disillusionment pushed him to action. If she

wanted affection, or a bit of seduction, that's what he would give her.

He slid one hand behind her back, just above the small bustle of her gown, and pulled her toward him. His other hand—he'd removed his gloves before their card game—came up to cup the silken jut of her jaw. He caressed her flushed cheek with the pad of his thumb.

Her full lips parted on a sharp intake of breath that brought a smile to his face. At least she wasn't immune to him. At least he was man enough to excite her.

"You are very beautiful, Vienne," he murmured. "I find I don't mind losing to you—once."

She smiled at that, blue-green eyes brightening. "That sounds like a challenge, Lord Trystan."

"I suppose it is." He lowered his head. "I'm going to kiss you now, so I expect you to claim your prize with decorum."

Trystan's mouth touched hers, softly at first, but the moment her lips parted some of his control slipped . . . and she tasted of champagne and seduction. Her tongue met his inside. There was nothing hurried about the act. She simply tasted him as leisurely as he tasted her.

His fingers traced the line of her neck down to her shoulder. She was so warm and soft, just as he remembered. She had the most incredible skin—like silk beneath his hand. She shivered gently against him. He would have smiled, but then he would have to stop kissing her.

One of her arms came up around his neck, fingers sliding through his hair. Her other arm went around his waist, her slender hand stroking slowly over his back. Trystan silently groaned and pulled her closer. Damn all the layers of skirts women wore. He wanted to press the hardness of his erection against her, but there was so much fabric between them.

He moved her back in a kind of dance, still kissing her. They were in the shadows, partially illuminated by the lamp on the table, and he had her against the wall. The hand that had been at her back was now at her hip, sliding upward to cup the swell of her breast as it threatened to spill from the neckline of her gown. Corsets might be damnable contraptions at times, but they did offer up breasts in the most tantalizing way. She fit perfectly in his hand—and when he brushed his thumb over the little nipple pressing against the silk of her gown, she moaned.

This kiss was quickly spiraling into something else. He knew he should stop, that he was probably doing exactly as she wanted, but he wanted it as well. She pushed herself against his hand, and he obliged her by toying with her nipple some more. He could push the neckline aside and touch her naked flesh, but teasing her—both of them—was so good.

Her teeth caught his lower lip in a playful bite that struck him like a fist to the chest. He was hard, practically aching to have her; and when her hand slid from his back around to his front and down between them, he couldn't stop his hips from arching. Her fingers cupped the length of him through his trousers, squeezed and rubbed. He groaned into her mouth. *Christ.* She was going to drive him over the edge.

He tugged on her gown, pulling the fabric aside. His fingers slid inside, dipping into the top of her corset to lift her right breast out. He tore his lips from hers, kissing a hot damp trail along her jaw and down her neck. When he closed his mouth over her nipple, he was rewarded with the sweetest moan he'd ever heard. She was pebble hard against his tongue, warm and tight. The fingers in his hair tightened, holding his head so he couldn't stop. As if he would.

Trystan ran his hands down her sides, over the curve of her hips. His fingers clutched the thick layers of skirts and began pulling them up, bunching them and pushing them aside until he could slide one hand beneath.

Vienne didn't stop him. In fact, she lifted one leg and braced her foot on a nearby chair so that he could easily slip his fingers between her thighs and touch the dampness there. She wasn't wearing drawers and the discovery almost unmanned him then and there.

He ran his middle finger along the moist cleft, driven on by her soft sounds of delight.

Then there was a shout followed by raucous laughter, so abrupt and harsh it sliced through the sensual haze—just barely.

Vienne pushed at his shoulders, her thighs suddenly clamping shut on his hand. "Trystan." She pushed against him again. "We have to stop. Someone might see."

He lifted his head. Arousal had made his mind foggy, but he managed to turn and see the open doorway where anyone could have stumbled upon them or been watching them. What the hell was he thinking? It was one thing to be caught in a kiss, but this could not be passed off as a mere kiss.

It was only sheer luck that they hadn't been discovered. For all he knew someone might have been spying on them anyway. It wasn't as though Vienne was a young debutante whose father would force Trystan to marry her. This would just be fodder for the gossips. An embarrassment for his family.

Christ. He prided himself on being the one Kane male who didn't court scandal like a permanent mistress. All Vienne had to do was kiss him and he threw all caution to the breeze.

Damn it. She made it so easy for him to lose

control. He was like an ox with a ring through its nose—ready to go wherever she wanted to lead.

"You have to stop playing games with me, Vienne," he told her from between clenched teeth. "I'm your associate, not a boy you order about as you please. One of these days you're going to take it too far."

She gaped at him, one hand pressed against the neckline of her gown, which was now back in place. "Trystan, I . . ."

He held up his hand. "Don't. I have no desire to hear anything you have to say. Not tonight. I'm afraid I won't be available for breakfast tomorrow morning. I have another engagement, but I will meet you at the site later. Good night, Vienne. I hope you sleep well."

With that acidic farewell hanging in the air between them, Trystan turned on his heel and strode from the room. He didn't return to the ball. Instead, he made his way to the foyer, thankful that his arousal had cooled as quickly as it had ignited, else he would have had to stay in that room longer. He was too humiliated, too angry at himself for that.

When the footman looked up, Trystan asked him to have his carriage brought around. He was going home. He had enough society for one evening.

But the most maddening realization was that he hadn't had enough of Vienne. And he was afraid he never would.

Chapter 8

"Do you believe I'm someone who must always be in control?" Vienne asked Sadie two days later as they enjoyed a leisurely picnic lunch on the grass behind Saint's Row, where, at night, softly lit by torches, guests could sneak away for trysts or find their way to hidden grottos made for such assignations.

Her friend nearly choked on a strawberry. "Do you want me to lie or tell the truth?"

Vienne shot her a droll glance. "Trystan accused me of trying to control him, or rather our relationship."

"Relationship." Sadie practically sang the word. "And just what kind of *relationship* do the two of you have now?"

Vienne picked a small chunk of cheese from the piece in her hand, and popped the deliciously sharp morsel into her mouth. "I honestly do not know. He acts as though he wants to be lovers, but then becomes angry with me for it. I would like to be friends, but I do not know if that's possible."

"*Friends . . .*" The other woman sounded dubious. "Vienne, I've seen how the two of you look at one another, and believe me when I say that the two of you will never be friends. Perhaps Trystan is angry because he thinks you want a sexual relationship and he wants something more."

Vienne frowned. "How is that possible? He despised me after I ended our affair. Sometimes I think he still does."

"Well, he went through an awful lot of trouble to insure the two of you had to work together, so that must say something."

Vienne mulled that over with another bite of cheese. Was it possible that Trystan had legitimate feelings for her? Not dislike or an urge for some kind of revenge, but truly romantic feelings? The thought turned her stomach. She didn't know what to think of that. She had come to look forward to seeing him everyday. She enjoyed his company when he wasn't accusing her of being manipulative—which she knew very well was one of her many character flaws. She would hate for him to fall in love. . .

Then she would have to break his heart again.

Wouldn't she? What was truly terrifying was that

a very small part of her insisted heartbreak needn't take place.

"He deserves better," she confessed without an ounce of self-pity. "I don't know if I could ever fully trust him, Sadie. I've had my trust betrayed by so many men in the past." Her father and Marcel were but two of them—the worst of the lot.

"If you came down with influenza and couldn't work for a few days, would you trust Trystan to continue work on your shops?"

Vienne nodded, tilting her head so her hat shielded her face from the surprisingly bright afternoon sun. "Of course, provided he gave me daily updates."

"If the two of you were in a dangerous situation, would you trust him to get you out of it?"

"I would trust that both of us together could get us out of it."

Vienne smiled. "That is what I love about you, Vienne. Your confidence."

"I'm not stupid nor am I helpless."

"I would never accuse you of either."

"Many men think I'm cold and unfeminine because I trust my own instincts. Trystan claims to like it, but then he turns around and accuses me of trying to seduce him into docility."

"Are you?" Sadie asked in all seriousness. "Are you trying to manipulate him?"

Vienne glanced down at the blanket and began picking at a loose thread. "I did try at first, but now . . . I'm not sure what it is he's up to, but I do not want to control him. He has come up with so many wonderful plans and ideas, I would hate to stifle that."

Sadie smiled like a child who knows a secret she's not supposed to tell. "Sounds to me as though you like him. A lot."

"I do. Sadie, I respect him. That's odd isn't it? Especially since I do not know if I can trust him outside of business."

"It's not odd. You are a woman who has been treated poorly and has come to expect it from every man she meets. It's how you protect that wonderfully big heart of yours."

She snorted. "Oh yes, I am such a warm and loving person."

"You are. Look at how much you give to charity. You helped me when I needed it. Your friends are very fortunate people, Vienne. They are merely low in number."

Such praise. No one had ever said such things to her before. "My friends are very dear to me," she replied hoarsely. "Sadie, I want you to know that if anything should happen to me, I have left the club and everything I own to you and Indara."

Her friend started, her face going stark white.

"Vienne, don't say such things. I don't want to hear it."

She reached over and patted Sadie's slender hand. "I don't mean to distress you, I just wanted to tell you."

"Is there something else you need to tell me?" There was a slightly frantic note to her voice. "Are you ill."

"No, but I received this yesterday afternoon." She took a letter from a pocket in her jacket and passed it to her friend.

Sadie opened the letter and read, "'Cease construction or suffer the consequences, Jezebel.' Good lord, Vienne. This is a threat."

She nodded. "Yes. It would seem Trystan wasn't the object of the pranks after all."

"This is not a prank." Sadie waved the letter. "This is frightening."

Vienne took the note from her and slipped it back into her pocket. "Indeed. That is why I shared it not only with our private security but with Scotland Yard as well. They're investigating it now."

"What did Trystan say?"

Suddenly the pattern of the blanket was vastly intriguing. "I haven't told him."

"You have to! Why, you both could be in danger. For all you know he received a similar missive."

Her smile was a wry one. "If so, then he hasn't

seen fit to share it with me either." She sighed. "I will tell him next time I see him." Truthfully, she would have told him yesterday. But the stony silence he gave her at the construction site, the day finishing touches were being put on the first-floor shops, made her wary. He had canceled their breakfast meeting in the morning as well—and that hurt just enough that she decided not to go after him out of spite. In fact, she had yet to step foot on location today, coward that she was.

She doubted he even cared. With her out of the way, he would be free to do whatever he wanted to the emporium. For a second—and only one—she wondered if perhaps that was the plan, but then she realized that if Trystan wanted her dead, she would be dead.

No, this was the work of someone wanting to scare her. They were moving on from hurting her employees to threatening her. Perhaps Trystan had gotten a similar note.

"My dear friend." Sadie's expression and tone was all sympathy. "You do not know what to do with yourself, do you?"

"No." Vienne shook her head as humiliating tears burned threateningly at the back of her eyes. "I feel as though I don't quite know myself. I know I should stay away from Trystan, but I contrived to kiss him because I couldn't stand it any longer. I want him, but I am afraid of having him. He is not a man who will be content to have what we did before."

"There's nothing wrong with that."

She met her friend's wide gaze. "He could hurt me, Sadie. He could hurt me very, very badly. And I would not blame him if he did."

Sadie inched closer on the blanket to put her arm around Vienne's shoulders and Vienne welcomed the contact. "I hate to see you so uncertain. Why can you not see yourself as a good person?"

"Because I am not. I have done awful things, the least of which was breaking Trystan's heart." Perhaps that wasn't the least, because right now it seemed like a terrible thing indeed.

"Look at what Jack and I did to one another. We caused each other so much hurt, and yet we managed to forgive one another."

Vienne pulled back enough to look her in the eye. "Yes, but you two love each other. You always have."

Sadie's smile seemed pitying . . . or Vienne might simply be paranoid. "Didn't you once tell me that Lord Trystan declared his feelings for you?"

"Years ago."

"It takes a lot more than a few years to destroy true love."

Vienne's stomach rolled. "Don't say such things. I beg you."

"Why is it so awful for you to think that someone might love you?"

"Because I don't deserve it? Because they might expect it in return from me? I don't know, Sadie! Can we talk of something else? The idea of Trystan Kane being in love with me makes me want to be ill."

Her friend stared at her as though she had never seen her before. "You poor thing. You're in so deep you don't even see it, do you?"

"What?" Vienne demanded. "What don't I see?"

Sadie shook her head, causing the huge hat upon her head to jiggle. "Nothing. We will talk of something else then. Did you hear that Lady Gosling has ordered a red gown to wear to her husband's funeral?"

That brought a smile to Vienne's lips. The old lord had died the day before and no one was very sad to see him go, especially not his wife. "I had not heard that. What other gossip have you heard?"

Sadie began to chatter, filling Vienne in on the most scandalous and ridiculous *en dits* from the Upper Ten Thousand. She listened and smiled, even laughed in places, but her mind never strayed too far from the note in her pocket and the fact that she wished Trystan were there to tell her everything was going to be all right.

The fact that so many days had passed without incident at the construction site made Trystan feel a strange blend of hopefulness and paranoia. Just because nothing had happened didn't mean it would continue to go so smoothly. More than likely their culprit was simply lying in wait, hoping they'd think he was done before springing something disastrous on them.

On this afternoon that had started out sunny but was starting to gray, Trystan had just finished checking in on another of his projects and was enjoying a cigar and a glass of scotch with his brothers at Brooks's. It had been ages since he'd visited a gentlemen's club and now he remembered why.

"Can't believe you'd get behind such a sordid scheme, Trystan m'boy," Earl Chase lamented. "Why, it'll turn our virtuous ladies into debauched bawds, you mark my words."

He could humor the older man, perhaps even pity his drunken state, balding head, and unfortunate teeth, but Trystan wasn't in a mood to do either. He'd been in a foul temper ever since he'd left Vienne at Angelwood's ball, and the reason did not elude him.

"How do you suppose a convenient shopping experience will do that, sir?" he asked, despite being kicked by Archer under the table. Grey watched with barely concealed amusement.

The earl seemed to think it should be obvious. "Why, it will expose them to all sorts of untrustworthy gentlemen! Encourage them to spend their husband's money on frivolous things and turn them into ill-mannered harridans!"

"They're 'exposed' to unsavory gentlemen every time they attend a ball. Most of the time their husband's money is the dowry the lady brought to the union—and the only thing that will turn them into ill-mannered creatures is if they take up getting drunk in the middle of the afternoon and spouting off about things of which they know *nothing*."

The aging aristocrat stared at him, sputtering, and his brothers were trying—not very successfully—to hide their laughter. Trystan, however, wasn't finished. "It's not that I do not appreciate your concerns, Chase. I simply think you're a misogynistic antique who believes all women are pretty idiots. Out of sympathy for your poor wife, I shall have to extend Lady Chase a generous line of credit. Good day."

The earl was as red as a freshly boiled lobster. He pointed a hairy finger at Trystan. "You insolent cur. I ought to trounce you within an inch of your life."

"With what?" Trystan taunted him. "The strongest thing on you is your breath."

The earl drew back his hand, as though he planned to slap Trystan across the face. Trystan waited, hoping the old man would do it, just so he could hit back.

Instead, Grey stood and caught the other man's arm. "I believe my brother said good day, Chase. Do run along before I have to you escorted out."

The old man sneered at Grey, then at Trystan, but he walked away without another word.

"I wish you hadn't done that," Trystan remarked peevishly.

Grey took a puff on his cigar. "Yes, because knocking about an old man will make you so very popular in society."

He had a point, damn him. Trystan tossed back the remainder of his drink and reached for the bottle to pour another.

"So," chirped Archer, "what's crawled up your arse and died?"

"I don't want to talk about it," he replied sullenly.

His brothers exchanged glances across the table. "La Rieux," they said in unison.

Trystan pressed his forehead against the table-top. "What did I ever do to deserve you two sods for brothers?"

"I dunno," Archer replied. "Must have been a lottery or something. Look, Tryst, I'm the last person who should be giving relationship advice, but it seems that ever since you tangled up with that French bird again you've bounced between ecstatic and suicidal. It's obvious there's something going on that you need to do something about, and fast. Because quite frankly, we can't stand being around you when you're like this."

He lifted his head and glared at his brother. "That's rich, coming from you."

Archer shrugged. "I admit that I'm normally the dramatic one in the family—I do have the most flair—but Grey and I are worried about you."

"You needn't be. I'm perfectly fine." He was looking at Archer so he didn't see Grey move. The slap to the back of his head almost sent him crashing into the table nose first.

"Ow!" he cried, shooting his brother an incredulous and furious glance. "What did you do that for?"

Grey shrugged. "Thought it needed to be done."

Archer raised his glass. "Well played, Your Grace."

Trystan rubbed the back of his skull. "I think it's time for me to leave London again," he said, only half joking.

His eldest brother scowled at him. "It's time for you to grow the hell up and go after what you want.

If that's La Rieux, go get her. If not, find someone else— because this side of your personality is pissing me off."

Grey's words could have easily sent him into a tantrum of epic proportions, but that in itself was a sobering thought. His brother was right. He needed to grow up. He thought he had, but really he hadn't. Where Vienne was concerned, he was still acting like the spoiled boy he'd been when she first took him to her bed. He blamed her for this mess, when really he had started the whole thing by insinuating himself in her life. He wanted her to see him differently, but he continued to treat her as a woman who had broken his heart and cast him aside. He expected her to trust and believe in him, when he wasn't willing to give her the same courtesy.

What if she hadn't been playing games at Angelwood's party? What if her reaction to him was real, driven only by attraction? What if she honestly wanted him as much as he, admittedly, wanted her?

What if he had been given a second chance to win her heart? It wouldn't be easy, as distrusting as she was. She would fight him tooth and claw, but he had already established how well they worked together, and maybe this time she wouldn't be so quick to run away. He would have to treat her like a feral cat and coax her to him with patience and care.

Or with a butterfly net. He smiled at that thought.

"He's gone mad," Archer remarked to Grey.

"Have not," he responded. The whiskey had gone to his head, but he still had all his faculties about him. "I just had an epiphany."

"I do hope it's not contagious," Archer replied with mock seriousness.

"No," Trystan answered, clapping him on the shoulder. "Unfortunately for you, Arch, common sense cannot be passed on."

"Haven't seen anyone skulking about, Mrs. La Rieux. Been quiet as a church 'round here."

Vienne did not correct the head of Trystan's hired private guard. He could assume she was, or had been, married if he wanted. Though it was the *Englishness* of it that irked her mostly.

"Thank you," she told him. "I appreciate how diligent you and your men are." That diligence was no doubt why she got the threatening note, because the villain couldn't get close to the site.

He doffed his cap to her, bid her a good day, and went on his way. She assumed he and his men slept during the day in order to patrol the entire night. When he was gone, she went back to inspecting wallpaper for the ladies' powder room. Pale gold with turquoise and green birds, or a pale cream with pastel flowers? Her natural inclination was to the gold, so she decided on the cream instead.

"I like the gold," came a voice from the door.

Vienne squeaked and then silently cursed herself for doing so. She rarely ever startled, but she hadn't been paying attention.

She glanced over her shoulder. Trystan stood in the doorway, bright eyed and freshly shaven in a dark blue coat and tan trousers. Had he decided to grace her with his presence and attention? She looked away. "I've decided on the cream," she replied civilly.

He chuckled. "Of course you have. You missed breakfast."

She shrugged and set the wallpaper swatches on a nearby workman's sawhorse. "I assumed you were no more available this morning than you have been the past few."

"I should have sent 'round a note. My apologies."

Her brow drew together, and she hesitated a moment before turning to face him. "An apology. How very novel."

He stepped into the room. "Actually, I was thinking that you and I spend a foolish amount of energy misunderstanding one another and then apologizing for it. It would be so much less taxing if we simply talked, wouldn't it?"

That was not the reply she had anticipated. "Yes. I suppose it would be."

"Excellent. I'll go first. Vienne, I apologize for thinking you're trying to manipulate me. I assume that since you rejected me years ago your only interest in me is to have me under your control, especially since I was so . . . underhanded in how I became your partner."

She gaped at him. When he said they should talk, he meant it. "I accept your apology. I will admit that at first I wanted to be the one in charge, but now I find there's a certain degree of comfort in having someone to help shoulder responsibility. To be honest, I must confess to suspecting that your reasons for wanting to work with me were based on revenge for me breaking your heart . . ."

He smiled. "You think a lot of yourself, don't you?"

There was no malice in his tone, but she wasn't quite certain how to take his remark. A rueful grin curved her lips. "Sometimes. But so do you."

"True enough." He moved closer and leaned his shoulder against the wall where she stood. "Vienne, I like you. I like working with you. I think you're a beautiful woman and I would like nothing more than to share your bed or have you in mine, but I don't want to ruin our business relationship, which is what I think would happen if you were to decide to end the affair. And you would end it. I think we both know that."

Vienne glanced down at her feet, unable to bear staring into his nonjudgmental eyes. "I decided a long time ago that trusting people only led to heartache, and I do try so very hard to protect myself from hurt. I cannot argue with you, Trystan. You are right, I would probably end things. Better yet, I would hope to stop it before it ever started, and not because I worry about getting hurt, but because you have become one of the last people I would ever want to injure, and I would injure you. I do not think I could avoid it. We are from entirely different worlds, are entirely different people."

"But you want me, don't you?" He slipped a finger under her chin and forced her to meet his gaze. "Tell me I'm not the only one who wants to say to hell with it and have you right here and now."

Oh. His admission sent a shiver through her entire body. "No. You are not the only one."

His answering smile was rueful. "Then we will have to help each other stay strong and resist temptation. I know how attractive I am, do you think you can stand firm against me?"

Stand and *firm* might not have been the best words to use in the situation, but Vienne went along with his jesting manner. "I believe I might be able to keep my hands off you—with your assistance, of course."

His eyes sparkled. "Of course."

It was the perfect solution, and it felt as though they had just taken their relationship to a new level, so why did she feel like crying? It was a hollow victory. She would have rather he'd come in here and ranted and raved and then kissed her again, so she'd have the excuse to kiss him back.

She would never admit it, but she wanted him so badly she suspected she would be willing to risk their partnership and friendship for even just one night with him. Or an afternoon. Honestly, she wasn't fussy.

"I ran into Menkins when I came in. He said things have been fairly quiet around here."

Vienne swallowed. She had been dreading this moment almost as much as she had dreaded seeing him. She withdrew the note from her pocket. "Around here, yes. But not so much elsewhere. I received this the other day."

Frowning, Trystan took the paper from her and quickly read it. "Bastard," he muttered before handing it back. "He's gone too far. Why didn't you show me this before?"

She gave him what she knew had to be an incredulous look. "Perhaps because you were being a total buffoon? It's not as though it happened weeks ago.

I've only had that a matter of days. I'm telling you now, and that will have to be good enough."

She could tell from his expression that he didn't know whether to kiss her or strangle her. "Did you go to the police?"

"Yes. And I showed it to your inquiry agent. I'm not stupid, Trystan."

"Good Lord, woman. I've never thought otherwise."

They stared at each other a moment before giving in to the urge to chuckle. It was too absurd not to.

"Forgive me," she said. "It is unfair, but I am accustomed to most men treating me as though I do not know what I'm talking about."

Trystan grinned. "I don't know how you modern women do it. Were the roles reversed, I think I might have shot someone by now."

She shrugged. "I have."

He chuckled. "Touché. I was at Brooks's yesterday with my brothers when Earl Chase came up to me and asked how I could be part of a scheme that would basically lead to the downfall of the entire female gender."

"Oh, he's one of those ones who believes being able to buy everything in one place will lead righteous women down the path of greed and debauchery?"

"Something to that effect, yes."

She made a scoffing sound. "Perhaps he is the one who sent me the note."

"Did it smell like bourbon when you opened it?"

"No."

"Wasn't Chase, then. Though, it was someone like him, wasn't it? Which means he's of middle or upper class."

"You assume it's a man. It could be a woman."

Trystan thought about it. "Not to be prejudiced, but I suspect there aren't too many women who know how to construct a false step."

"Not many aristocrats either," she shot back. "Could you?"

"I confess I might be able to give it a go, but it wouldn't look as convincing. However, our man—person—might have hired someone to make the step, and even put it in place. The smartest criminals know better than to get their own hands dirty."

"Known many criminal sorts?"

"You don't want to know." He grinned. "Enough of this jabbering. We'll go to Scotland Yard tomorrow and see what they can tell us."

She raised a brow. "Now look who's trying to take control."

He rolled his eyes—in a manner that reminded her of herself. Obviously they were spending far too much time together. "Shall we go to the Yard tomorrow?"

"*D'accord.* That wasn't so difficult was it?"

Shaking his head, Trystan offered his gloved hand. "Come with me. I want to show you the chandelier for the upstairs foyer."

Vienne clapped her hands excitedly—like a child. "They delivered it? When?"

"Yesterday. Apparently the men installed it before heading home. I'm surprised you didn't see it."

"I was only here for a short time yesterday. I had club business that needed attending. Not all of us can afford to ignore our other concerns."

Another grin. He smiled so easily—she loved it. "I have minions to take care of things for me. Shall we?"

She took his arm and allowed him to lead her from the room. They walked slowly, discussing how pleased they were with things, or what needed to be changed. She asked his opinion on carpet for the men's hat-and-gloves section and he picked her favorite. It was a silly thing, but it pleased her to no end.

They had to climb the stairs to the first floor as the lift had yet to be installed. Vienne was more than willing to allow Trystan to go first. The memory of the fear she'd felt when the step gave way was still too fresh; and after receiving that damned note, she was far more anxious than she could ever be comfortable with. She despised being afraid, and if she ever found the man—or woman—responsible she would be tempted to give them a wound to match William's.

"While we're being honest with one another," she began, ascending the steps behind him. "Did you by chance have any involvement in making my mess with my winged footman disappear?"

Trystan paused on the step, one foot braced against the next, hand on the banister. He glanced down, between his arm and body to look at her. "I might have. Would you be angry if I said yes?"

"No," she replied honestly. "To be honest, I'm flattered. For the past eighteen years, I've had only myself to rely on. I'm humbled by someone caring enough to take action on my behalf."

His expression turned thoughtful and slightly dumbstruck, as if he'd just seen a pig fly or a dog talk. "I've never thought of it that way. I'm always offended when my brothers try to protect me—as though they still think of me as a child."

She followed after him as he began to climb again. "To them you will always be their younger brother. They would do anything for you. I envy that."

"But you have older siblings, don't you? I remember you telling me about them years ago."

A small lump of dread landed in her belly. It was the same feeling she always had when she thought of her family. "We're not very close."

Obviously, he sensed that she didn't want to talk about it, because he didn't press. They made it up the stairs unscathed, and when they got to the top, she saw the beautiful crystal chandelier hanging from the high ceiling over the first-floor foyer. It would look so amazing when it was lit.

"It's lovely," she announced breathlessly. "I adore it."

"I thought you might," Trystan replied with a slightly smug expression. "Given the ladders, I would say the boys are either polishing or repositioning it, so be careful where you stand. I need to ask Gordon when it will be convenient to have the carpet delivered. I'll be right back."

Vienne smiled. "I'm quite capable of entertaining myself in your absence."

He flashed that charming grin again and walked away. Oddly enough, Vienne actually found herself missing his presence. What foolishness. Cursing herself, she walked over to one of the ladders. It was tempting to climb up and take a closer look.

"Pardon me," she called to a small group of men in

an adjoining room. "Would one of you mind holding the ladder for me?"

They all volunteered, of course, but she chose the one—she couldn't remember his name—who had told her about his wife and children. He was a devoted husband and father, so she felt reasonably safe that he wouldn't try to see up her skirts.

"We secured these ladders last evening, Madame La Rieux," he informed her as she started to climb. "They're tied up to posts with wire so they won't fall."

"Good to know," she replied, her heart beating a little faster with every increase in height. She wasn't afraid; rather, she was somewhat eager. She felt very daring climbing up this high to inspect a chandelier. She'd wager none of Trystan's little washed-out debutantes had ever done such a thing.

Near the top she stopped and turned her torso so that she might get a better look at the crystal-and-brass monstrosity. It was even more impressive up close.

The ladder wavered a little as she twisted around, and she was just about to ask the man to hold it still when she heard a slight twanging sound followed by the distinctive sound of metal being pulled from wood and a loose wire striking wood.

She whirled around, but it was too late, the ladder

had already pulled away from the wall. She tried to reach for the wall, a molding, or the window ledge, but the ladder continued to move despite her leaning in the opposite direction. Below her she heard the workman give a shout.

She tried to climb down, but the ladder was simply too unsteady. For a second she stood straight—like a stilt walker, and then the ladder tipped back. She slid down, desperately trying to keep from falling, and then she was falling back through the air, riding the ladder all the way to the polished wood floor. She couldn't stop it anymore than she could the scream that tore from her throat.

Vienne heard Trystan yell her name as she hurtled toward the floor. She hit with a thud that shook every inch of her body. Her head hit a fraction of a second later.

And then everything went black.

Chapter 9

Trystan ran to Vienne, but he wasn't fast enough. He could only watch helplessly as the ladder she was on crashed to the floor, taking her with it. Everyone rushed to her, but he was the first.

He fell to his knees beside her, shoving the ladder out of his way. The first thing he did was check her throat for a pulse. It was there but felt weak against his trembling fingers. She had a pulse and was breathing—that was good. But there was blood seeping from beneath her head. And though he knew that even the slightest head wound could bleed like mad, his heart damned near stopped at the sight of it.

"Fetch a surgeon," he commanded. "Now!"

Two of the workmen raced off. "They're familiar with this area, sir," Gordon told him, his face white behind his bushy ginger moustache. "They'll bring back the best."

Trystan could only nod in response. He hated leaving Vienne on the floor like this, but he was afraid to move her in case she was injured internally. He hated feeling useless, so he did what he could: checked for broken bones, and thankfully found nothing. Then he removed his coat and covered her with it. After that there was nothing he could do but sit beside her and hold her hand.

Silently, he prayed for her to wake up, but either God wasn't listening or it was simply out of His control.

Trystan thought her indestructible. She was so resolute and strong. He'd never known her to have so much as a sniffle—and now, here she was, sprawled on the hard floor at his knees like some broken china doll.

Blinking back the hot wetness that threatened to spill from his eyes, he adjusted her skirts so her ankles were covered. She would no doubt laugh at his concern for her modesty, but it seemed wrong to leave them exposed.

How long Trystan knelt there, holding her hand and praying, he didn't know. Vienne began to stir when the workmen arrived with the surgeon. Trystan shushed her when she tried to speak, and demanded that she lie still and let the man examine her. He hovered nearby, waiting again.

"I do not suspect any internal harm has been done," the surgeon said finally, rising to his feet after examining Vienne and wrapping gauze around her head to staunch the blood flowing from her wound. "She has taken a fairly good blow to the head and is concussed; she will be in quite a lot of pain for the next few days, but otherwise she seems perfectly fit. A lucky lady indeed."

"I told you I was fine," Vienne said, voice weak as she stared up at Trystan. "Now, help me up. We have much to do."

"All you have to do is go home," he informed her, and the surgeon agreed that she should rest—also that someone should stay with her and keep her awake. Concussions were apparently tricky things.

"But—" she protested.

"But nothing," Trystan cut her off. "I'm taking you back to Saint's Row and I'm going to send word to both Sadie and Miss Ferrars. Surely one of them can come stay with you."

She fought him, of course, but he turned a deaf ear and sent for his carriage. Then he picked her up and carried her to his vehicle as though she were a child. Vienne's cheeks were pink as they descended the stairs.

"Trystan, put me down. This is most improper."

"Look at you, caring about what's proper."

"People will talk."

"Yes, about the fact that you could have been

killed." The thought had put a chill in his bones that was there even now.

Her eyes widened. "You do not believe this was an accident, do you?"

"We'll talk about it once you've rested."

"We will discuss it now," she insisted. "Tell me what you suspect."

Stubborn wench. He glanced at her as he tried to concentrate on reaching the bottom of the stairs without his arms or weakened knees giving out. Vienne was not a plump woman, but she was fit and wearing at least twenty pounds of gown and undergarments. And she had given him quite a scare.

"I find it odd that the workmen secured that ladder only to have it fall when you climbed it."

"Do you think someone deliberately tampered with it?"

"I do. Though I do not believe you were the intended target. I believe the same fate would have awaited anyone who used the ladder."

She closed her eyes, alarming him for a split second before she opened them again. "Trystan, what are we going to do? This cannot continue."

"Let me worry about that right now. You concentrate on healing." As soon as he was certain she was tucked safely in bed, he was going to pay a visit to Scotland Yard. Vienne was right, this mischief could not continue. He wanted nothing more than to catch the bastard, or bastards, responsible so he could personally have a word—with his fists.

His carriage was out front, and he managed to get Vienne into it without drawing attention. Trystan held her the entire ride to Saint's Row, chatting away and asking questions to make sure she stayed alert.

"You're fussing over me like a nursemaid," she grumbled. "I told you, you irritating Englishman, I'm fine."

"Vienne," he began calmly, though his nerves were as raw as a bad burn, "have you ever been kicked by a horse?"

She scowled at him. "No."

"You're going to feel like it by tomorrow morning. Like you've been kicked repeatedly. You're going to need someone to help you do the most mundane things." Then he added, "You'd better not attempt to come to the site tomorrow or I'll personally truss you up and deliver you home."

She made an exasperated sound. "Really, you are worse than a nursemaid. You're an old woman."

"Compliments. How delightful. Do be quiet, Vienne. The surgeon said you should be silent and still."

"I think part of you enjoys lording over me."

He put a finger to his lips. *"Ssssh."* Her mouth tightened, but she did not say another word for the rest of the trip. She did, however, hold on to his hand, which was draped over her as she leaned into him.

As luck would have it, Sadie was at Saint's Row when they arrived. Apparently she was doing an end-of-Season charity event that evening and she would be reading leaves. Her face turned pale when she saw Trystan walk in holding Vienne in his arms.

"They told me she'd been hurt," she said, immediately directing him to Vienne's private rooms.

"Would have been a lot worse if her head wasn't so thick," he joked as he carried his charge up the narrow stairs. Vienne wasn't the only one who was going to feel it the next day. His biceps were going to despise him.

"Mon Dieu, I will be glad to see the backside of you," Vienne lamented.

Trystan smiled at her. "You've always admired my backside."

Ahead of him he heard Sadie snicker as Vienne flushed and glared at him. Personally, he was just so damned happy she was all right, he wouldn't care if she hit him.

He followed Sadie into Vienne's apartments, noticing that the tranquil sage color suited her perfectly. Vienne could be subtle, but she was also very bold and knew exactly how to balance the two when it came to her club, her wardrobe, and personal space. So, while she came across as strong, she wasn't intimidating or obnoxious.

Trystan placed her on the large bed. His mind went back in time, remembering how many times he had done this during their affair. He used to sweep her up into his arms and carry her to bed all the time. She liked it.

His gaze locked with hers, and he knew she was thinking of those times as well. For a moment they simply stared at one another, lost in the shared past.

Sadie cleared her throat, tearing Trystan back to the present. He pulled his arms from beneath Vienne and addressed her friend. "She's going to start stiffening up soon, so she'll need someone here regularly to help her with things. By this evening, you should be able to give her something for the pain." Then to Vienne, "You do what you're told. I'll be by later to check in."

She arched a brow, but didn't argue. Satisfied that she was in good hands, he turned to leave.

"Trystan?"

At the threshold, he glanced over his shoulder. "Yes?"

Vienne smiled at him. "Thank you."

His heart gave a queer twist. "You're welcome."

* * *

As much as she hated to admit it, Trystan was right. That night Vienne was so sore and stiff she could scarcely move, and she knew it would be worse the next morning. There was nothing to be done for it, however. She had to get up and take herself downstairs. Tonight was a charity gathering at the club—she had to be there to greet her guests, and persuade them to dig deep in their purses for a good cause.

"Vienne, lie down," Sadie commanded. "Your club is in good hands."

"There are no hands more adept than mine at running this place."

Her friend placed a firm but gentle hand on her shoulder. "Trystan has everything under control. Between him and I and Indara, we are more than capable of making certain this evening is a success."

Trystan. He was perhaps the only person whose name could physically soothe her. If he was taking care of things, then the club really was in good hands, especially if Sadie helped him. Sadie had been with her long enough and had been present at enough of these events to make certain everything was done properly—but she also had to operate her tea-leaf reading booth, and Indara was her assistant. That left Trystan alone out on the floor.

"He doesn't know who the ones with deep pockets

are," she insisted, trying to sit up once more. Damn her soft bed all to hell. It was like trying to right oneself in the center of a cloud.

Sadie pushed her back down—it didn't take much as she hadn't gotten very far. "He got a thousand out of Lord Farqward."

A thousand out of tightfisted Farqward? *Impossible!*

"And he raised just a little more than that by himself."

A sense of dread washed over her. "More? What did he do?"

Sadie hesitated, then smiled. "He auctioned himself off: dinner with him in private rooms at the Barrington, and an evening at the theater. It went over so well that he's trying to round up other bachelors to do the same. I believe Lord Archer was about to offer himself as an artist's model in the classical style."

Even through her shock, she had to smile at that. "Lord Archer will do anything for an excuse to disrobe. It seems the club is just fine without me, then." A wave of self-pity washed over her. Was there nothing Trystan Kane could not do, and do better than she?

Sadie's smile turned sympathetic. "Not quite, my friend. Simply everyone has inquired after you, even Bertie."

That warmed her a little. "How sweet of the Prince of Wales. Is Mrs. Langtry with him?"

"She sends her regards as well."

"You had better get back down there," she suggested. "I'm certain your adoring public will soon mutiny if they do not soon have their tea leaves read."

Her dear friend looked torn. "Are you certain you do not need anything?"

Vienne nodded, feeling very well loved at that moment, and grateful for it. "I am fine, and I have this little bell I can ring if I need anything. I do have a maid, you know."

Sadie smiled and kissed her on the forehead, just as a mother might. "I'll check in on you again later."

As soon as she was gone, Vienne engaged in the struggle to sit up once more. This time she managed, though it took a lot of swearing and strength she didn't know she had to accomplish it. And, dear God, it *hurt*!

Slowly, she slipped her legs over the side of the bed and rose gingerly—oh, so gingerly—to her feet. She hobbled to the vanity, using the bed and other furniture for support. The hem of the nightgown Sadie had helped her into brushed against the top of her feet as she walked bent over like an old woman.

At the mirror she stopped and turned, craning her head over her shoulder as she lowered the top of the gown to expose her back. What she saw made her gasp.

There was very little of her back that was the color it should be. Most of her skin was varying shades of purple and magenta, so dark in spots she looked like an overripe plum. The sight, coupled with the pain, brought tears to her eyes.

She knew she was lucky to be alive, that it wasn't as awful as it looked, but still . . . she looked terrible.

There was a knock on her door, and it opened before she could speak or completely cover herself once more. As luck would have it, it was Trystan. The color drained from his face when he saw her—and her back.

"Oh, Vienne. I'm so sorry."

Her hand shook as she struggled with the neckline of her nightgown. The damn thing would not come back up.

"Easy," he said as he walked toward her. "Let me help you."

"I can do it." She pulled harder—her battered body screaming in protest.

"For the love of God, woman. Stop!" Gentle hands took hold of hers. "I thought you might be hurting, so I brought you some of what my nanny called an old family recipe. Come, lie down and I'll put some on you." He gently tugged her toward the bed . . . and didn't even try to peek down her sagging top.

Perhaps she truly had lost her appeal.

"Trystan, you shouldn't be here."

"Not going to give me the 'it isn't proper' speech, are you?"

"Hang propriety, you need to be downstairs taking care of guests, convincing them to be charitable."

"Relax, Frenchy. Everyone has been very generous, and Sadie told me that my tally is even better than the last time you hosted one of these shindigs. Everything is good."

"Of course your tally is better," she remarked a little more bitterly than she intended. "Do not call me Frenchy. You know how I feel about that." During their affair he had teasingly called her that. To hear it now was like mockery.

His brows lifted. "Do I detect a hint of bitterness?"

She scowled at him, the pain making her heedless of how she sounded. "Of course I'm bitter. Everything you touch seems to turn to gold. You appear to be better at running my business than I am, and I'm not the least bit surprised!"

"Has it not occurred to you that my success this evening has more to do with wanting to impress you or because I don't want to let you down?" They reached the bed and he continued to hold her hands as she slowly sat down.

She glanced up at him, gritting her teeth through the pain. "Why in the name of God would you want to impress me?"

He shrugged. "At the moment? Damned if I know. Lie down."

Most men, she would tell to go to hell. There was no way she would put herself on her belly and make herself vulnerable when she had no protection except a thin layer of cotton, but Trystan had more honor than that.

She trusted him—with her livelihood. Her mind wanted to invent all manner of horrible things he could be doing, paranoid that he was out to ruin her and drive her business into the ground, but some other part of her—a stronger part—wouldn't have it.

It took all her strength to do it, and not cry, but she managed to settle onto her stomach. Trystan's hands were warm as they pulled down one sleeve and then the other. She hadn't bothered to retie the neckline, so it gave way easily under his fingers.

He took the top off a jar, scooped out some ointment, and rubbed it between his palms to warm it. Of course he would think to do that. Everything he did was done exactly the right way.

"Smells nice," she commented, a little anxious.

"Effective too," he replied. "This will have you better in no time. I don't want to hurt you, but I have to rub it on, all right?"

She nodded, cheek rubbing against the pillow. "I trust you."

He hesitated. "Thank you."

How could two simple words turn her heart to pudding?

His touch was so gentle, but even still she sucked in a breath when he began to lightly massage the ointment into her skin. Never before had she ached like this.

"I hear you sold for more than one thousand pounds," she remarked, distracting herself with conversation.

"News travels fast."

"Saint's Row is known for discretion, but I know everything that happens under this roof or on my property."

"Of course you do. It would be bad business if you didn't. And to put a finer point on it, I sold for one thousand six."

"To whom?" Did she sound disinterested? She wanted to sound as though it made no never mind what he did, or how much some desperate woman paid him to do it.

"Lady Gosling," he replied. "Caused quite the ruckus what with her husband barely in the ground. Not one for mourning, Lady G."

Vienne closed her eyes. Of course it would be that slag Gosling. The woman was in a constant state of heat. "I know what she's hoping to have for dinner. You'd best take a chair and a whip with you just in case."

He laughed, and some of the sick feeling in her stomach eased. "No need. I've no desire to sample what the lady has to offer; and if she thinks I'm offering anymore than a pleasant evening, she will be in for a shock."

"A pleasant evening is exactly what she has in mind, Trystan."

His hands stilled. She opened her eyes to find him watching her with a strange smile on his lips. "Why, Vienne. Are you jealous?"

She snorted. "Do not be ridiculous. I simply do not believe you know what you are getting yourself into."

His lovely hands began to move again. "No, you're trying to make certain I don't 'get into' anything, or anyone."

She coughed, choking on a breath. "You are the most self-satisfied man I know. You think every woman wants you."

"You have met my brother Archer, have you not? And I am not the one accusing Lady Gosling of having seduction on her mind. If either of us believes all women want me, it's you."

He had her there. "I do not believe every woman wants you." She should follow with a declaration that she didn't want him, but she couldn't quite do that.

"That's all right, Vienne. I won't tell anyone that you find me so terribly attractive you think all women must as well. Honestly, I'm flattered."

"You're delusional, that's what you are."

Trystan chuckled. "Perhaps. There, all done." Gently he tugged her gown as much into place as he could with her on her stomach. "You should notice a big difference in the morning. Have your maid or Sadie put more on you then, and another application tomorrow evening."

She looked up at him. "Thank you."

His gaze had a warmth to it she hadn't seen in years. "You're welcome. I'll check in on you tomorrow afternoon, if that is all right."

"I hope to be at the site by then."

"You won't be," he informed her. "You will be right here, in bed recovering."

"I've lain abed long enough."

"No, you haven't, and you'll figure that out when

you wake up tomorrow morning stiffer than you are now."

"I thought you said I would notice an improvement."

"In the pain and bruising, but you're still going to be sore. Now, try to get some rest. Just because I can make do without you for a few days, does not mean I like it."

He pulled the blankets up over her. "Do you need anything?"

Laudanum would take away the slight ache in her skull, and probably lull her away from the pain that plagued her entire body, but she didn't like to feel fuzzyheaded and out of control. "I'm fine. Thank you."

He patted her hand. "You are very welcome. Good night, Vienne."

"Good night, Trystan."

She listened as his left the bed and walked across the carpet to the door. He paused on the threshold. "Say, Vienne . . . do you suppose we should offer an evening with me as a service in one of our shops? We'd make back our investment in no time. Just think about it."

She was still laughing when she heard the door click shut behind him.

* * *

Trystan was right, of course. He always was, the infuriating man. Vienne wasn't as sore the next morning, but she was stiffer than a stale baguette. There was no way she could get herself to the construction site. No hope of leaving the premises at all.

Idleness was not something she liked. She much preferred to be busy, doing something. Lounging in bed gave her too much time to think about her past and all the regrets that lingered there. There was only so much reading she could do before her mind started to wander. If she read a historical account or periodical, her mind wandered to thoughts of Trystan and how things were progressing at the site. If she read a novel, she began to imagine herself and Trystan as characters in the narrative.

There was nothing for it. She missed him. Missed his teasing and his ideas. Most of all she missed his optimism and how he treated her—as though he had her best interests at heart. She even missed how he ordered her about. Who knew that Trystan Kane could put his foot down, or that it would be such a firm, resolute foot at that? There was no arguing when he got his mind set on something.

She had forgotten what it was like to have someone looking out for her. Which was why three days after her accident she had to make a brief detour on her way to the emporium. To return the favor.

She was shown into a parlor where the dark-haired lady she'd come to see waited upon her. Vienne moved like a woman whose corset was tied too tightly, but she was recovered enough to do this.

"Madame La Rieux," cooed a smooth voice. "This is an unexpected pleasure. What brings you to my humble abode?"

This house was as humble as a two-cent whore trying to make rent. "I hope you will indulge me, Lady Gosling, but I have something of importance I wish to discuss with you."

The beautiful woman's dark green eyes flashed with interest. "What might that be?"

Vienne seated herself in a chair across from her hostess and smiled easily. "Trystan Kane."

Despite the fact that he was expecting female company, Trystan didn't take any longer to dress the evening of his dinner with Lady Gosling than he would have any other night. After all, he didn't want her to get the wrong impression. Vienne might be correct that the lady had more than dinner and theater on her mind, but that was all she was going to get.

If nothing else, the meal would be exquisite, as

the Barrington chef was in a class of his own. And the theater would be entertaining because the Season was almost officially over and this was to be the last performance.

To be fair, Lady Gosling wasn't as bad as some made her out to be. She was outrageous and not terribly discreet about her lovers, but she was intelligent and capable of much more educated conversation than many of her contemporaries.

Plus, the money she paid to spend the evening with him would help Vienne's charity for girls and women who needed assistance escaping unpleasant personal situations. He wouldn't let himself wonder if the charity was so special to Vienne because she herself had escaped something—or someone—in her past. The thought made him quite angry, and there was nothing he could do to fix it now.

He had wanted to see more of her today, but work had gotten in the way; and then his mother had summoned him to luncheon because she wanted to know if he'd chosen a potential bride yet. Time was apparently wasting.

Shortly after seven he left for the theater, where he was to meet Lady Gosling in the box Grey owned and had loaned him for the evening. Traffic was considerably lighter than it had recently been, due to the aristocracy beginning to trickle back to their country homes, to their dogs, and to the promise of hunting parties. Yet he arrived right on time.

"Your guest has already arrived, Lord Trystan," he was told by the theater manager when he stepped inside. "I took the liberty of escorting the lovely lady to His Grace's box myself."

Trystan thanked the man and slipped him a few notes for his consideration. Lady Gosling was not only punctual but early. How odd for a woman of her rank. Hopefully it was a personality quirk and not a sign of how eager she was to be alone with him.

Wouldn't Vienne laugh at him for thinking such things? She'd accuse him of having a high opinion of himself and delusions of his attractiveness. She hadn't seemed to find him unattractive that night at Angelwood's. He'd almost manage to put it completely out of his mind, but now there it was, back again and making him wonder if maybe—just maybe—he and Vienne might still have a chance.

Of course it was all a lot of nonsense and wishful thinking. And why should he wish it when it was fairly common knowledge that she had tossed him over once already?

He climbed the crimson-carpeted stairs to the first floor and quickly navigated the wide corridor toward his brother's private box. People milled about, some aimless and some with purpose. He wove a path among and around them until he reached the door he sought.

Trystan took a moment to gather himself and to send up a quick prayer that all would go smoothly, then turned the knob and opened the door.

"I hope you haven't been waiting long," he said as he stepped inside and closed the door behind him.

The lady turned, a smile on her full lips. Trystan's heart skipped a beat. She was the most beautiful creature he had ever seen in russet silk and glittering citrine jewelry.

"Vienne, what are you doing here?"

She took a sip from a glass of champagne. There was a bottle in a bucket of ice nearby, and another glass on a tray. "Right now I imagine you're feeling a fraction of the same surprise I felt when you told me you had won my marker from Angelwood."

Surprise was only the tip of what he felt. There were so many other emotions vying for dominance. "Did you win this evening from Lady Gosling?"

"Actually, I offered her a great deal of money for it."

His sense of self-worth inched upward. "How much?"

"Two thousand. Fortunately for my accounts, she refused."

And plummeted once more. "If she refused, how did you come to be here?" He glanced over his shoulder, as though Lady Gosling might come bursting through the door at any moment.

"She traded me the evening for a favor."

This was certainly shaping up to be one curiously strange evening. Now Trystan glanced out to see if anyone in the audience was watching the goings on in the Duke of Ryeton's box. It didn't appear that anyone had any interest in them whatsoever.

He turned his full attention to Vienne. "What sort of favor?"

She smiled. "Nothing you need concern yourself with." She gestured to the chairs before them. "Shall we sit?"

Trystan waited until she had seated herself and then took the chair to her left. "I beg to differ. I think the favor you promised concerns me very much."

She took another sip from her glass. He watched her throat as she swallowed. "I agreed to spend time with her."

The most wanton and delicious images flickered through his perverted mind. "How so?"

Her head turned, pinning him with her sharp gaze. "You will take your mind from the gutter, Trystan Kane. I'm merely going to spend time with Lady Gosling as a friend."

Heat burned in Trystan's cheeks. How had she known what he was thinking? "Friends?"

"Yes. She doesn't have any, you know. Theone—
Lady Gosling—believes I might be the *only* woman
in London confident enough to be a friend to her. I
told her I was not so sure about that, but she insisted
and so here I am."

He shook his head as the noise of the crowd grew.
The play was about to begin. "I don't understand
why you would go through so much trouble for one
evening with me. You could have just asked."

She smiled. "Where's the fun in that? Besides, I
rather enjoy catching you off guard."

His gaze locked with hers. He would not blink.
He would not look away. "Just tell me why, Vienne."

She sighed and refilled her glass from the chilled
bottle. "Because I wanted to. Is that good enough
for you?"

No, it wasn't, but it would do for now. Later, he
would find out why she orchestrated all of this.

Suddenly Trystan found himself hoping that his
companion for the evening expected more than a
play and dinner.

Much, much more.

Chapter 10

She would undoubtedly regret it at a later date, but Vienne was determined to seduce Trystan before the evening was over.

It was not a good idea to mix business and pleasure, but in this case she was beginning to think she might go mad if she didn't do just that. She was jealous of other women, wondered where he was when he wasn't with her. She wanted his attention directed at her and her alone.

And she needed to know that he still desired her—that, even though she was creeping toward her mid-thirties, she was still attractive.

It was a mere four years between them, but it had seemed so much greater during their affair. Back then, he was still a young man whose experiences with the world were all the indulgence and adventure that wealth could afford. Vienne on the other hand, had felt ancient right down to her bones. Even then. Life had aged her inside, and she felt the difference between them might as well have been thirty years. Until Trystan started making her feel young again—and that was when she'd gotten scared.

She was scared now as well. Obviously she had never quite gotten over him. That old attraction had reared its head the first night he had sauntered into her club and flirted shamelessly with Sadie. Being with him had begun to consume her thoughts until she was convinced having sex with him was the only way to end the foolish obsession.

After all, sex took the shine off every relationship. Once the prey was brought to ground, men moved on. It was a lesson she had learned from Marcel—one she practiced in her own relationships, leaving before she could be cast aside like rubbish.

Once Trystan had scratched her itch, they could get back to being business partners and nothing else. She hoped. If that didn't work, she had no idea what could possibly be done.

The theater had been mildly diverting—at least the actors seemed to be having a good time. Several times she and Trystan had burst out laughing at their antics.

Dinner was lovely. He had it brought up to his apartments rather than a private dining room. Perhaps he had an itch that needed scratching as well. They dined on surprisingly light but delicious fare:

salads and lobster in a delicate garlic-wine sauce followed by champagne and succulent ripe fruits they ate with their hands.

"Your taste has improved," she commented teasingly before biting into a plump dark cherry. "I remember you being strictly a beefsteak-and-potato sort."

Trystan grinned and popped a grape into his mouth. "When you travel as much as I have, and love to eat as much as I do, there is little else to do but jump in and sample local cuisine."

"Which were your favorites?" Other than growing up in France, she hadn't done much traveling. She always meant to, but she was so busy there never seemed a good time.

"Italy is impressive, of course. And there were several dishes I fell in love with in India. If I had to choose one country with the best food, it would probably be Greece. Wonderful olives, meat, and desserts, which, I am convinced, come straight from the gods. Have you ever heard of baklava?"

She shook her head. "What is it?"

"Heaven," he replied in all seriousness. "Layers of crisp pastry filled with nuts and dripping in honey. Messy, and the only time I've ever licked my fingers in public."

A little shiver raced across Vienne's shoulders,

which were fully covered by her gown because of the fading bruises. An image flashed in her mind of Trystan hovering over her, lifting glistening fingers to his mouth.

"Vienne?"

She jerked her head up. "What?"

He was frowning at her from across the table. "Are you all right? You seemed far away and your color became very high."

A strangled giggle bubbled up from her throat. She sounded like a madwoman. "I'm fine. Forgive me. You make me want to visit Greece."

"You should. You'd love it there."

Anyone else and she would dismiss that comment with the thought that they had no idea what she might like . . . but not this time. If Trystan said she would enjoy Greece, she probably would. That alone should make her run as fast and as far as she could. The last time she'd trusted a man as much as she was trusting Trystan Kane, it had gone very, very badly—ending in ruination in every way possible.

That she didn't want to run scared her even more. She wanted to stay and poke this dangerous relationship with a stick just to see what might happen.

They had not discussed business all evening, and it was lovely.

"Jack tells me you threatened him with physical harm if he hurt Sadie."

Vienne perused the platter of fruit, searching for something interesting and exotic to try. She'd never tasted mango before, so she selected a slice that was a rich orange color and juicy. "I did, yes. She is my dearest friend." She popped the fruit in her mouth. It was delicious! Tangy but sweet at the same time.

Trystan smiled. "Enjoying the mango?" She nodded. "Good. So when you 'swapped' this evening with Lady Gosling you did so to . . . protect me?"

"In a manner of speaking, yes." She plucked up another slice of mango. "Lady Gosling is too much for you. Let someone like your brother Archer have her."

A strange expression came over Trystan's face, transforming it from good-natured to dangerous with the most subtle of change. "Too much? I am not man enough for her, is that what you're saying?"

Vienne actually drew back. She did not like that look. "Of course not." She didn't add that any man was "man enough" for the woman. "What I mean is that you are not . . . You are an honorable person and . . . *Damn it, Trystan!* She is the kind of woman who would take everything you offered and give nothing in return, and you deserve better."

His expression turned droll. Thank God that

"look" was almost completely gone. "But my brother does not?"

She waved her hand. "Lord Archer has played the game long enough to know how to insure his needs are met." She could not believe she was discussing his brother in this manner.

Trystan leaned one arm across the table and poked the back of her hand with one long finger. "You and I have not communicated in years. You have no idea how good I've become at playing games."

She swallowed, her throat suddenly very dry. "You are right, of course. But I would like to believe that you still treat women with respect. It is rare in my experience that a man finds almost as much pleasure in a woman's satisfaction as he does in his own. I would hate to discover you had lost that gift."

The tips of his fingers trailed along the backs of hers. In the soft light his eyes looked almost violet. "Tell me the real reason you are here tonight, Vienne. You did not go through this much effort to protect me from Lady Gosling. You did this because you don't want me to make love to any other woman but you. Isn't that right?"

His touch did strange things to her head, making it impossible to think straight. Perhaps it was the champagne, but she was unsteady inside herself. And when he put the question to her in such a blunt way, with that delicious voice of his and those pretty, pretty eyes. . .

"Yes," she rasped. "You must think me the most horrible woman on the earth after the way I treated you those many years ago, but I am selfish, Trystan. I want you all to myself, and I keep hoping that if I just give in perhaps I will stop thinking about it so very much." It wasn't until she finished speaking that she realized she had been speaking in French. Good God, was she going to have to repeat it in English? She had done well simply to get through it the first time!

But Trystan's fingers curled around hers. His thumb stroked the back of her hand with featherlight pressure. *"D'accord,"* he said.

She blinked at him, not just because he'd spoken in French and presumably understood what she had said, but because his reply was the equivalent of saying "all right." As though she had asked him if he wanted a cup of tea.

"D'accord"—she lifted both brows, as high as they would go, it seemed—"That is all you have to say?"

His fingers tightened. He pulled her forward, so that their faces were but inches apart. There was nothing but his face—his eyes. The rest of the world faded away. "We've spent more than enough time talking."

Vienne's lips parted as a sharp thrill raced through her veins. It was just as she remembered but more acute, deeper. The only man who had ever truly quickened her blood and made her want to believe in fairy tales, and she was about to play with fire once more.

She was either incredibly stupid or a changed woman because she did not get up and run away. In fact, she lifted herself out of her chair and closed the distance between them to press her lips to his. He opened his mouth for her and she didn't hesitate to slip her tongue inside. He tasted of champagne and mango . . . *Delicious*.

Trystan stood, pulling her with him, neither of them breaking their kiss. His tongue stroked hers; his teeth nipped at her lower lip. She shuddered in his arms, pressing herself against the long, lean length of him.

His hands moved to her shoulders, then down her sides, avoiding the areas on her back where she was still a little sore and slightly bruised. Her heart swelled at his consideration.

Vienne was impatient. It had been so long since she'd last been with him, and that night at the An-gelwood party only heightened her appetite for him. Her fingers crept up to his cravat and untied the elegant knot. Slowly, she unwound the length of silk and pulled it away from his neck, dropping it to the floor. Next she moved on to the buttons on his coat and pushed the fine black wool off his shoulders and down his arms. Eyes closed, she tossed it to the side.

Trystan chuckled against her mouth, warm breath mingling with hers. "Madam, you have absolutely no regard for my clothing."

She shrugged, and flicked her tongue along his full lower lip. "No, sir. I do not. Feel free to have as little regard for mine."

To her intense relief, he kissed her again and put his nimble fingers to work unfastening the myriad buttons on the back of her gown. Why couldn't she have been sensible and worn a gown that perhaps wasn't as pretty but was easier to remove? Her mother always said her vanity would bring her nothing but trouble.

He took his time, teasing her by being so infuriatingly slow. She moved on to his waistcoat, and after ridding him of that, pulled his shirt from his trousers. The faster she rid him of his clothing, the sooner she could assist in removing her own. It didn't matter who was naked first, just so long as they both ended up bare as the day they were born.

He was still working on her buttons, so she slid her hands beneath his shirt and slid her palms up his smooth, muscled back. His skin was so warm.

Vienne pressed against him. It wasn't close enough.

Finally the top of her gown sagged around her shoulders and Trystan's skillful hands pushed the fragile silk down her arms. She pulled back so that the gown could simply crumple about her feet, leaving her still wearing entirely too many clothes—corset, shift, and stockings.

She pulled his shirt up. He obliged by lifting his arms so she could pull the fine linen off altogether. Then she took a moment to admire his naked upper body.

As a young man, Trystan had been English pale and whipchord lean. Somehow over the years he'd gained a little color, and his skin had a faint tan cast. He was also bigger than he had been, which only made sense considering he was now a man and not a boy. His shoulders were broad, the bones standing out beneath his skin. His arms were thicker and more defined, the upper half curved with muscle. But it was his chest that fascinated her the most. She had seen a few chests in her lifetime; some of them quite impressive, but none like this. Trystan looked as though an Italian master had sculpted him into being. His pectorals were well defined above slashes of muscle and ribs, and his stomach would have been almost concave were it not for the ropey muscle there.

"*Magnifique*," she whispered, tracing her fingers

down that satiny flesh, marred by only a fine trail of hair that disappeared beneath the waist of his trousers.

"*Merci,*" he replied, a smile in his voice. He had loosened the laces of her corset while she admired him, and now set to work popping the hooks in the front. "This is very pretty."

It was pale yellow satin embroidered with tiny flowers. She wore it because it displayed her breasts to best advantage. She gasped when Trystan caressed the top of one breast before peeling the corset away. "Thank you."

He tossed the corset aside as she had his coat, not bothering to see where it landed. It was on the floor, and would remain there until she had need of it again. That was all she had to know.

Vienne stood perfectly still as Trystan's hands settled first on her shoulders, then slid down her arms. His fingers bunched the gauzy material of her shift and pulled it taut against her body. Instinctively her nipples hardened and a thrill of sensual pleasure struck between her thighs, moistening the delicate flesh there.

She drew a deep breath, pushing her breasts against the thin material. He made a low sound deep in his throat. "I want to rip this thing right off you." His voice was a growl.

"Do it," she challenged. So long she'd been the one in charge and now she wanted—no, she *needed*—someone to take charge of her. "Rip it off me. Take me to your bed and do what you will to me. I want you to."

His gaze locked with hers. There, in the fathomless depths of his beautiful eyes, she saw the precise moment he passed the point of no return. Something primitive sparked there, and it sparked in her as well, although in a region considerably lower than her eyes.

He pulled. There was a rending of fabric, so loud in the stillness of the room it sounded like a shriek. And then she was standing there, her ruined shift hanging in tatters from her shoulders, exposed from breast to thigh—*sans* drawers.

Trystan pushed the rags from her arms and tossed them to the floor, his gaze seeming to drink in every inch of her. His expression was akin to wondrous, and his fingers trembled slightly as they reached out toward her. Vienne held her breath, trembled from head to foot.

"Please," she whispered, "touch me."

Again his eyes met hers. At the same time his hands came up to cup her breasts, thumbs sliding over the tight, sensitive peaks. Her knees weakened and her entire body seemed to throb in response.

He wasn't rough and he wasn't overly gentle. The one thing that hadn't changed about him was the fact that Trystan Kane seemed to instinctively know exactly how to touch her, how to pleasure her.

Vienne sighed in delight. And when he lowered his head, she combed her fingers through this thick, silky sable hair. She damn near sobbed when his tongue spent a hot, wet stroke over her desperate nipple.

His hands moved again, one holding her around her waist, the other sliding down her stomach to ease between her thighs. She parted her legs to give him easier access and felt the cool rush of moisture on her skin. All he had to do was lick her nipple and she was wet.

Long, talented fingers slid between the folds, immediately finding the knot of flesh that begged for his attention. One firm stroke made her shudder. The second jerked her hips upward and had her moaning aloud. Once more and she pulled his hair, on the verge of climaxing.

And then he removed his hand, leaving her on the verge, aching and about to implode. He stopped tonguing her breast as well.

Vienne looked at him from beneath her lashes. "If you leave me like this, I will kill you."

Trystan grinned and reached around her to grab

one of the chairs from the table. "Sit," he commanded. And she did.

He was still wearing his trousers, the front of which bulged impressively. Vienne reached out and caressed that bulge. Trystan groaned, wrapping his fingers around her wrist so he could push her hand against his erection. She squeezed, anticipation mounting. It wouldn't take much for her to sink to her knees on the carpet and release his glorious length from its cloth prison. She could take him in her mouth and make him beg for release.

Before she could do any of that, he released her wrist and slowly eased down onto his own knees in front of her. He took the champagne bottle from the bucket beside the table and set it on the floor beside him. Then he wrapped his hands around the back of her knees and pulled her forward so that her backside rested on the very edge of the chair.

"Spread your legs," he commanded.

There wasn't a single part of her that would dream of denying him, not when that undeniable tone of his voice made want her to shove her hand between her legs and finish herself off. She spread her thighs wide, until she could see a flash of pink through the ginger curls of her sex. Her hands went behind to grip the edge of the chair, bracing her weight so she could arch her hips invitingly.

Trystan trailed a finger along the sensitive flesh she offered him. Then he raised the champagne bottle so that the mouth of it hovered just above her quim, and tipped it.

Vienne cried out as the cold liquid made contact with her body's heat. Shock and pleasure mingled, making her hips jerk and churn. Before she could recover, Trystan wrapped his arms around her legs so that the back of her thighs rested near his shoulders, and fastened his mouth on her.

"Oh!" She lifted her pelvis, bracing her weight on her hands and his arms so she could offer herself up like a feast on a platter. Trystan's tongue lapped at the bubbles of champagne that tingled on her flesh. The sweet ache of arousal deepened and she could not contain the cooing sounds slipping from between her parted lips. She ground herself against his mouth, begging him in French to give her the release she sought. Higher and higher he took her, winding the spring inside so tightly she thought she might cry if he didn't soon let her come.

And then he did. With one forceful lap of his tongue, Trystan sent her over the edge. Pleasure rushed up and seized her, obliterating all thought or reason, shaking her entire body for what seemed an eternity. She cried out—a long, keening cry the likes of which had not escaped her lips for far, far too long.

She sagged in the chair. He licked her again and she jerked, still so very sensitive. Panting for breath and feeling as though she'd just had her bones turned to pudding, Vienne watched as Trystan rose to his feet with a smug smile on his glistening mouth.

"I'm going to assume you liked that."

"You know I did, you vain man. You should give lessons."

"And share my secrets? I think not." His fingers went to the front of his trousers, which he unfastened and slid down his lean hips. "I'm not done with you, woman."

"I should hope not," she replied saucily as he straightened, kicking trousers, stockings, and shoes out of the way. She had always admired the lean but shapely length of his legs, and still did—though now the muscle there was a little heavier and more pronounced. His hips were still narrow, the bones jutting slightly beneath his skin, but those weren't what caught her attention.

Trystan Kane had what she personally believed to be the most magnificent cockstand in all of Britain, perhaps the Continent as well. Neither too long nor too short, too thick or too thin—it seemed as though it had been perfectly designed with her pleasure in mind, a fact for which she planned to thank God for once she'd had it inside her.

She slid to the floor, ending up kneeling at his feet like a penitent sinner. She slid her hands up the back of his calves, the hair tickling her palms. When she reached his thighs, she tugged him closer, opened her mouth and took the hard length of him inside. He groaned in encouragement, his hands gently cupping the back of her head. Vienne took him deep and then released him, hollowing her cheeks to form tight suction as she took him all the way once more.

"You are so very, very good at this," he murmured, the compliment ending on a groan.

Inwardly Vienne smiled as he patted her on the head. One more stroke and she set him free. She rose to her feet and met his hungry gaze with her own. "Next time I will make you come that way, but right now I want that beautiful cock inside me."

Trystan's eyes glittered with mirth and seductive promise. "As you wish."

She turned him around and then pushed against the hard wall of his chest so that he sat down on the same chair she had been in. Then she straddled him and wrapped her fingers around his hardness, guiding him into place so she could take him inside with one slick descent. Her body stretched to accommodate his, both of them shuddering and moaning at the incredibly intense sensation.

For a moment, Vienne sat on his lap, the two of

them connected like pieces of a puzzle. Then she braced her toes against the carpet and pushed herself up. Down. Up.

Trystan held her hips, but he let her set the pace of their coupling. She gripped his broad shoulders as she moved, never taking her gaze from his face. At that moment, she had never seen a more beautiful or perfect man. Even though his nose was slightly crooked and a little large, and his mouth a little too wide, he was exceptional in his beauty. She loved the lines around his eyes and mouth and the light smatter of freckles across the bridge of his nose—she could look at them for hours and never suffer boredom.

She lowered her head and kissed him, slowly savoring the warm pliancy of his lips. She would never regret this night. No matter what came after, she would always be thankful that she had the chance to hold him again, feel him against her and inside her one more time.

One of his hands came up and began pulling pins from her hair as she rode him—languidly. Having already climaxed once, she wasn't in a desperate hurry to do it again, although the urge was definitely building. When her hair tumbled freely down her back, she shook her head so the strands fell over her shoulders and breasts. He liked seeing her hair loose, falling between them as they made love. She knew this because he had told her years ago and she never forgot.

He smiled at her and she smiled back. Never had she looked a man in the eye as often and without shame as she did Trystan. He had seen her at both her best and worst, and still he was here with her now. Was she incredibly fortunate, or did he have some sort of mental defect when it came to her?

He ran his fingers through her hair, plucking up a strand and tickling her nipples with the ends. She squirmed, which only served to plant him as deep inside her as he could possibly go.

"You're killing me," he groaned.

Vienne grinned. "I am the one on top. I make the rules."

He arched a brow, and then suddenly she found herself standing, empty and slightly bewildered. Trystan stood as well, his erection still high and firm. He took her by the waist and turned her around so that she faced the table.

"Put your hands on it," he ordered.

Vienne did, aware that doing so set her hips and backside at a very provocative angle. Trystan ran gentle hands along her back; and when she felt his lips touch where his hands had been, she knew he was kissing what bruises remained. The knowledge tugged at her heart.

He nudged her legs apart and filled her with one thrust. His fingers splayed across her hips, holding her still as he teased her with shallow strokes. Gritting her teeth, Vienne bent her arms, lowering her torso onto the table so her hips were even higher.

It felt so good, what he did to her. It was so arousing to be completely at his mercy, all of her control stripped away. Every slick thrust brought her closer to a second climax, made her muscles tense. The only sounds in the room were their harsh breaths, little incoherent words of encouragement, and pleasure.

How did it feel for him, she wondered? Did the feel of her tight wetness make him half as mad as his hardness made her? Did he wish this could go on forever yet push all the harder toward the inevitable spending?

One of his hands slid beneath her, his fingers tweaking her nipple. Sensation flared and she gasped in sweet delight. She clutched at the tablecloth, their movements jostling dishes and silverware. Thankfully it was a sturdy table, so there was little worry of anything breaking should things become a little more intense—as they were, slowly.

His other hand left her hip to seize a handful of

her hair. The gentle tug made her moan aloud. Was there nothing he did not remember about her sexually? With his fingers pulling and pinching at hair and breast respectively, and his glorious cock filling her, orgasm would not be far off. She widened her stance, taking him deeper. He grunted and began to thrust faster, pulling harder on her hair—but still not enough to hurt—and tormenting her breasts to the point where pleasure almost became pain but was still too good to stop.

"Yes," she murmured, practically hissing. "Oh, Trystan . . . Yes, please . . ."

"Tell me you want it." His voice was a hoarse growl.

"I want it." Her eyes squeezed shut as she concentrated on the mounting tension inside her. "I need it."

"What do you need?"

"You," she gasped. She meant to say "your cock" but her mouth seemed to have other plans. "I need you."

Obviously those were the right words to say because he began thrusting faster, harder. The pressure inside her swelled and tightened, building higher and higher until she came with a force that drove her up onto her toes, forehead braced on her fists as she cried out in the sheer bliss of it all. She felt Trystan stiffen, heard him stifle a shout as he came as well, pulsing inside her.

They stayed like that for a few seconds, until both their limbs decided to give up supporting them. Then they sagged to the floor and lay together on the carpet, still gasping for breath.

Neither of them said anything, but Vienne was hardly worried. It never had been their habit to talk after sex. Usually they had curled up together and fell asleep in each other's arms. That wasn't going to happen on the floor of Trystan's home, not when there was a perfectly good bed only a couple of rooms away.

A quarter of an hour and some heavy petting later, Trystan was hard again. This time he took her to bed, and sprawled on the mattress so she might climb on top of him. He let her take charge and set the pace. For Vienne the victory wasn't so much in being in control but watching his face when he came just after she did. At first he looked as though he was in pain, but then his expression changed to one of joy; and after he stiffened, he grinned and began to chuckle. She understood how he felt—it truly was that good.

She collapsed beside him on the bed, wrapping her arm and one leg over him in case he tried to pull away before she was ready to let him go. He wrapped his arms around her and held her tight against his chest, and she knew he wasn't going anywhere.

He kissed her forehead and traced gentle circles on the small of her spine. She could hear the beating of his heart as she placed her head on his warm, slightly damp chest. In that one perfect moment, hearing his heart mimic the beating of her own, it was as though everything made sense. Everything was where it belonged.

And so was she.

Chapter 11

He'd been awake for at least half an hour, watching Vienne as she slept. She looked so peaceful—like an angel at rest—he couldn't bring himself to wake her, even though the longer she stayed, the more scandal they courted.

What was this feeling fluttering in his chest? This wasn't how he'd felt about her the first time. Back then everything seemed so dramatic and earth shattering. Now there was just a happy sort of peace filling him up inside. Trystan didn't need to think too hard upon it; he recognized the emotion for what it was—all he had to do was open himself to the inevitability.

He was in love with Vienne La Rieux.

It was entirely possible that he'd never fallen out of love with her, despite all her efforts to encourage just that. It would not be easy to convince her to do otherwise now either. She would resist him with as much fervor as she could, simply to protect herself.

He would be able to gauge the depths of her emotions by how frightened she was. It wouldn't happen right away. In a few days, once she began to realize what she had done, and those feelings began to take hold, she'd fight him.

Only this time he was ready for the battle. He wouldn't be cast aside like a stupid boy who didn't know a frightened woman when he saw one. This time he would do everything in his power to make her realize she was not alone.

He realized now that this had been the plan all along. He told himself he wanted to be her equal and have her acknowledge that, and this was still true. But what he truly wanted was for her to realize they were good for one another—perhaps even perfect. He wanted her to allow him to help clean out that internal cupboard of hers and toss out the ancient skeletons she hid there.

What had driven this home to him? When he saw her fall from that ladder and realized he would rather take an injury than see it happen to her. If he could take away all her pain, both physical and emotional, he would do it. Even if it meant he would have to experience it all himself.

His mother insisted that he find himself a wife, and he had found her. All that stood in his way was the chosen bride. She would not surrender without a fight, he thought, a smile curving his lips. It was good, then, that he was more than up for the challenge.

Vienne's auburn lashes fluttered and opened. Her gaze was unfocused as it met his and she blinked before rubbing the sleep from her eyes with her knuckles. When she looked at him again, her vision was clear.

"Good morning," he said.

She frowned. "What time is it?"

"Vienne." He placed just enough amused censure in his tone to make her blush. He loved that he, of all people, could bring a flush to the usually so cool and composed Madame La Rieux.

Sheepishly, she smiled and stretched. The sheets tried valiantly to conceal her nakedness to no avail. Trystan's morning was made—with a peek of pale coral nipple.

"*Bon matin,*" she said, squirming closer so she could wrap one long silken leg over his. "Did you sleep well?"

Trystan grinned. "Oddly enough, yes. I would have thought having such a delectable woman beside me would prove a distraction, but it seems that you are better than a sleeping powder."

"If only I could manage to bottle and sell it, I would be rich beyond words."

He put his arm around her and pulled her tight against his chest. Her breasts were warm against him. "I do not think I would want to share your powers with the rest of the world."

She eyed him for a moment, and the teasing light in her gaze faded into something that reminded him of wonder. "You really wouldn't, would you? After everything I've done, you would want me all to yourself?"

There was no point in denying it, even though he knew admitting such would probably frighten her. He lifted a lock of her hair from the pillow and stroked the shiny, copper length. "I would, yes. Does that bother you?"

Vienne propped her head up in her hand. She couldn't be too upset by the admission because her free hand stroked the edges of his ribs, and she didn't try to shield her nudity from his gaze. "A little," she confessed. "I am not accustomed to men wanting me all to themselves."

The reminder that she'd had other lovers shouldn't have cut as deep as it did. He'd always known she was experienced, though far from what he would consider promiscuous. It wasn't the fact that there had been other men; it was the idea that he might not measure up under comparison.

"You are jealous." Her tone was lightly teasing,

but there was an edge to it as well, as though she expected this might grow into an argument.

Trystan smiled, pushing the negative emotion aside. It didn't matter if he was the best lover she ever had, so long as he was the last. "So accuses the woman who bartered her time and friendship to prevent another woman from spending the evening with me."

She pinched his arm. "It isn't polite to throw a lady's words back at her."

He stroked a hand up the back of her thigh. "I suppose it isn't polite to do this either." As he spoke, he gently eased a finger inside her. She was warm and slick, and clenched sweetly at the intrusion.

Vienne gasped. "No, it certainly is not."

Trystan slowly withdrew his finger and then slid it inside her again. "How fortunate for both of us, then, that I am such a rude man."

She chuckled. "Indeed."

This time when he removed his finger, he replaced it with his erection. They made love on their sides, facing one another. To watch her face as passion took over was amazing—seeing how she flushed as her eyelids became heavy and lips parted with every soft breath.

He wanted to do this for the rest of his life. With *her*.

Afterward, he held her against his chest and

kissed her forehead. She was a disheveled mess as opposed to her normal perfectly turned-out self, and she was gorgeous.

"Trystan?" she murmured against his chest.

"Mm-hm?"

"What time is it?"

Laughing, he checked the small clock on his bedside table. He winced. "It's a quarter of ten."

She bolted upright. "What? Oh, *mon Dieu!*" Then she went off in a torrent of such fast and furious French, he could only make out the odd word. She was not pleased, as was evident when she tossed back the blankets and stomped around the room snatching up her clothing.

"Vienne." She ignored him. "Vienne!"

"What?" She whirled on him, hair streaming around her shoulders, clothes clasped to her front. "There's no way I can sneak out of here quietly, Trystan. Someone will see me leaving this place wearing evening clothes—and the gossip will be so very, very annoying."

Most women he knew would find the idea of people talking about her personal life a catastrophe—ruination. Vienne found it annoying. Like a fly buzzing about her head.

"I sent Havers 'round to Saint's Row earlier with a letter for your maid requesting she send a change of clothing for you in a discreet bag. You can change into day wear, fix your hair, and leave here this morning looking as though you arrived for a breakfast meeting."

She stared at him. "Are you serious?"

He nodded. "I am. He should be here any moment."

She dropped the clothes and came back to the bed gloriously naked. "You are very useful man, Trystan Kane."

He smiled. "I put a great deal of effort into being just that." He wasn't the least bit offended that she didn't want people to know they'd spent the night together—he didn't either; it was no one's damned business.

True to his prediction, Havers knocked on the door a few moments later, just before breakfast was brought up. Meanwhile, Vienne was safely wrapped up in his spare dressing gown while he wore the other.

They shared a leisurely breakfast, something neither of them often did. Usually he read the paper and she went over plans for the day; and they tended to speak of business concerns, but not this morning. Today, they talked about frivolous things, and some personal things.

"Your brother the duke will try to run me out of town, if he finds out about this." She gestured to the bed.

Trystan helped himself to another slice of bacon. "Don't worry about him. Grey will do well to keep his nose out of my business."

"You are very fortunate to have family who love you so much."

He snorted. "I cannot say I agree with that sentiment, but I thank you for it. What about your family? You rarely speak of them."

She shrugged—the French could convey so much with that very simple action. "There is not much to say. They are in France and I am here."

She closed herself off in such a way that he knew she did not want to talk about her family, or her past. He knew, then, that family played a part in whatever had happened to make her afraid of forming attachments.

Whatever Grey and Archer's faults, he could not imagine what would have to happen for him to leave them behind and never speak to, or of, them ever again.

"Scotland Yard wants to meet with us later this afternoon to talk about the incidents at the site. Do you feel up to that?"

She arched a brow at him over her coffee cup. "Yes. You did not exhaust me so thoroughly that I feel the need to recuperate for the rest of the day."

"Ouch. You wound me."

Vienne grinned and tossed a croissant at his head. "Not bloody likely, Englishman."

He laughed at the way she said "bloody"—*bluh-DEE*.

After breakfast they bathed together, which led to further delay. Then he sat and watched her fix her hair before playing lady's maid and helping her into her teal day gown. It felt very domestic, very comfortable and very *right*.

"Will I see you at the site later?" he asked, trying not to sound overly eager.

"Yes. I have luncheon with Sadie, but I will be there. You know, we really do need to decide on a name for it. I'm tired of calling it 'the site' or 'the emporium.' It should have a name of its own."

"We could call it Kane's," he suggested with a smile.

She rolled her eyes before patting him gently on the cheek. "No." She paused. "Although perhaps both our vanities might be appeased by something such as Trystienne's?"

He thought about it. Combining their names seemed almost silly, but he had to admit he liked the sound of it. The two of them, together forever—at least as a shopping destination. "I think it just might do," he said.

She smiled happily, as though she had won a major victory. He had to chuckle at just how much she loved to win.

"How could I not like it when my name comes first?"

Her smile faltered just a little bit, but she took his teasing in stride. And then she kissed him good-bye, and he felt he couldn't wait for nightfall, thought of spending the evening with her and . . . all the evenings after, if she would let him. But he couldn't push; that would be the quickest way to drive her away.

He had driven her away last time. He would not lose her again.

Vienne was still at her desk tackling the day's correspondence when Sadie arrived. Her friend sailed into the room in a bright violet day gown trimmed with chartreuse and a large, wide-brimmed hat with feathers dyed to match. Only Sadie could get away with such an ensemble and make it look like the height of fashion.

Setting aside her pen, Vienne pushed away from her desk and stood, smiling at the sight of her friend.

Sadie, however, took one look at her and stopped dead in her tracks on the richly patterned carpet. "Jesus, Mary and Joseph," she said in astonishment. "You slept with him."

Heat crawled up Vienne's cheeks. She felt it seep under her eyebrows. "Who?" Questions were always the best way to avoid having to answer them one-self. She skirted around Sadie to close the door to her office, lest eager ears overhear. Her friend followed her movement.

"You know very well who. Trystan Kane, the man whose heart even you say you smashed."

This certainly wasn't what she had expected from Sadie. Perhaps a little ribbing, or even full-on teas-ing, but she hadn't thought her past actions would be thrown into her face. "That was a long time ago."

"You haven't changed."

Not by much, no. "Trystan has. He doesn't have those same romantic notions about us anymore."

"Are you sure about that? Did you by any chance think of asking him before you jumped into his bed? What did you do, arrive at the hotel while he was having dinner with Lady Gosling?"

The fire in her cheeks roared to life again. She didn't have to say anything; Sadie's eyes widened. "You fixed it so they didn't have an appointment at all, didn't you? Arranged it so you could have him all to yourself . . . and you don't think he might get all kinds of 'romantic notions' in his head because of it? For the love of all that's holy, Vienne. What were you thinking?"

"I wasn't!" she shot back. "I just knew I couldn't let her or anyone else have him. I couldn't bear it." She slumped onto the sofa and pressed a palm to her forehead. "It never occurred to me that he might take it as some sort of declaration."

"Of course not," her friend replied with more than a touch of sarcasm. "Who would?"

With a sigh, Sadie plopped down beside her. "You have feelings for him?"

Removing her hand, Vienne narrowed her eyes. "Of course I do. I'm not entirely a heartless predator."

"Committee's still out on that one, dearest." Her expression turned sympathetic. "Oh, Vienne. You cannot seem to help yourself where he is concerned."

"No," she admitted. "I cannot. I wanted him and I have him, and I'm going to enjoy having him for as long as it lasts."

"And if he wants more than just an affair?"

It wasn't "just" an affair. They were partners. "I see no reason why we can't go forward as lovers."

"Men like him cannot be satisfied with a lover, Vienne. They want wives to share their lives with."

Vienne knew she spoke from experience. Sadie had thought to give Jack up when he inherited his grandfather's title and became a viscount, but Jack would have none of it. He could have found himself a fancy wife, but he wanted Sadie. Vienne thought the better of him for it.

But what if she was right? What if Trystan wanted more than she could give? And just how much was that? A few weeks ago, she would have had a ready answer. But now . . . now she only knew that she would fight anyone who tried to take him away; and if he told her tomorrow that he was to be married, it would break her heart. How fitting that she, who had hurt him so badly so long ago, was now in a position to have the same done to her.

She wouldn't allow it. She would leave him before she risked her heart. It wasn't that she was afraid— well, perhaps a little—but she had been through that pain and betrayal. She could not stand to offer herself and be hurt or, worse, have someone offer himself to her and find herself unable to love him. Because that was part of the deeper issue: she didn't know if there was any love left in her to give; and if there was, and she gave it and got crushed in return, she truly would be nothing more than an empty, unwanted shell.

Isn't that what Marcel had said to her? That there was nothing about her that was lovable except perhaps her female parts. She was too vain and too selfish. Just all around less of a woman than she should be.

Others had seen this in her. She knew because

many men had told her what a bitch she was, or how cold and unfeeling. She wasn't whole—and Trystan deserved better.

But it was a lovely fantasy, thinking of the two of them together, in a perfect world where she wasn't past her prime and could give herself to someone without fear of being rejected. She always left first, that way she was never the one cast aside.

"Vienne?"

She blinked and looked up. Sadie watched her strangely. "You wandered off."

"My apologies, my friend. My thoughts ran away with me. Yes, I know Trystan wants a wife. His mother has been pushing him to find one."

"And he hasn't."

"No." That gave her so much more joy than she would admit.

"Because of you."

She refused to take the blame. "Because he has not fallen in love."

Sadie tilted her head to one side. It was astounding that her enormous hat didn't force her head to keep going. "Has he not?"

Vienne laughed in disbelief. "Of course not. Trystan is a sweet, wonderful man, but he is not stupid, Sadie. He knows falling in love with me would be a horrible idea. Believe me, if anyone knows better than to offer me his heart, it is Trystan Kane."

So why the bitter taste in her mouth? Why the sudden anger twisting in her soul? She was angry . . . angry at herself for not being what he wanted. Not being good enough for the only man who made her feel like, perhaps . . . well, feel as though she was good enough for him after all.

"I know you mean well," she said to her friend, "but I don't want to discuss Trystan or our relationship right now."

"All right." Sadie took a pin from her hat and remove the large accessory. "But you did sleep with him?"

Vienne nodded. "If you must know—yes. I did."

Sadie grinned—a wide flash of straight teeth. "How was it?"

"Did I not just tell you I didn't want to talk about him?"

Her friend rolled her eyes. "I don't need to know how you feel about it, I just want the sordid details. I told you about Jack. Eventually."

There would be no peace unless she divulged at least something, and truth be told she wanted to tell. She wanted to giggle over it like a foolish young girl, and blush over the details. "It was amazing," she confessed, giving into the temptation. "Oh, Sadie. I have never known a man who compares to Trystan."

Sadie's big eyes grew even wider. "Honestly? Not one?"

Vienne could take offense at the suggestion that she'd had a number of lovers, but she didn't. It was true, she had known many men in the biblical sense, but to deny that would diminish Trystan's talents. "Not a one." She chuckled. "How did you guess that I spent the night with him? Did you see it in your leaves?"

"Not at all. It wasn't hard to surmise. You have this slightly idiotic look to you, like you could get kicked by a horse and it wouldn't hurt."

Kicked by a horse. Trystan had likened how she would feel after her fall to such a thing. She was still tender and a little stiff from it. Then again, she was a little tender from last night—and this morning. Just the thought of it was enough to make her tingle inside. "I'm fairly certain it would hurt a great deal. However, I will admit to feeling more relaxed today than I have in a very long time. Now, why don't we retire to my apartments and see what delights Cook has prepared for us. You can help me select a gown for this evening."

"Oh?" Sadie asked, as she picked up her hat and joined Vienne in quitting the room. "Are you doing something particularly special?"

Vienne grinned. *"Someone."*

They laughed all the way to the stairs.

* * *

Following a brief meeting with Grey concerning several of his investments, Trystan joined his brother for a brandy in his study. After all, he had some time before he had to meet the Scotland Yard man with Vienne.

The thought of her brought a smile to his face.

They had just sat down when Archer arrived. He strolled into the room looking dapper in a dark gray suit, even if he was slightly bleary-eyed. God only knew what he had gotten himself up to the night before.

"Good day, my dear brothers"—and helped himself to a glass of brandy—"I do hope I'm interrupting a terribly boring conversation."

"You are indeed," Grey replied. "We were just talking about you."

Archer made a face, his gaze flitting between the two of them before he sat down on the loveseat across from the sofa where Trystan sat. Grey was in a large wingback to the side.

"Are you certain you weren't discussing the fact that Trystan has fallen prey to La Rieux again?"

"What?" Trystan and Grey both exclaimed. "Where in the hell did you hear that?" And Trystan scowled.

"There's speculation all over town," Archer replied nonchalantly. "I didn't pay heed to any of it, of course, not until I walked in here and saw that moony-eyed look on your face. Christ, man! You might as well wear a sign around your neck that reads, Recently Well-Shagged."

Trystan opened his mouth to protest, not completely certain how to phrase it, but was interrupted by Grey, who shot him a very pointed look.

"Is it true?" his eldest brother demanded, his eyes flat as pewter.

If ever there was a good time in his life to lie to his brothers, now would be it. Just like the time he lied about breaking their mother's favorite vase when he was but eleven. Of course, she figured out the truth when he bought her a replacement with the first bit of money he earned on his own, but that was beside the point.

"My personal life is none of your damn business," he retorted instead.

The Duke of Ryeton had always been a good brother, but a protective one. Telling him that something wasn't his business was akin to waving a red flag in front of a bull. As far as he was concerned, everything that happened to any member of his family, no matter how minute or intimate, was *his* business.

And of course he always knew when his younger siblings were trying to hide something. "It is true . . .

Christ on a bicycle, boy," Grey said. "Have you not a lick of sense?"

Trystan clenched his jaw. "I'm *not* a boy."

"*No*," Archer agreed amiably. "You're an *idiot*."

"That's a bit of the pot and the kettle, don't you think?" he shot back.

"Why in God's name would you get involved with her when you know it will lead to no good?" Grey demanded. "Are you looking for revenge?"

"No!" Good Lord, what was it with people thinking he wanted vengeance on Vienne? Even in the throes of heartbreak, he hadn't wanted revenge. He only ever wanted her to see him as special and to regret she had treated him shabbily. "Look, Vienne and I are different people now. I'm a grown man I can be involved with whomever I want."

"Until we have to pick you up and slap you back together again," Archer remarked with more venom than Trystan had ever heard him use. "If she breaks your heart, you will have no one but yourself to blame."

He nodded. "I know, and that's a risk I'm prepared to take. She's the one, Arch."

His brother drained his glass in one gulp. "Deliver me from such drama."

"Leave him alone, Arch," Grey ordered, leveling an unreadable gaze at Trystan. "He's right. It's his life and his decision. If La Rieux is what he wants, then we should respect him enough to know what he's getting into."

"He's already gotten into it," Archer replied hotly. "That's the problem."

Trystan sighed. "Look, I appreciate that the two of you don't want to see me get hurt. But if I don't at least try to win her heart, I'll regret it for the rest of my life."

His brothers exchanged glances. Archer shrugged. "Fine. I suppose I understand regret."

Grey nodded. "As do I. We support you in this Tryst. We don't like it, but we will stand by your decision."

"Even if it is frigging idiotic," Archer added.

Trystan smiled. Vienne was right, he was lucky to have two brothers who cared so much about him. "Thank you."

A knock at the door further diminished the tension between the three of them. It was Rose, looking lovely in a pale blue gown that made her skin glow prettily—or perhaps it was her pregnancy that caused the inner light. She wasn't far along—barely a couple of months—and hadn't yet begun to show. Grey lit up like a candle when he saw her. Lucky bastard, he was.

If a man like Grey, who at one time was as debauched as they come, could settle down, surely a woman like Vienne could as well. He knew it wasn't a fair comparison, but that didn't stop him from hoping that he might persuade Vienne to take a chance on love just as Rose had persuaded his brother.

"Hello, boys," she greeted with a smile. "My apologies, but I'm ravenous and Cook has prepared a tea to feed an army. Would you care to join me?"

Since none of the Kane boys ever lacked in appetite, the three of them agreed and rose to their feet. Rose turned her doe eyes in Trystan's direction. He watched as those big eyes got even bigger.

"Trystan." Her voice had a strange stiffness to it. "You look in good spirits today."

"I am, thank you."

But she wasn't done with him. She seemed to study him, her earnest gaze traveling over ever pore in his face. Then she stood back with her hands on her hips and beamed at him. "You're in love!" She clapped her hands. "*Oh*, won't your mama be so excited!"

"*Whoa!*" Grey barked as Trystan and Archer protested as well. "You do not say a word of this to Mama, Rose."

"God, no," Archer joined in.

Grey's duchess was obviously confused, but there came a moment when understanding dawned, and she turned to Trystan with a look that could only be described as pleasantly shrewd. "It's Madame La Rieux, isn't it? I knew it! Eve said she thought you were going to make an offer for Annalise Beaumont, but I knew your affections were engaged elsewhere."

Archer peered over her head at Trystan. "She knew."

Trystan rubbed the back of his neck. He was beginning to develop a headache. "Rose, this really isn't something I want to talk about."

She looked disappointed. "But I'm your sister-in-law."

Grey took her hand in his and smiled gently. "That doesn't make you his confessor, darling."

She was unconvinced, turning a bright smile on Trystan once again. "I'm female. I can help. I can give you advice as to the best way to court someone like Madame La Rieux."

"No," Grey told her. "You can't. But I can."

Trystan started. This was a switch. A new tactic, perhaps, to persuade him to change his mind? . . . *"You?"*

"Of course . . . I've often thought La Rieux and I were very similar underneath the skin—kindred spirits of a sort."

At first Trystan wanted to disagree, but then he thought about it. Grey had been attacked years earlier and left with a nasty scar on the left side of his face. The attack had been rumored to be the work of an ex-lover, and it affected Grey deeply. He withdrew from the world. Something had happened to Vienne to make her protect herself so fiercely. Perhaps his brother was right.

"How?" he asked as the four of them prepared to leave the room.

Grey placed a hand on the small of his wife's back and shot him a rueful smile. "Relentlessly."

Chapter 12

Inspector Jacobs from Scotland Yard was an average man in appearance, but beyond that he was anything but. He was neither tall nor short, neither fat nor thin. His hair was the same ordinary shade of brown as his suit and his eyes were a common hue of hazel. His features were entirely ordinary, which would make it rather difficult to give an accurate description. He was, in short, the sort of man who could go about unnoticed, and that made him both highly useful and extremely dangerous, depending upon how you looked at it.

Trystan was pleased to have him investigating their concerns. No one else seemed prepared to take it all that seriously, chalking the mishaps up as simple accidents. Inspector Jacobs, however, seemed inclined to agree with Trystan and Vienne—these were not accidents.

"When did these incidents first begin?" he asked, opening his notebook to a fresh page. He sat in one of

Vienne's wingback chairs with his legs crossed. On the table beside him was a glass of water, the only refreshment he accepted.

Trystan turned to Vienne. "There were letters, weren't there?"

"Yes," she responded, her attention focused on the inspector. "I dismissed them as harmless. I might still were it not for how events have escalated."

The inspector nodded. "What exactly were in these letters?"

"Warnings to stop construction, that Trysti-enne's—that is the name we've considered so far for our venture—would lead to the downfall of virtuous women. I kept a few if you would like to see them."

"I would, yes. So you didn't suspect any malicious intent behind these letters?"

Vienne shrugged. "No. They did not say anything the fuddy-duddies in the papers didn't already suggest."

The inspector smiled at her use of *fuddy-duddies*. Trystan did as well. He felt compelled to add his own thoughts. "It's been a shared opinion of some of the more old-fashioned and conservative minds in this country that if women can shop for everything under one roof, they will go mad with temptation and spend their husbands dry."

Jacobs nodded, scribbling in his book. "Never

mind that, at least she will have something to show for her spending, as opposed to her husband, who probably gambles."

"Exactly," Vienne agreed, shooting a pleased glance in Trystan's direction. "We offer accessibility and convenience, certainly not sin and *not* debauchery."

The inspector looked up with a faint curve of his lips. "It occurs to me, Madame La Rieux, that you have set yourself up to take not only the wife's money but the husband's as well. Very shrewd of you."

Vienne puffed up like a peacock under his praise. Trystan watched with interest. The inspector was an older man, intelligent and seemingly open-minded. He was exactly the sort that would draw her interest—not necessarily sexual, but still intimately. She courted approval from such gentlemen.

"So it began with letters, then a workman was injured?"

Vienne nodded. "Two, though the first was so common I wonder if perhaps it's not a simple coincidence."

"But then you took a nasty fall"—he consulted a few pages back in his book—"from a ladder that was supposedly secure."

"Yes." Trystan reached over and squeezed her hand—a gesture the inspector noticed.

"So these incidents began before Lord Trystan became your partner."

Trystan frowned. "Yes. What are you implying, Inspector?"

The man raised his head, a bemused expression on his face. "Nothing at all, sir. I'm merely eliminating you as a target."

But not as a suspect, Trystan thought to himself. "Both Madame La Rieux and I have sunk a tremendous amount of funds and time into this project, Inspector. These incidents have cost us considerably. I am concerned that next time someone might be seriously injured—or worse."

Inspector Jacobs nodded. "I'm afraid that is a viable concern. Often this sort of criminal will escalate his attacks if lesser measures do not succeed in achieving his goal, which is to obviously make certain"—he consulted his book again—" 'that Trystienne's never opens its doors to the public.' "

Vienne's sharp breath caught his attention. He squeezed her hand again. "That won't happen," Trystan promised before turning his head to find the inspector watching them with an unreadable gaze.

"Do either of you have any enemies or competitors who might want to do you harm?"

"I cannot imagine any of them going to such lengths," Trystan replied. "I've tried to make as few enemies as possible. However, I'm sure there might be one or two."

Vienne nodded. "There are always those who think a woman has no place in business. A few clientele have expressed their disappointment at losing money at my tables. I am, unfortunately, aware that there are people who would like to do me harm."

To hear her speak so, in such a cavalier tone, chilled Trystan to the bone.

Inspector Jacobs seemed to have no trouble believing it. "I will need names from both of you so I may investigate further. Meanwhile, I will have men stationed at the site around the clock, as well as covert inquiry agents talking to various dissidents around the city. This may not be revenge related at all, but the work of an unwell mind."

That didn't make Trystan feel any better about the situation, but he appreciated that Jacobs at least seemed determined to get to the root of the issue.

He rose to his feet and the smaller man followed suit. Trystan offered his hand. "Thank you, Inspector. You will be in touch?"

Jacobs accepted the handshake with a firm grip. "You may depend upon it, Lord Trystan. Have those names sent 'round to me as soon as possible. If you think of anything else, please don't hesitate to contact me."

They thanked him and insured him they would do just that. Then they stood together in silence and watched as he left the room. Trystan waited a few moments before speaking, wanting to make certain they were indeed alone. "He's going to investigate me."

Vienne didn't seem the least bit surprised by his claim. "*Moi, aussi.*"

"You?" Trystan scowled at her. "He thought you were wonderful. Besides, you were a victim of one of the incidents."

"Yes, and escaped relatively unscathed." She angled her body toward him. "I'm not saying Monsieur Inspector believes either of us responsible, but he's going to do a thorough job of making sure we are not."

"Agreed. I suppose we should be thankful. That is his job, after all."

"Indeed." She smiled at him. "And now we find ourselves alone."

Trystan returned the playful smile. "We could go to the site together."

"A wonderful notion, Lord Trystan," she agreed as she walked across the room to close the door. He heard the lock click. As she came back toward him, her smile took on a seductive quality. "I thought perhaps first we might have a business meeting—between partners."

He took her into his arms without hesitation, enjoying this playful side of her nature. "I think that an excellent idea. Where would you like to begin?"

She tugged on his cravat. "Suitable business attire. I'm sorry, sir, but you are wearing entirely too many clothes. I've had complaints."

"Perhaps you could assist me in finding a more appropriate state of dress," he suggested, and then lowered his head to hers.

A few days later, her back aching from the onslaught of her menses, Vienne began to feel the urge to run.

It wasn't Trystan's fault. He was perfect—the perfect business partner, the perfect lover. He knew when to take charge and when to let her make the decisions. He knew when to give her room to breathe and when to sweep her off her feet. Occasionally he got under her skin, but then she did the same to him. They were two individuals who spent the better part of their days and their nights together. Anyone else and she would have killed him already.

It was the fact that she didn't want to kill Trystan that frightened her. Normally by this part of the affair she would have settled into a routine of her design, and her lover would have no choice but to follow that routine as well. But with Trystan she was more than content to give his schedule as much consideration as her own. She was not the end-all, be-all of his life.

And she missed him when he wasn't there. She looked forward to seeing him. She trusted his judgment and found herself asking his opinion even in moments when she normally would have made the decision on her own. It wasn't that she was dependent on him; it was that she wanted to share these things and hear his thoughts.

Was it any wonder she was terrified? The man was becoming entirely too large a facet of her day-to-day life. When Trystienne's opened, there would be little need for them to spend quite so much time together. He would no doubt want to begin traveling again, and both of them would develop other projects. He would find a wife and their affair would come to an end.

Vienne would rather end it now than be tossed over for a younger, fresher replacement. Unfortunately, she couldn't bring herself to end it. She told herself that it wouldn't be good for their partnership if she left him. But it was necessary to put a little distance between them, just to prove to herself that she didn't need to have him around all the time. It was unbecoming in a woman of her age and position to be so attached to a man like him.

It was the same issue she'd run into years ago. She liked Trystan. He was the kind of a man a woman could give herself to wholly. The kind of man who made her want to believe she could live the fairy tale, happily ever after.

But she didn't believe in happy endings. If they did exist, they were for women more trusting and better—for she was fairly certain she did not deserve to be loved after what she did.

Her monthly cycle provided the perfect excuse for a little time spent apart. Unfortunately, it also made her more inclined to feel particularly dramatic about the whole thing. Trystan, of course, understood.

Damn him.

Today she was interviewing potential employees, a task Trystan left entirely in her hands. He knew she would give him no end of grief if he hired someone who turned out to be ill suited for the work. He was used to investing and improving business, while she had more experience dealing with the public. The upper classes were high spenders, but they could also be colossal pains in the arse, as Sadie was fond of saying.

"Of course, we will not be open for several more months," she explained to the young woman sipping a cup of tea across the table from her. She'd had re-freshments sent over from Sadie's tearoom on Bond

Street for the interviewing process. "But I will need assistance from all the new employees in readying each boutique for opening day."

The young woman nodded her pretty blond head. "I currently work at a hat shop and we regularly make up displays and such things as to draw the customer's attention. It's one of my favorite aspects of the job, to be honest."

Vienne made note of that in her book of candidates. "Which shop do you work in?"

"Le Chapeau Moderne."

Her pronunciation was good for an English person. Vienne nodded. "I've seen the displays. I quite enjoyed the one with a lady's top hat amid playing cards and Ascot adverts. Very provocative."

The young woman beamed. "That was one of mine, madam. Some thought it might be a little too risqué, but isn't that the point?"

Vienne looked her in the eye. "Miss Gayle, I do not believe you are suited for the position of clerk at Trystienne's." Before the blonde could look too crestfallen, she hastened to add, "You are clearly much better suited to window dressing. You will decide how items are to be displayed and have another girl beneath you to assist. You will also work with me on advertising. How does two pounds a week sound?"

Cornflower blue eyes widened. *Oh no, was that*

a tear? Vienne did not do well with tears. Crying women frightened her.

"Madam, I . . . I do not know what to say!"

"Say yes. You'll work for every shilling, I assure you—and you will have to spend time with me, which will lead you to one day demand at least an extra twenty pence a week, I'm certain." She extended her hand. "Do we have an agreement?"

A firm hand gripped hers. "We do. When would you like me to start?"

"Three weeks from tomorrow. I have a modiste from Paris coming to discuss fashions for next season. You will join us. I will have a note sent around to your address with a time and place."

She walked the happy young woman to the door. Trystan came in just as they reached the exit. He tipped his hat to both of them before continuing up to the next floor.

Miss Gayle turned coyly to Vienne. "Will you tolerate a little brazenness in your employees, Madame La Rieux?"

Vienne raised her brows. "On most days I demand it."

The other woman nodded in the direction Trystan had gone. "That Lord Trystan is a very fine figure of a fellow."

Vienne chuckled. She should reprimand the impertinence, but didn't have the heart or the inclination. "That's not brazen, Miss Gayle. That's God's own truth."

When her new employee had left, Vienne leaned her back against the door and let her gaze drift up the wide staircase. There would be a lift installed as well, but the stairs would be a focal point of the entryway. Hand-carved oak, polished to a rich sheen, with a runner of navy, salmon, and cream carpet down the center.

Miss Gayle had been her last interview of the day, so there was nothing keeping her there. She should return to Saint's Row and look after that business instead of hanging about this one, especially now that Trystan had arrived.

She was halfway up the stairs before she realized what she was doing. Turning around didn't seem to be an option as she continued the climb. Workmen bustled around the first floor and she could hear them on the one above as well.

There hadn't been other incidents since Inspector Jacobs took over as their champion, but that didn't mean she let her guard down. Enough had happened that she fully expected their foe to strike again, especially since there had been a story in the paper just yesterday morning as to the danger of copious spending among married ladies.

Apparently spinsters, widows, and young misses spent just enough, she thought bitterly. Had the writer of the piece never seen what a young girl in her first Season cost her papa in clothing alone?

On the first-floor landing, she stopped and looked up at the great chandelier. It seemed a lifetime ago that she had climbed the ladder and crashed to the floor. Glancing about, one would never know any such accident had happened on this very spot. Why, her blood hadn't even stained the wood.

"May I be of assistance, Madame La Rieux?"

Vienne's chin came down. A scruffy but friendly-looking workman was watching her expectantly.

"Have you seen Lord Trystan?" she inquired.

"Indeed I have, ma'am. He's up on the next floor, in what's to be the shop for linens and what-not, with another gentleman."

"Thank you." She smiled as he tipped his hat and then lifted her skirts to climb the next set of stairs. Who might this other gentleman be? She hadn't seen anyone arrive, but then she had been interviewing shopgirls, all morning.

After this she needed a little chocolate, or perhaps an entire pot. And a hot water bottle for her belly. Maybe a nice warm bath and a nap.

Or a fight. She could just as easily jump feet-first

into a good debate, or even a little hair pulling. It was just that sort of day.

At the top of the stairs on the second-floor landing she turned left, pausing only a moment to admire the chandelier that hung there as well. It was similar to the one on the first floor, but with a different design in the metal. This floor was coming along nicely. It really was amazing the difference that an experienced workman, paid exorbitant wages, could make.

She found Trystan and his company exactly where the workman said she would, which was good because she never would have heard them to follow their voices—standing face-to-face, speaking in very quiet voices, as they were. Vienne's heart quickened at the sight of Trystan—Miss Gayle was right about him being a very fine fellow—but that eager pounding stopped abruptly when she saw who it was he was speaking to.

Ira Fletcher. Tall, blunt-featured and thick as a bull, he was soft spoken and allegedly a very good dancer. He was also one of the most notorious crime lords in all of London. He had approached Vienne shortly after she opened Saint's Row about providing protection for her business. She politely refused. When someone beat one of her footmen senseless, she went to Fletcher's place of business and stabbed one his men through the foot with a rather pointy parasol. It was a move that could have gotten her killed, but it earned her the criminal's respect instead.

What the hell was he doing here? *With Trystan?* What possible business could they have? Unless. . .

It was a terrible thought. But once her suspicious mind thought it, there was no taking it back. She knew it was impossible . . . but what if Trystan *was* involved with the mischief that had plagued her for all these weeks?

No. She refused to entertain the stupid notion. She felt dirty having thought it. Was she such an awful person that she automatically suspected it in others as well? No, Trystan Kane was a good and honorable man.

A good and honorable man who just happened to be talking very quietly to a notorious criminal in her—*their*—place of business. She might wonder whether Trystan would ever hurt her—and perhaps *nearly* believe that he wouldn't be stupid enough to jeopardize an enterprise in which he had sunk so much of his own money. There was one thing, though, that she was certain of—

There was no such thing as doing good and honorable business with Ira Fletcher.

* * *

Trystan didn't fancy himself necessarily an intellectual sort of man, but he was smart enough to know when someone was avoiding him, and Vienne was avoiding him.

After his meeting with Ira Fletcher—the man owed him a favor for the investment advice Trystan had given him—he went looking for Vienne to tell her what he'd found out, only to be told that she had left just a few minutes earlier.

Why hadn't she come to say good-bye? Maybe he was being what Archer called clingy, but *he* would have informed her he was leaving for the day. Perhaps she had started to do just that, and then saw him talking to one of London's most infamous citizens.

He swore under his breath. God only knew where that mind of hers had gone after that. He should have known better than to meet Fletcher at the site; she was bound to use it against him. But Trystan wanted those who might be watching—or the people, or person, responsible for the incidents—to know that he was asking questions; and wanted to frighten whomever it was enough to back down, or feel poked enough to try something else so Inspector Jacobs might catch him, her, or them red-handed.

Chasing after Vienne wasn't the best strategy, but

it was better than giving her time to think herself out of their relationship. Besides, what Fletcher had told him was important—the sort of thing she would want to know.

So he surprised Havers by climbing into the carriage at an unscheduled time and instructed his driver to deliver him to Saint's Row—and to wait outside for him. He didn't plan to be there long; he'd explain and then leave. If he stayed any longer, she'd think of something to fight about—he'd been around her during "that time of the month" before.

At Saint's Row he didn't knock. They all were used to him by now. He climbed the stairs to Vienne's apartments without bothering to check her office first. If she was upset, she would go to her room first and perhaps have a drink or some chocolate. If she wasn't feeling well, she might lie down. Regardless, he likened it to walking into the den of an injured lioness. He'd be lucky to escape unscathed. Yet for all that, he really only wanted to make certain she didn't think ill of him, and to be assured that she was all right.

He knocked once and then let himself into her private living space. She stood in the middle of the carpet, a box of chocolates in her hands. She started at his entrance, chewing on a bite of what appeared to be a nougat.

She swallowed. "Trystan. What are you doing here?"

"You left without saying good-bye," he replied, all innocence. "May I have one of those?"

She set the box on her writing desk. He knew better than to cross the invisible line and try to take one for himself. "Trystan, if you are going to be so . . . needy that you follow me across the city just to say good-bye—"

"And you say I think too much of myself," he interrupted, earning himself a scowl. "I'm here because I know why you ran off. You saw me with Fletcher and you couldn't wait to run home and stew on it."

She glared at him . . . and Trystan didn't have the heart to tell her that the effect was ruined by a spot of chocolate on the corner of her mouth. "I am not *stewing* on anything. Who you choose to converse with is your own affair, though I do wish you had picked a more suitable venue."

All that was missing from her indignant speech was a well-placed sniff. "Have you made me into a villain yet? Am I killing puppies, or perhaps busy engineering another 'accident' at the site?"

A guilty flush filled her cheeks. It was so expected, he couldn't even be disappointed at it. "You're so afraid to trust that you would rather make me a villain then believe in what we have."

Her chin came up. "Don't you dare presume to know what I think!"

"Oh, Vienne. Darling. It's positively transparent what you think, don't you know that? I know you, and I know that a part of you rejoiced at seeing me with Fletcher, because now you can talk yourself into a reason to end things between us."

That was the spark that finally set her ablaze. He knew it wouldn't take much. She was as hungry for a fight as she was for those chocolates. "You brought that man into my business! My house!"

"*Our* business." He might as well provoke her; there would be no reasoning with her.

"Don't you dare try that tactic with me. I am not the one who has done anything wrong!"

"Neither am I!" Perhaps he understood why she behaved the way she did, but that didn't mean he had to like it or put up with it. "Fletcher owed me a favor for investment advice. I asked him to ask around about anyone who might be involved in the incidents at the shops."

Arms folded under her breasts, she raised an expectant brow. "What did he say?"

At least she retained some degree of common sense. "He said that he had heard of a fellow making trouble for merchants earlier this year. A man whose wife apparently went on a spree and drove him deep into debt."

She looked interested. "What's his name?"

"I don't know. Fletcher's going to find out, and then we can give the name to Jacobs." He couldn't help but smile faintly. "Feel free to thank me."

She looked as though she'd rather eat glass. "Thank you. You should have told me before you met him. I might have been prepared. He injured one of my men, you know."

"And you stabbed one of his in the foot, isn't that right?" That was it, provoke and tease her. That will go over so very well.

She shrugged. "I don't like being bullied."

He sighed. "There are so many things you don't like, Vienne. Why not concentrate on the things you do."

"Such as?"

"Us. You like *us*, but any moment now you're going to open that pretty mouth of yours and tell me it isn't working, or that you think we shouldn't spend so much time together."

Her jaw tightened. "You presume to know me very well."

"I do know you very well, and you know me. You knew that I wasn't up to anything with Fletcher. It was just an excuse. Now you have to look for a new one. You know . . . you could just be honest."

"Fine. I think we should end our affair."

Expecting a blow did not generally make it hurt any less. He forced himself to remain stoic. "Why?"

"Does there have to be a why?"

"There does when you don't want to end this anymore than I do. What are you afraid of?"

"You," she amazed him by answering. "I am afraid of you and the damage you could do if I trust you with my heart. *Mon Dieu*, I have a difficult time trusting people with my coat, let alone my heart."

He smiled—pitifully. "That doesn't surprise me. You trust me with your business, Vienne. You know I would never hurt you."

"No, not on purpose, I don't think you would. But you might by accident. Or, God forbid, Trystan, I could hurt you. Surely you know the capacity I have for doing harm."

He did. There was no arguing that nor was there any comfort for the ravaged look on her face.

She continued. "Everything I love turns awful and bitter. Turns against me. I have hurt so many people and been hurt so many times in kind, I think that is all I am capable of. I do not want to hurt you, but I would rather never see you again than give you the opportunity to see me for what I really am.

I would rather die than see the day when you look at me with disgust in your eyes . . . and it would happen. I know it would."

"Vienne . . ." He started toward her, but she stopped him.

"Please do not touch me." Her voice was a frail whisper. "You want to tell me I am wrong. You want to insist that I am lovable, but I am not. Worse than that, I am not capable of that emotion anymore. I will not allow myself to feel it. Do you understand what it is I'm saying to you?"

He stared at her. "That it doesn't matter if I love you. It doesn't even matter if you love me, you refuse to take a chance because one of us might get hurt."

She nodded. "Yes."

"Are you out of your goddamn mind?" Disbelief and rage came pouring out of him. "That is the most ridiculous excuse I've ever frigging heard!"

Vienne took a step back, staring at him as though he had suddenly sprouted a second head. "It is not an excuse! It is true."

"It's bullshit and we both know it. You love Sadie. You love your employees."

"I shot one of my footmen!"

"Winged him, and the bastard deserved it. What this boils down to is that you are scared and too much of a coward to let whatever we have take its course. You would rather end it now and deny both of us whatever joy we might have had. You would rather go on to be a bitter old woman."

"While you can go on to marry a sweet young debutante."

"Oh ho!" A bark of sardonic laughter burst from his chest. *Can men become hysterical?* "I wondered how long it would take before you martyred yourself on the altar of age and experience! You are only four years older than I, Vienne! That's nothing."

"It is something in the eyes of society."

"Hang society. I don't interfere with their love lives. Those years are not the gap they once were. You told me then that you were so much older than me emotionally because you had lived and seen something of the world and its ugliness. Well, let me tell you something Miss I've-only-seen-France-and-London—I've seen a helluva lot more of this world than you have, and I don't give a rat's arse about your past, except for the fact that something in it obviously kept you from being able to have adult relationships."

Vienne gasped. "You wait just one minute—"

"No." He moved closer, driven by the force of his emotions. "Everyone on this earth has regrets, Vienne. Lord knows I've made enough mistakes of my own—some might even say that you were one of them. But I've learned from them and I've moved on.

You should too. You cannot hide from life or dictate to it like you do your employees. Neither life nor love is a business transaction. That's prostitution."

She slapped him. He barely saw it coming—just a flick of her hand and then his left cheek was on fire.

"How dare you," she seethed.

His gaze locked with hers. "Did that make you feel better? Are you righteous and indignant now?"

"You are trying to make me angry because you are. You want me to hurt you so you can hurt me in return."

Trystan snorted. "You have no idea what I want."

"I cannot know you?" Her expression was pure mockery. "Yet you claim to know me so very well. You truly have no idea what kind of woman I am, Trystan. If it's true that my life has been a kind of prostitution, then I am indeed a whore. A high-priced one at that."

It struck him then that this self-loathing of hers wasn't merely a façade or convenient excuse to hide behind. She truly believed herself to be an awful person. How could he possibly fight against that? He couldn't, not when he had no idea just what had happened to her.

He honestly did not have a chance where she was concerned, and this thought cut him as deeply as it made him angry. So very, very angry.

"Grey told me the only way to court you was relentlessly, but I'm tired of trying to prove myself worthy of your attention, Vienne. Do you know why I worked so hard and pulled so many strings to become your partner? Because I wanted you to see me as a man." He laughed—bitterly. "All these years all I've wanted is to prove myself to you, so you would see that I was worthy of your love after all. Christ, I can't believe what a fool I was. What a fool I am. It doesn't matter what I do. It never did and it never will. I'm not the one who is broken. You are."

The color fled from her cheeks, but God help him, he did not regret his words. "You are such a wonderful woman, Vienne. You are smart and funny and generous to a fault, but you are like a child afraid to go to sleep in the dark because of what *might* lurk in the shadows. You'd rather the curtains catch fire. I've already wasted years of my life trying to be good enough for you, and I simply cannot do it anymore."

"I never asked it of you."

"No, you didn't. I brought all of this on myself, and for that I should have my arse kicked. Lord, help me. But I can't even bring myself to regret it. But you will, Vienne. Someday you will regret that you pushed me away."

She didn't say anything, and her silence was

worse than any word or insult she might have uttered. Trystan pressed a kiss to her forehead and squeezed his eyes shut. He would not unman himself by crying.

"I love you," he told her. "But I am done living my life for you alone. If you find the courage to love me back, let me know. In the meantime, I assure you this will have no effect on our business relationship. Good-bye, Vienne."

He turned then, before he could see pity in her eyes. He had just humbled himself more than he ever had to anyone ever before, and it stung like a scratch from an angry cat—raw and red.

And it hurt like hell.

Chapter 13

Vienne never realized how empty her life was before that first day she spent without Trystan in it. Emptiness was something she'd never noticed before he came whirling back into her life. Now, though, when most of the aristocracy had left town for the country and society was spotty at best, she felt alone.

She still had Sadie, of course, though her friend did have her own life to live. Indara came around once in a while for tea. She even had dinner with Lady Gosling one evening—the widow who scandalized the nation by refusing to wear black for her joyfully departed husband. She enjoyed the evening immensely, but that enjoyment lost some of its shine when she remembered that she couldn't share it with Trystan.

She saw him on an almost daily basis, but it wasn't the same. His eyes didn't light up when he saw her, and his conversation was all business. She kept expecting the Duke of Ryeton to call and make good on his promise to ruin her, but he never did. And now he and his duchess must surely have taken up residence in their country home as well.

Work on Trystienne's progressed nicely; and though there was little word from Inspector Jacobs or the dark counterpart, Ira Fletcher, there was no new mischief. The workers seemed to think the worst was over, but Vienne felt as though the giant sword of Damocles hung over their heads, and she was waiting for it to drop.

On this warm late August morning she was on the first floor, watching the plastering of the walls in the corsetry and lingerie section. The walls were going to be a soft salmon color, which would look incredibly elegant with the delicate scrollwork on the ceiling and molding.

Someone cleared his throat behind her. "Vienne? Might I bother you a moment?"

Her heart jumped into her throat at the sound of that voice, despite the stiffness of tone. She swallowed and turned, willing herself into some state of composure. "Of course, Trystan."

He gestured to the door, so she moved toward him, preceding him out of the room and into the next shop, which was empty of workmen. "What is it you wished to discuss?" she asked once they were alone.

Her heart pounded painfully as part of her hoped he would renew his declarations of love.

He tugged on the cuffs of his dark blue morning coat. "It has occurred to me that continuing to work together might be something neither of us wishes to endure once Trystienne's is completed."

She couldn't have been more surprised if he slapped her. "Oh?"

He nodded. "So, I want to advise you that I am in the process of finding you new investors. I know a partner was never something you desired, so as soon as I can find a handful of suitable people I will sell off my share of the venture, and you will be solely in charge as you originally wanted."

Originally was the operative word in that declaration was it not? At one time she wanted this project to be hers and hers alone, but now she couldn't imagine running it without Trystan's assistance. It was obvious, however, that Trystan did not share her vision any longer.

He wanted nothing to do with her.

"If that is what you want, Trystan, I have no objection."

Was it her wishful thinking or did he stiffen ever so slightly. "Excellent. I will begin immediately." He bowed his head. "Good day, Vienne."

"Good day, Trystan." She watched his straight back

as he left the room, her chest about to cave in under the intense pressure weighing upon it. She pressed a hand to her breast to keep whatever wanted out, inside; she slapped her other hand against the wall for support as she turned toward the windows and stared out unseeing into the day.

It hurt so very badly. Too much for her to keep inside. A sob wrenched its way out of her throat despite the invisible vise that gripped her. Hot tears filled her eyes and she could not stop them from spilling over. Her shoulders heaved—it was all she could do to keep the pain inside—and yet she was sobbing as though her world was ending, but made barely a sound.

Once out in the hall, Trystan heard Vienne weep. It was such a heartbreaking sound that his own body reacted—there was an almost crippling tightness in his chest and throat. He could go back and try to comfort her, but to what end? It would only make matters worse between them, more muddled and confusing.

He loved her. He had for years, and wasn't ashamed to admit it, but he couldn't force her to be something she wasn't or to give him something she didn't think herself capable of giving. It was time to be practical and move on with his life.

But first he had to see this project through to the end. He had invested so much of himself into it, he couldn't just up and walk away. Plus, there was the note that had been delivered to him yesterday at the Barrington. It was written in a decent script, indicating that the writer had some degree of education. Short and to the point, it merely stated that if he did not put a stop to the emporium scheme, and chose to become a corruptor of women, that he would suffer a worse "accident" than Madame La Rieux.

He couldn't give up just yet, and allow someone else—possibly Vienne—to be injured because of him. He had to take this note to Inspector Jacobs and he had to continue doing what he was doing, despite the fact that being so close to Vienne caused him no shortage of pain.

That was why he had to get out of there now. Her crying—*what did it take to make such a woman sob?*—cut him; and if he couldn't comfort her there and then, he knew he must leave. It was hell to look at her and not be able to touch her, to joke with her. He had to escape; and since he had an appointment with Inspector Jacobs later that day, he may as well leave immediately.

He instructed Havers to take him to Ryeton House in Mayfair. Tomorrow, Grey and Rose would leave for the country, where they could spend some much-deserved time alone, and Grey could watch his wife grow fat with child without society yammering about it. He would no doubt make a trip to visit them later this fall, but he wanted to say good-bye before they left.

And if he were totally honest, he needed his brother to give him a pat on the head or something—just so he knew everything was going to be all right. For his whole life, he'd been taught that anything he wanted was his for the taking if he worked hard enough, and was charming and smart enough. He was the youngest boy, spoiled by his family, unaccustomed to being denied whatever he asked for.

Until Vienne.

He did not know how to react to this loss. She was not something he could simply work harder at obtaining. He could not "fix" whatever plagued her. Unless she let him in, he could not help her heal—and there would be no forcing her into compliance. He didn't want to force her to do anything.

He must accept defeat and move on, though he had no idea how to do either.

The trip to Mayfair was shortened by the fact that there wasn't nearly as much traffic on the streets during these late summer days. A few weeks ago the streets would have been congested; it was the way of expanding cities with narrow streets.

Grey and Rose were sitting down to a luncheon on the back terrace with Archer when he arrived.

"I had hoped you might join us." Rose greeted him with a broad smile. "I had a place set just in case."

What sort of heart would not lighten at such a greeting? Trystan put on a happy countenance.

Grey raised a glass of lemonade in salute, but his gaze narrowed when it settled on Trystan's face. Thankfully, he did not remark upon it.

Neither did Archer, though Trystan thought he saw both his brothers exchange a knowing glance. At least he could take comfort in the fact that his mother had returned to the country with Bronte and Alexander. He would not have to face her disappointment at not finding him a bride this Season, or listen as she planned a strategy for next.

"What time do you depart tomorrow?" he inquired as Rose poured him a glass of cold lemonade.

"Before noon," Grey replied. "I haven't decided where we'll spend the night yet. Rose wants it to be an adventure, so we've made no plans." He smiled indulgently at his wife.

"What of you?" Trystan asked Archer.

His older brother shrugged. "Since I have taken over Friday's rooms at the Barrington, I believe I'll stay in London. Though, I have planned at least one visit to the country this fall—and Christmas, of course. You?"

"I'll remain here, of course. It's been too long since we've all spent a Christmas together. In the spring I'll return to New York—plenty of work to do there. Perhaps I'll land one of those brash American heiresses," he said it with a grin, but his family didn't seem to get the joke.

Rose frowned. "But I thought . . ."

Grey silenced her by placing his hand over hers. "My brother has never been one to sit still for long, love."

"Speaking of that"—Trystan cleared his throat—"I'm going to sell my shares in Trystienne's once it opens. Either of you interested in buying in before it becomes an incredible moneymaking machine?"

Another shared glance. The two of them were as subtle as dogs lifting their legs on a tree stump.

"Sounds too good to pass up," Grey commented, helping himself to several slices of cold ham. "Let me know when you want to sell. My solicitor here in town can take care of the details."

Archer seized the small silver bowl of sliced cucumber. "Your business advice has never steered me down a regretful path before. I'm in as well."

Trystan smiled. "Excellent." He only needed

his brothers to buy into a small amount, and then he would no longer hold a full half interest in the scheme. He and Vienne would no longer be partners, but he could still profit from all their combined hard work.

Unfortunately, he would forever be reminded of what might have been by the name of the damn place. It would be hung above the door and on all the bills and packages that came out of the building. *Trystienne's* would mock him for the rest of his days.

Yes, a return to New York might be just the thing. He felt more the thing already, just for having a plan. He always felt better when he had a goal in mind.

"Pass the rolls, will you, Arch? I'm suddenly starving."

Word about town was that Trystan Kane planned to return to America by the spring. Word also was that he was spending a great deal of his evenings at Chez Cherie's, the most exclusive whorehouse in the city. Then again, the gossips also said that Vienne was sleeping with Nathan Xavier, a magician who occasionally appeared on stage at Saint's Row. That was complete nonsense, so perhaps the rumor about Trystan was unfounded as well. Although, it certainly was none of her concern.

She missed Sadie. Her friend would probably tell her to gather her courage and go after Trystan, but she longed for her company all the same. Lady Gosling might prove to be a good friend one day, but they didn't have the sort of intimate relationship that made Vienne think the countess would act as advisor.

Most of all, she missed Trystan, who, somewhere along the way, had become her best friend as well as her partner and confidante. But she was not the kind of woman to allow herself to wallow. She put things behind and moved forward, and she would do the same with her feelings for Trystan.

Because of the rumors, however, Vienne had received overtures from three wealthy gentlemen interested in Trystan's shares in the emporium—since he was, supposedly, returning to America. She thanked them for their interest and promised to keep them in mind if Trystan decided to sell.

If she knew him, and she was fairly certain she did, he'd let his brothers have the first opportunity to buy in. She was going to lose him completely, and had no one to blame but herself.

Now that the Season was over, she had more time on her hands to devote to the completion of Trystienne's. She threw herself into the project relentlessly, to the point that she often missed meals because she was working. Indara started coming by the site at least once a day to bring her food.

"You are wasting away," she scolded in her Bombay-spiced accent.

Vienne merely shrugged. "It won't take me long to fill out again."

They continued on like this for several days. In fact it was just after one of these lunches when Greyden Kane, Duke of Ryeton, stepped into the still-empty but prettily painted shop where Vienne was sitting on the floor, going over carpet swatches for runners.

She looked up when he tapped his knuckles against the doorframe. "Your Grace, whatever are you doing here?"

"I had to return to the city on business and thought I'd stop by." came the reply as he rolled his hat in his hands. "May I come in? Or is this a bad time?"

Wary of his pleasant demeanor, she nodded. "Of course. It's not a bad time at all. How are you at choosing carpet?"

"Brilliant," he answered with a hint of a smile. He moved into the room with the grace of a big, lazy cat. Trystan had a similar way of moving, but without the predatory nature. He startled her even further by sinking down onto the bare floor beside her.

He looked through the samples, then at the walls, then back to the samples. "This one." He held up a

William Morris print of black, white, gold, green, and salmon—vines and flowers.

"You weren't jesting," Vienne remarked, impressed. "You are brilliant."

He shot her a very pointed glance. "Good taste runs in the family."

"Was that a compliment?"

The duke tipped his head. "Could be, yes."

Vienne set aside the swatches. "Why are you here, Your Grace? You didn't come all this way to solve my decorating dilemmas."

He leaned back on his hands. "I want to talk about you and Trystan."

She sucked in a breath. So he knew. Of course he knew; Trystan would have told his siblings just as she would have if her sisters still spoke to her.

"I don't know what he told you, but he is not something I wish to discuss."

"He didn't tell me anything except that I could buy more shares in this place if I wanted." He glanced about. "Now that I've seen it, I think I'll have to do just that. You've done a wonderful job."

"Thank you, but I have not been alone in its construction."

He tore his attention away from the scrollwork on the ceiling. "No, my brother has left his mark here as well. The two of you make a good pair."

"At least in business," she allowed. The anticipation was getting to be too much. "Are you here to tell me that you plan to make good on your promise to ruin me?"

The duke shook his head, dark hair falling over his forehead. He looked so much like an older version of Trystan that it hurt to look at him. She forced herself not to look away. "I have no interest in ruining you, Madame La Rieux. Hurting you would only hurt my brother, and I would rather take my own eyes out."

Her eyes widened. This was not what she had expected. Where was his ranting diatribe? His threats? Why didn't he call her every name she deserved to be called, and had already been called by herself?

"Then why are you here?" She didn't mean it to come out so mystified, but this was very unexpected.

He smiled crookedly, which accentuated the jagged scar that ran down the left side of his face. "I came to offer you some advice—if you'll take it. Advice from someone who has a fairly good idea of what's been going through your head lately."

Vienne arched a brow. "I assure you, Your Grace, that you have no idea whatsoever of what's been going through my head."

He only chuckled. The Duke of Ryeton found her no more intimidating than a butterfly. "You don't think you're good enough for my brother. You think you've done him a favor by breaking his heart—again. And you think you saved him from being disappointed by you sometime in the future. In short, you've put up a cross and nailed yourself to it good."

She stared at him, jaw slightly slack. Aside from the blasphemous bit about the cross, what he said was true. "I do not believe Trystan would appreciate you discussing this with me."

The duke's gaze hardened just a little bit. "And I don't appreciate you treating one of the best men I know like his feelings and opinions have no more worth than a pair of torn stockings."

Vienne swallowed. "Of course his feelings matter, but I'm not going to continue our . . . *relationship* when it's not good for either of us."

"That's where you and I have a difference of opinion. I happen to think you're one of the best things to ever happen to Tryst. He used to be a lazy bastard—no direction. Then you broke his heart and suddenly he had a purpose." Vienne remembered what Trystan had said to her about wanting to prove himself.

"Then he comes back to London and the two of you made this magnificent place together. I'm not sure what you think is so wrong about the two of you, but I'll bet my entire fortune it's not worth turning your back on something so special."

"With all due respect—"

"You're an ornery bit of baggage, aren't you?" he interrupted, scowling. "Did I not explain to you that the purpose of this visit is for me to talk and for you to sit there and listen?"

She shook her head.

The duke shrugged. "Now you know. Here's what I've learned over the last few months since giving in to my Rose. I've discovered that love does not care if you think you deserve it or not. In fact, this sadistic emotion seems to take great pleasure in plaguing those of us who know we do not deserve it by sending us the most amazing people, who seem to know better.

"The true test for people like us, Madame La Rieux, is whether or not we can abandon our dear mantle of misery and nurture that love. I have discovered that it takes a much better and stronger person to accept love and hold it than to deny it."

"I appreciate your concern, Your Grace—"

"There you go, talking again. Listen to me, you foolish twit. My brother is the best man you will ever—*ever*—find. I have a few ideas of what he sees in you; and if he likes you, then I suppose you can't be as cold and amoral as I thought. I don't know what mistake you made in the past and I don't want to hear it. What I do know is that no matter what it is, it is not worth missing out on the life Trystan can give you. If a man can forgive you for breaking his heart, anything else you've done won't matter."

Vienne didn't think she'd ever heard the duke say so much at one time. When he rose to his feet, she just sat there, staring at him.

He pointed at the swatch in her hand. "I really do like that one. Good day, Madame La Rieux. I hope to see you at Christmas."

She watched him leave in stunned silence. What had just happened? Had she been lectured on love by a man rumored to have once bed a mother *and* her daughter? At the same time no less. And what did Christmas have to do with any of it?

He certainly gave her something to think about. Ryeton had done worse things than she in his past. He had to have, otherwise she really was the worst person in the world. If he deserved happiness enough to have found it, shouldn't the same apply to her?

It certainly gave her something to think about.

The man responsible for the incidents at the construction site was most likely a man named Francis Gibbs, according to Ira Fletcher's sources. Inspector Jacob's investigation pointed in the same direction.

Trystan wouldn't know Gibbs if the man walked up to him and poked him in the eye. It was a bitter and hard medicine to swallow to think that Vienne could have been severely injured by someone with whom she'd never had contact—and he knew for a fact they'd never met because Jacobs had checked thoroughly for any ties that might possibly provide a better reason for why Gibbs was so barking mad.

The only explanation the lawman could give was that Gibbs had once been fairly well-to-do and had married a young lady with a large dowry. All had been good between them until the lady began shopping at an emporium. Then she began spending huge amounts of money and ran off with a store clerk. That was Gibbs's story. According the wife, she had spent her own money, and Gibbs had gambled away the rest. She ran off with the glovemaker because she loved him, and Gibbs was a complete tosser.

Gibbs was the head of an organization that called themselves the Coalition for the Preservation of Morals and Virtue. Over the past three years, the members protested anything they felt might lead women and men down a vice-ridden path, from shopping to dancing to excessive fresh air.

"Have you arrested him yet?" he asked Jacobs as they sat together in a coffeehouse not far from the construction site.

"Not yet," the inspector replied. "I've only just collected enough evidence against him to charge him and make it stick. One of my men has been watching his residence and is to let me know where he goes."

"Good." Trystan couldn't quite bring himself to sigh in relief just yet. Once this Gibbs was arrested and in jail, then he would believe Vienne and everyone else involved was safe.

He took another sip of coffee. That was all the time that elapsed between his thoughts of safety and Jacobs's man rushing into the coffeehouse.

The inspector's back went rigid. *"Abrams!* Good lord, man. *Whatever* has happened?"

"It's Gibbs, sir," the young man replied, flushed and gasping for air. "He's gone to Lord Trystan's business. I think he might be armed."

Trystan's heart literally stopped.

Vienne.

He bolted out of his chair at the same time that Jacobs leapt to his feet. The three of them raced out of the shop with the rest of the patrons staring out the windows after them.

Trystan bellowed at Havers and practically threw himself into the carriage as it lunged into motion. His driver pushed the team to top speed and steered the carriage through traffic like a madman—a very skilled madman.

He just prayed they were fast enough to get there before another madman—a very dangerous one— hurt Vienne again.

When Trystan burst through the door, Vienne didn't know whether to kiss him for coming for her, or kill him for being so foolish as to put himself at risk. Where the devil was Jacobs?

Mr. Gibbs whirled around, swinging the gun in his hand toward Trystan. "Ah, his lordship has arrived." He jerked the pistol toward Vienne. "Go stand by your woman."

Holding his hands up by his shoulders, Trystan did just that. "I'm not here to hurt you, Gibbs."

"Of course you are!" The small bespectacled man had a wild look in his eye. "If I didn't have a weapon, you would have tried to rip me apart by now."

"Mr. Gibbs," Vienne began in a placating tone, "why don't we talk about this? Surely you don't want to hurt anyone."

"It's the only way your kind ever listens," he told her hotly. "You don't respond to morals or reason, but enough people get hurt and start to cost you money and suddenly you're all ears. After today, no one will ever have to worry that this pit of debauchery will ruin any other lives, because it will cease to be. Once word gets out that people actually died here, no one will work for you. Hard to work for a dead woman. Or man."

Vienne swallowed, trying to moisten her parched throat. "You have a very strong hate for my business, sir. Might I ask why? I have never personally harmed you, have I?"

"Of course not." He glared at her. "Nor has he, but you do everyone whose wife or mother will shop here a gross disservice indeed."

"So your gripe is not with us, but with this building?" He truly was just a fanatic, then. Not a foe or competitor. He was simply a loon.

The pistol wavered slightly. "My wife bled me dry because of a place like this. She ran off with a glovemaker!"

"I'm sorry for you, but your wife obviously wasn't the woman you thought she was."

"She was a good and virtuous woman before that damned stack of shops drove her to the devil. The two of you didn't listen to me before, but you'll listen to me once I take away someone you care about." He leveled the pistol at Vienne.

Fear knocked her knees together. She did not want to die, but she would if it would save Trystan. "Yes," she said. "I'm the one to blame. I want women to come in here and spend as much money as they possibly can."

"Vienne!" Trystan shot her a look that was half anger, half terror. "Do shut up."

The man with the gun paid him no mind. "Jezebel."

The poor fellow was clearly unhinged and more than a little melodramatic. Vienne smiled. "Calling me names won't bring your wife back. But to be safe, I will make certain I hire a female glovemaker."

The gun cocked. The man squeezed the trigger and fired. It all happened in excruciatingly slow motion. Vienne heard a shout and then she fell to the floor as something heavy slammed into her.

It was Trystan. He had knocked her out of the way.

He had been hit by the bullet meant for her. Blood seeped through his waistcoat. Vienne would have cried out had she been capable of making a sound. Instead, she acted on pure instinct. Trystan's coat was opened and she saw that he had a pistol at his side. Vienne grabbed it, lifted it, and pointed it at Mr. Gibbs.

She pulled the trigger, hitting him in the exact spot she'd shot William. It was fortunate she was such a good shot, because he had been aiming to shoot her next, only his hand shook too badly.

With Gibbs down, she turned to one of the workmen. "Get Havers." Then she lifted her skirts and pulled a wide strip off her petticoat to use as a sort of bandage to put pressure on Trystan's wound.

"Vienne?"

Her gaze leapt to his face. Trystan was pale—too pale. "I'm here, Trystan. I am here."

His hand fumbled for one of hers. She let him take the one that wasn't trying to keep all of his blood from pouring out. "Are you unhurt?"

"I am, thanks to you, you great stupid article. What were you thinking, jumping in front of me like that? You could have been killed!"

He smiled faintly. "I knew you cared."

"You truly are too full of yourself. Now stop talking and rest. Havers is going to get you to the hospital."

"You shot him, didn't you? With my gun?"

"I did. And if you say another word, I will gag you. I mean it."

Havers rushed in then, and he and another man lifted Trystan from the floor—there was a puddle of blood where he'd lain. Vienne blanched at it, but Havers gave her a blunt nod. "'Tis a good sign, ma'am. Means the bullet went through him and isn't still stuck inside."

She supposed that was a good thing.

Trystan turned his head. "Vienne."

Her heart fluttered. God help her, she was going to fall apart right there, in front of all these people.

In front of *him*. "I'm here, Trystan. I'm here."

He stretched out his hand and she took it, even though she had blood on hers. He squeezed, and she was glad that his grip was that strong. "Come with me," he said as they left the building.

As if anyone could stop her. She stayed with him all the way to the carriage, and once inside, she held his hand. She continued to hold it even after he lost consciousness. That was when Vienne La Rieux had her first conversation with God in more than fifteen years. It was a brief conversation and consisted of a mere five words.

Please do not take him.

Chapter 14

Havers, it turned out, was right. The fact that the bullet had gone through Trystan's body was actually a good thing, as the surgeon didn't need to dig the shot out. Still, despite this bit of luck, the wound became infected; not badly, though, just enough to make him run a fever and scare the life out of Vienne as she watched him fade in and out of consciousness for two days.

After taking him to the surgeon's office, he was moved to his rooms at the Barrington, where he could rest more comfortably. That's where he was when the fever hit, and also where Vienne had come face-to-face with Archer Kane. She thought he would blame her for this, but he took one look at her, with her disheveled hair and bloodstained hands and clothes, and did the most surprising thing. He hugged her.

Vienne struggled free of his embrace, eyes burning. "Don't," she choked out. "He wouldn't be hurt if not for me."

"Unless you pulled the trigger yourself, I don't see how that's possible," Lord Archer replied, his usual caustic tone softened by rare compassion. "You have injured my brother in many ways, Madame La Rieux, but this is thankfully not one of them."

Vienne stared at him. He said it so matter-of-factly—it was not an insult but simple truth. Somehow, she would have rather had him angry at her. Anger would have made her feel less despicable.

"I'm staying with him," she announced, lifting her chin. She expected him to argue but he merely nodded.

"You should send Havers 'round to your place for fresh clothing—blood is very much not your color. Go. I'll sit with Tryst for the few moments you are gone."

She didn't argue, but made off straightaway to find the coachman. It was easier than she thought because he was downstairs in the lobby of the hotel, talking to Inspector Jacobs. Both men looked up as she approached, as did several guests. She could only imagine how she looked. Dear God, the gossips would have such a party with this! Thankfully, it would take word a while to reach the countryside.

Perhaps she would be able to get out of England before the Duke of Ryeton heard the news and killed her himself.

"Inspector, Mr. Havers . . . I beg your pardon, but, Mr. Havers, I wondered if I could trouble you to fetch some clean clothes for me from my home?"

The older man smiled, forming deep creases around his eyes and mouth. He had a kind face, kissed by the sun and wind rather than beaten by it. "Of course." Then to the Scotland Yard man, "Are we done, sir?"

"Yes. If I have anymore questions, I know where to find you. Madame La Rieux, but might we have a word now?"

Vienne's mind wasn't working quite the way it should. "I would prefer to return to Trystan."

"I don't mind accompanying you."

She was about to refuse him when she remembered that she had wounded the man who shot Trystan. He would want to know about that. He might also have news about the bastard, which she wanted to know.

"All right. Lord Trystan's brother is with him right now, but I am certain he will want to hear what happened as well."

They rode up to the private floor in the small, elegant lift run by a young man in a smart Barrington uniform of black and gold. They didn't speak, and the young man made a special point of not looking at Vienne's soiled clothing. He had to know what had happened—the entire staff must surely know by now.

As they departed the cage, the young man spoke, "Ma'am?"

Vienne turned to glance at him and saw the question in his wide eyes—the hope there. "He's going to be fine," she replied with more conviction than she felt. She even managed to add a smile.

The young man sagged in relief. "Thank the lord. And thank you, ma'am."

She nodded warily and then led Inspector Jacobs to Trystan's door. Once they were inside, Archer came out of the bedroom. He seemed composed but his eyes looked red. Had he been crying? Now she was the one tempted to hug him. She would have if they didn't have an audience.

"Lord Archer, this is Inspector Jacobs of Scotland Yard. Inspector, may I introduce Lord Archer Kane, Lord Trystan's brother."

The two men exchanged handshakes before the three of them sat down in the sitting area. Vienne would have offered refreshment, but she had no idea how to go about doing so. Trystan didn't have any servants, so she would have to go downstairs again and she really just wanted to get this interview over with.

"What of Gibbs?" she asked the inspector. Then

to Archer, "He is the man who shot Trystan and was behind the sabotage."

"It will be a while before he regains use of that arm," the lawman informed her with what sounded like respect. "You're a crack shot, Madame La Rieux."

"You shot the villain?" Archer's tone and expression were as surprised as they were impressed. "Well done."

Vienne smiled slightly. "Is it true that Gibbs's only motivation for attacking us was because of his wife's deception?"

Jacobs nodded. "It appears so. It was nothing personal against either you or Lord Trystan. You were just most newsworthy."

She thought of all the stories in the papers about her, the club, and Trystienne's. Add that to the gossip printed about her and Trystan, not to mention Trystan's accomplishments, and it was no wonder Gibbs targeted them. Their project was simply the best known.

"What you are saying, then, Inspector, is that my brother was shot for no other reason than he is co-owner of a bunch of shops?"

"Yes. I'm afraid so, Lord Archer."

Trystan's brother swore. Vienne heartily agreed with his assessment.

"If it is of any relief at all, I can tell you that Gibbs

will most likely die in prison," Jacobs informed them. "He's going to be there a great many years."

"It is something of a relief, monsieur. Thank you." It *was* a relief, even though Trystan was injured. At least Gibbs would not be able to torment them any longer.

Since he had arrived on the scene after Trystan, the inspector stayed a little while longer, getting Vienne to tell her account of the events—how Gibbs had simply walked onto the site and pulled a weapon on her. She relayed how he had gone on and on about his wife and the damage Vienne was about to do to society in general, the fairer sex in particular. Then Trystan had arrived and took the shot meant for her.

When she was done, she dared to glance at Lord Archer, who was in turn watching her expressionlessly.

"I will keep you no longer," Inspector Jacobs announced and rose to his feet, tucking his notebook and pencil inside his coat. "Thank you for your time."

Alone with Archer now, Vienne went to the liquor cabinet. "Would you like a drink, Lord Archer?"

"Hell, yes. A stiff one."

She poured them each a whiskey and returned to her chair. Her stomach felt as though it was tied up in knots, she was so nervous about facing him.

He reclined in the chair like a long, lean tomcat. "Let me get this straight—you're angry at Trystan for saving your life."

"I'm not angry. I simply wish he had not acted so rashly. I was Gibbs's target."

"And then you shot the man in retaliation."

It wasn't a question but she responded as such. "Yes."

"I appreciate what you did for him, and the care you took to make certain he lived. I'm sure you have my entire family's gratitude. I know I should ask you to leave, but I cannot be that cruel, even though I fear you will only break his heart again."

Vienne swallowed. Such a blunt lot these Kane men were. "I would like to stay, so thank you."

But Archer was not done with her. "I do not understand it. Trystan is the best man I've ever known, brother or not. How can you reject him?"

"It's not really any of your concern, sir."

He suddenly leaned forward in his chair—like a cobra about to strike. "My brother put himself in front of a bullet for you, woman. He would have given his life to save yours, a trade I do not think would have been a fair one given your shit behavior. Do not dare tell me this is none of my concern."

"You do not mince words, do you?" She agreed with him, but his words still shook her.

"Not usually, no." He took a drink. "If Trystan finds you here when he wakes up, he's going to think you stayed because you care for him."

"He'll think I stayed out of guilt," she corrected. "He doesn't believe me capable of caring."

Her companion scowled in disgust. "He doesn't believe that, not truly. He wouldn't have tried so hard to win you if he did. The boy believes you to be something special. I have yet to see it myself, but if Trystan sees it, I have to believe it exists."

Vienne raised her own glass. "He's not a boy, sir. He is a man, and I *do* care for him. I am simply not the right woman for him. He will accept that."

Archer watched her from between narrow lids. "Will you?"

"Will I what?"

"Ever fully accept that you are not the right woman? Because I have to tell you, madam, your state of dishevel and the pallor in your cheeks suggest otherwise."

She swore. "My God! I am so very tired of you Kane men presuming to know my mind better than I! You do not, and I will thank you to keep your opinions to yourself!"

"Its 'thank' not 'tank'," he informed her blandly. "And I believe in releasing my opinions to the world

where they can be of benefit to others. I'm very phil-
anthropic that way."

There was no stopping the smile that tugged at
her lips. She wanted to stay angry with this obnoxious, arrogant man, but she could not. However, she
was firm when she said, "I'm going to stay until I am
certain he is recovered, and there's nothing you can
do to stop me short of physically removing me from
this place."

"All right."

That was it? He was fine with her staying even
though he had demanded she do otherwise? She
added *strange* to her mental list of Kane family traits.

It was good that she stayed, because of the infection that did set in. With the help of some potions
from the surgeon and regular cleaning of the wound,
Vienne saw a vast improvement within just a couple
of days—a good sign. Trystan's fever broke and he
began to have more lucid periods despite the pain
medication he took.

Vienne and Archer continued to take turns
caring for him. Archer had written to the duke to
tell him what happened, making certain Ryeton
knew Trystan was recovering nicely and that there
was no need for him to return again to London,
especially since Rose should get her rest. He knew

exactly what to say to convince His Grace not to come to town—much to Vienne's relief. The last thing she wanted or needed was another Kane around, especially the one member of the family that intimidated her.

Because of that, she and Archer formed a sort of truce. She wouldn't go so far as to say it was a friendship, but it wasn't as tense between them anymore.

Vienne was the one changing the dressing on Trystan's wound—now healing wonderfully—when he truly woke up. His eyes opened and focused on her. He was able to really see her now, unlike the foggy gaze he'd had while the infection and pain rode him.

"Vienne." There was such an expression of wonder on his face that she could have cried. "What are you doing here?"

She shrugged. "I had nothing else to do," she replied teasingly. "How do you feel?"

"Like I've been shot." His grin was tired, but true. He rubbed a hand over his jaw. "And I need a shave."

"Would you like me to fetch your shaving gear and a mirror?" There was no reason he couldn't shave himself. The bullet had gone through his side not his shoulder.

Trystan gave his head a shake and patted the bed beside him. "Come sit. Tell me everything I've missed. Did they arrest the bounder?"

Vienne sat down on the edge of the mattress, careful not to jostle him too much. "You shouldn't have jumped in front of me."

He took her hand. Little jolts of electricity shot up her arm. She hadn't realized how much she missed his touch until now. "You'll never make me regret it, Vienne. Don't bother trying. And don't you feel guilty either. Now, be a good girl and tell me what I want to hear."

With a sigh, Vienne abandoned all thought of chastising him and filled him in on everything he needed to know, right down to how work was continuing on Trystienne's. What she didn't tell him was that she had no intention of talking to other investors. She was going to fight him on that.

"Your brother said I should not be here when you regain consciousness. He said it might . . . confuse you in regards to my feelings."

He arched a brow. "What did you tell him? That I would think you stayed out of guilt?"

She started. He truly did know her better than anyone else. *That's why I love him*. The thought startled her even more. Good Lord, was it possible? How would she know if this was love or not? *Oh . . .* This was awful. It was wonderful. It was . . . she couldn't begin to think of the right words.

"Vienne?" He looked at her strangely. "Are you all right?"

"I'm fine," but her breathless tone proved that a fat lie. "Trystan, there is something I want to tell you."

He gave her a ghost of a smile. "I'm not going anywhere."

She nodded—hesitant. How to tell it truthfully? She wanted to tell it in such a way that he might see her charitably, but that wouldn't be the exact truth. She did not want him to see her at what had been her lowest, but it was why she was the way she was. It was something he had to hear before there could be anything more between them.

He might very well decide he wanted nothing more to do with her.

Vienne took a deep, calming breath. *Courage.* "It happened when I was fifteen."

Trystan was very glad to be alive. He was also very glad that Vienne was there when he woke up. Despite his remark about her feeling guilty, he hoped there was more to it than a feeling of obligation.

He refused to think otherwise. It was foolhardy, perhaps, but his heart seized the notion and ran with it. Damn stubborn thing. But lying in that bed, looking at her—so tired and beautifully fragile in her appearance—he couldn't help but love her. Couldn't help but hope that she might release her fear and let him in.

"My name—the name I was born to—is Vienne Moreau."

"I know." He shifted on the bed, pushing himself up so he could recline on the mountain of pillows. Christ, it hurt—brought a light layer of sweat to his brow—but he did it. And he managed not to miss the expression of shock on her fair face.

"You were born in a small village just outside of Paris. Your father, he was a publisher, right?"

She nodded, disbelief softening her features. "How did you know?"

"I like to research the people I do business with. Actually it was extremely difficult to uncover that much of your past. You are very good at hiding, Vienne. Is that what you wanted to tell me?"

She stared at him for a moment, seemingly dumbfounded. Then she gave her head a shake, sending little copper wisps dancing around her face. "No. That was but a part of it. This . . . this is very difficult for me. I have never told another person what I am about to tell you. I hope that declaration tells you how much I trust you."

But *not* with your heart, he thought rather uncharitably. His bitterness faded when he saw the trepidation in her eyes. Vienne afraid? Of him? This was not a good feeling, not at all.

She sighed and rubbed her fingers over her forehead as though trying to reach in and manually sort her thoughts. "My oldest sister, Marguerite, married a very handsome and well-known painter."

"What's his name? If I haven't heard of him, he's not that well known."

She looked at him as though she didn't understand why it mattered. To be honest, Trystan wasn't certain himself, but there was something in how she held herself and refused to meet his gaze that told him the painter's name was very important indeed.

"Marcel du Barrie."

He shook his head. "Never heard of him."

That put a faint smile on her lips. "Yes, well, he did quite well for himself."

There was just the slightest hint of *something* in her tone to make him wish this painter was there so he could perhaps break his fingers. "Go on."

If she noticed the edge in his voice, she ignored it. "Marcel was wonderful to we younger girls. He was always getting us to sit for him. He once painted me as Tatiana, the Faerie Queen."

Trystan merely nodded. He was lucky if he could draw a reasonably straight line. He hated this Marcel du Pretentious Bastard.

"Marcel was very handsome and romantic. We all envied Marguerite for marrying him. I think we all—there are another four girls—had a bit of a crush on him."

"I bet he loved that."

Vienne's head jerked up. Her hand came down on his, fingers squeezing. "Yes. I think he did. He certainly did nothing to discourage us. I'm not sure when my sister started to resent us, or when she perhaps stopped trusting in her husband's love, but she became withdrawn, spiteful. We didn't want to spend time with her because she was so unpleasant."

"Let me guess . . . The more unpleasant your sister became, the more affable Monsieur du Barrie became?"

She nodded almost eagerly, as though she was trying to will him to understand. Trystan wanted to tell her that there was nothing wrong with his understanding. In fact, he perhaps understood too well. Regardless, this was her story, her confession, and he was going to let her tell it.

"I thought I was Marcel's favorite. I never had a close relationship with my brothers; they were so much older. I was spoiled and indulged being the youngest. I sought Marcel's attention and enjoyed his flattery. I suspect he enjoyed my adoration as well."

Trystan turned his hand over so that his fingers could entwine with hers. A bitter taste coated his tongue. He didn't know how to describe what he was feeling. He was angry and sad and cold all at the same time. "Vienne, did he seduce you?"

"No." She pulled her hand free and used it to wring her other one. She turned her head, her expression anguished. "I seduced him."

A huff of laughter escaped him, bitter and harsh. "You were what, fifteen? How old was he?"

She shook her head. "You do not understand."

"Oh, I think I do. He was older, married to your sister, and the bastard should have known better than to take advantage of a young girl's infatuation."

"He tried," she insisted. "I kissed him and he told me it was wrong, but I decided I wanted him and I conspired to be alone with him on several occasions."

"He didn't have to be alone with you. He could have sent you away, but he didn't because he liked it. I suppose he told you that you were beautiful and that he cared so much for you, but it could never be."

Her eyes widened. Shock and innocence was a strange expression to see on Vienne's face. He was so accustomed to her being cool and composed, or furious. Passionate. This bewilderment unsettled him. "How did you know?" she asked.

He made a face. "Have you met my brothers? I grew up watching the two of them seduce house-maids, village girls. Christ, anything in a skirt. Grey's favorite as heir was to tell girls how much he loved them, but he had duties as a duke, etcetera. So, the painter fanned the flames of your fascination for him while putting up the pretense of resistance. Then he seduced you."

"You aren't listening to me. *I* seduced *him*. One night when Marguerite was away, I snuck into the old green house he had converted into a studio. I disrobed in front of him and offered myself to him."

"And he took what you offered." His words forced their way out between his clenched teeth.

Vienne looked down. "Yes. We were lovers for six months before Marguerite found us together."

Both of Trystan's brows rose. "That must have been awkward, at the very least."

She picked at a piece of lint on the quilt. "When she found out what I had done, she told the entire family. I was cast out in shame."

"Wait a moment." Surely he couldn't have heard her correctly. "Your family tossed you out? What of the painter?"

She glanced up, and gave him a look that said it ought to be obvious. "He and Marguerite were man and wife. When he told her what happened, she couldn't very well be angry with him."

Perhaps he was dimwitted, but he wanted to make sure he understood perfectly. "What exactly did he tell her happened?"

An exasperated sigh slipped from her lips. "Haven't you been listening? He told her how I seduced him."

He couldn't help it; he burst out laughing. When he saw the hurt look on her face, he stopped. "Vienne, surely you don't believe you were actually the one to blame? Perhaps back then, when you were young. But now?"

She frowned. "But I did. I seduced him. I set out to do it and I did."

"That's what all great seducers want their victims to believe."

"No." She gave her head a fervent shake. "My family cast me out because of my sin. My sister despised me for it. It was me. My fault."

"Your family is a bunch of sodding arses—and your sister obviously wanted someone to blame other than her husband. She was jealous of you, and pointing the finger at you made her feel better. If she blamed you then she didn't have to blame her husband, who was the real villain of the affair."

"No. It's not true."

"Vienne . . ." He reached for her, but she jerked away, stumbling to her feet.

"No! You are wrong! Because if you are not, that means they should have stood beside me. It means I shouldn't have had to become a courtesan to survive!"

Her words struck him like a fist. Good lord, what had she suffered? So young to go from a man she thought loved her to another who paid to bed her. Probably more than one man, at that. *Christ.*

"There!" She pointed a long finger at him. "There it is! I knew when I told you this you would judge me. How can you not?"

"Judge you?" He scowled. "Vienne, I once slept with a woman just to insure she bought into a scheme of mine. If either of us is going to be branded a whore, it should probably be me. I was the one with a choice."

"As did I. There's always a choice, Trystan."

She looked so frail and . . . broken. He had accused her of being just that. If he could beat himself silly, he would. "And sometimes we make the wrong one, or one that's hard to live with, but that only makes us human, sweetness."

"Do you understand now why we cannot be together?"

"No," he replied honestly. "I do not."

"I gave Marcel my heart, and afterward it was easy to give those men my body. I've used so many people, you included. I am sorry for that."

What was she trying to say? That she still loved the painter? Or was she saying good-bye? That's what it felt like.

"I'm sorry you went through that, Vienne. I truly am. If I could turn back time, I would do that for you. But I cannot."

"That's it? That's all you have to say?" She seemed surprised—angry even.

Sweet Christ. His side ached, he had to piss, and it tasted like something had died in his mouth. "What do you want from me, Vienne? Absolution? I don't think I'm the one who can give you what you want." She was the one who thought she had done something wrong. There would be no forgiveness until she realized that she had been a victim, and that she was strong enough to take care of herself in whatever way necessary.

She stiffened as though he'd torn the heart right out of her chest. Obviously he'd said something wrong, though for the life of him he didn't know what.

"You are right," she said softly. "Thank you, Trystan. If you will excuse me, I am needed at the site. Things are coming along brilliantly. I will have a progress report delivered to you first thing tomorrow morning. Good day."

Before he could say another word she walked out of the room and shut the door behind her, leaving him sitting there, aching and bewildered. Frustrated as well. He had let himself believe she was there because she cared, but now he was left wondering what he'd done wrong. Maybe he was just wrong. Perhaps Vienne was looking for a man like her painter, whom she had obviously never gotten over. *The bastard.*

That would teach him to get his hopes up. Where Vienne La Rieux née Moreau was concerned, that only led to heartache.

Vienne held back the tears until she was in the carriage on her way home. Only then, when she was alone and hidden from view, did she let them come. She had bared her soul to Trystan and he had acted as though it was nothing special.

He said he couldn't give her what she wanted. How could his feelings for her have changed so drastically? He had seemed like his usual self before she told her story. He hadn't seemed to think ill of her for having an affair with Marcel, so what had changed his mind? Was it the knowledge that she had been a courtesan? No . . . He had likened himself to a prostitute.

Maybe he had decided that being with her was simply more trouble than she was worth. Maybe he hadn't cared as much for her as he had claimed.

It had felt good to confess her past—like a heavy weight had been lifted off her shoulders. Half her tears were because of that release, the other because she had realized she loved Trystan too late. One thing the affair with Marcel had taught her was that love was not enough.

At least she knew she could love. She should be happy for that.

She cried all the harder.

Chapter 15

Over the next six weeks, things came together quickly at Trystienne's. Since Gibbs's capture, it was easier to find workers; and those Vienne and Trystan already had were so glad they were no longer in danger, *and* were getting paid higher wages, that they worked all the harder to get the place ready for its grand opening, which was going to be held sooner than expected.

The grand opening was going to be a huge affair. Despite the lack of society in town, it could still attract a large crowd as there were all those who remained in London year-round. Vienne was insanely busy trying to plan the party and train the shop-girls she'd hired. They all put in extremely long days unpacking stock from all over the world, pressing wrinkles out of delicate ready-to-wear dresses and undergarments, and putting together elegant yet provocative displays to catch the eye.

Sadie often worked with her, and arranged the

tearoom just the way she wanted it, making sure all the appliances were installed properly. The kitchen wasn't large, so the pastries and cakes would be made off site and delivered, but it was big enough to brew tea, wash dishes, and store what was needed. The walls had been painted a delicate peach and decorated with beautiful watercolors.

Trystan put in his share of hours as well. One morning Vienne arrived to find him still wearing the clothes he had on the day before.

"You have to sleep," she told him. "I need you rested."

At one time such a remark would have prompted him to say something intimate and romantic, but now he merely nodded. "I'm going to head home soon. I promise."

He seemed to be healing well, though he only mentioned it when she asked. The tension between them wasn't exactly uncomfortable, but it wasn't pleasant either. Hopefully, this would fade soon. If she couldn't have him as a lover, she would gladly have him as her friend, even though it hurt to look at him. She missed his friendship most of all. She missed the breakfasts they shared, the animated conversations about plans for the store and other individual projects.

It seemed now that he could barely look her in the eye. He claimed not to be at all bothered by her former relationship with Marcel, so it had to be the fact that she had been a mistress that made him so cold. But was he disgusted by her . . . or did he pity her? It was hard to decipher without asking, and she had too much pride to do that.

But she hadn't too much pride to entertain fantasies about him coming to her to tell her he couldn't live without her. What if she did that to him? Could she find the courage to walk right up to him and tell him she was sorry and that she wanted to be with him? It went against everything she had lived these past years. Her number one rule was to never put herself in a position where she cared too much. It was not only self-preservation: in this case, it could prevent her from inevitably destroying what affection Trystan had for her.

Trystan had told her she was wrong to blame herself for what happened with Marcel. She had been so young and clung to that blame like a piece of flotsam. If she didn't believe that she had been the villain, the one to blame, then she had to reconcile to the notion that her family had sided against her and wrongly cast her aside.

That idea gave made her heart ache. She didn't

want to consider it. Unfortunately, she had to. If she was ever going to be fine and right—whole—she had to take a good, hard look at herself.

She was not going to like everything she saw.

Vienne put in hours just as long as Trystan did during the day, then returned to the club at night, where she now was open for limited hours. Still, Saint's Row was open to the public, and it did good business. It was mostly just the gaming rooms and dining area, but people with money in London seemed to love risking it on games of chance or spending it on food that hadn't had the essence boiled out of it. English food made her French soul cringe.

The few hours a week she had to herself she often spent in the stables, caring for her sweet little mare. Unfortunately the sight of the gorgeous creature reminded her of Trystan.

One afternoon she accepted an invitation to luncheon from Lady Gosling—Theone. She was bored, grumpy, and in need of some companionship that would distract her from feeling sorry for herself.

Unfortunately, her new friend wanted to discuss the very things Vienne wished to avoid.

"Gossip has it that the ardor between yourself and Lord Trystan Kane has cooled."

Vienne took a sip of tea. "I suppose the gossips

would know. Honestly, I do not know where these people get their shameless fodder."

"Can you not?" The dark-haired beauty asked with blatantly false innocence. There would be no concealing her true feelings from Theone. The woman had the instincts of a hawk. "You know, Lord Trystan is the only Kane male I haven't sampled. Should I rectify that, do you think?"

Vienne was so surprised by the question that she sent the other woman a murderous gaze that would have cowed a person of lesser resolve. Theone merely chuckled. "I will take that as a no."

She shrugged. "It is none of my business who you take to your bed."

Theone set her delicate bone china cup on its saucer. Her teasing expression was tempered by the slightest degree of hurt. "Come now, Vienne. I was of the impression that we had become better friends than that."

Vienne met her forest green gaze. "Good enough friends that you would ask me if you should crawl into bed with my former lover?"

"So, it is over." Theone's tone was sympathetic. "I am sorry to hear that."

"Are you?" Vienne asked bitterly.

"I am, and if you're going to have that sort of attitude all afternoon, you can go the hell home."

The two of them stared at each other for what felt like eternity, then Vienne felt the beginning of a smile. She fought it, but when she saw Theone's wide lips twitch as well, she gave in. They shared a chuckle.

After their laughter faded, Theone poured more tea. "Do you want to talk about it?"

"There's very little to talk about. Trystan and I were lovers a long time ago. We were lovers again a few weeks ago. Now we are nothing. Business associates." She couldn't even refer to him as her partner because he made it clear he didn't want to be that either.

A delicate silver spoon, held by her long slender fingers, stirred the tea. "You are unhappy with this change in circumstances?"

"I am," Vienne admitted. It felt so good to say it aloud. "Very unhappy, but unfortunately I am at a loss as to how to change them again."

Theone set the spoon aside. "Strange as it may seem coming from me, I find honesty works best in this case. I've yet to meet a man who can refuse a genuine admission of lust from a woman."

"It's much more complicated than lust."

Dark green eyes lit with understanding. "You love him."

Vienne nodded, anxiety unfurling in her stomach.

The other woman had ammunition to use against her now.

"Then you had better do something about it. It is my belief that precious few of us are fortunate to find someone to love and hopefully love us in return. You get your claws into that man, Vienne, and don't you dare let go."

It was such a passionate speech that Vienne startled at it. "You did not love your husband, did you?"

Her friend's smile turned a combination of bitter and sad. "I imagine I did once. He seemed like my knight in shining armor when he first started sniffing around. I knew what he was when I married him, and went into the union willingly. But am I sad that he is dead? No. I'm glad for it. God help me, but I laughed when I found him at the bottom of the stairs. I laughed with the sheer joy of a slave tasting freedom."

Vienne could not imagine the feeling, but she didn't judge Theone for feeling as she had. She had no idea what the woman's marriage had been like. She had met women in her life whose husbands used them in the most awful ways, and Theone had the same look in her eyes as they—a haunted flatness.

"But he was nice in the beginning?"

Her friend paused in thought, then nodded. "He was, yes. He was married when I first met him.

Now I shudder to think of how that first wife might have died; her passing was rather convenient. He would come to the theater with gifts, saying pretty words. Before his wife died, he used to tell me how he wished we could be together, but that it could never be."

Those words sent a chill down Vienne's spine. Marcel had said the same thing to her.

"He was so charming and attentive. I truly believed he might care for me. Perhaps he did in his twisted, debauched way. Men will say anything to get what they want, I've learned. But they show their true colors when it comes down to making a choice. A man who is only in it for his own pleasure will simply walk away when things begin to disintegrate."

Like Marcel turned his back on her. She hadn't truly believed it when Trystan said as much, but hearing it from Theone . . . well, it was different hearing such truth from a woman so similar to herself, who had been through so much.

"Your husband came to my club on occasion. He seemed very charming."

Theone's mouth twisted as though she tasted something bitter. "Yes, he was good at that. Charming and flirtatious with everyone but me."

Had Marcel mistreated Marguerite? Was that why she acted as she had? Her mind couldn't wrap around that just yet, she was still trying to work through the facts that he might not have been the one in the wrong. Her family had sided with Marcel over her. What sort of people did that?

But if she was honest—no one forced her to leave home. They were angry and things were said in that anger, but her mother hadn't told her to leave, only that it would be easier if she went away. Her other sisters had been upset with her—very much so—but they had been upset with Marcel as well. Only Marguerite had been enraged enough to say she wished Vienne had never been born.

She had forgiven her sister those words because she had hurt her, and now she realized the older woman had only reacted to the discovery that not only had her husband betrayed her, but her sister as well. It must have been heartbreaking.

Marguerite had told her to get out of her sight, to stay away from her and from Marcel. Perhaps it hadn't been solely a punishment. Perhaps Marguerite was trying to protect her.

These assumptions were too much. She couldn't entertain them anymore. She had no way of knowing what her sister had tried to do, or how she felt. The only thing she could cling to was the realization that she was not the sole owner of the blame. That was enough for now.

"Vienne?"

She blinked and lifted her head. For a moment she forgot where she was, then she saw Theone's concerned face. "You knew someone like my husband, didn't you?"

She frowned and gave her head a shake to clear it. "Somewhat. A man I thought hung the moon and stars. Now I'm not so certain."

"In my experience, uncertainty is the same as no, but women such as we tend to say yes anyway. It's only when we are certain that we freeze or run in the opposite direction, because we're so very afraid someone might love us and then see how very unlovable we are."

"Yes," she agreed a little breathlessly. "Exactly."

A coy smile curved her new friend's lips. "May I let you in on a little secret, Vienne?"

"Of course."

"You and I are not awful people. Selfish at times, but not terrible. We are all about self-preservation and protecting ourselves, but we deserve love, Vienne. Don't you ever doubt that. Regardless of how much it terrifies me to think of someone depending on me, trusting in me, I truly want to find it someday. You're an intelligent woman—don't let fear keep you alone. This world is so much more pleasant when you have someone to share it with."

Good Lord, how many people were going to give her advice in the arena of love? Was it a conspiracy or a sign from the Almighty? Surely it could not be a coincidence. She didn't believe in coincidence.

But if it wasn't coincidence, that meant she had to take the advice and consider it carefully. It meant letting her guard down and trusting not only someone else but herself. She could do that in business, but wasn't so good at it in her personal life.

Still, she had let Trystan get away once. She would not do it again. The only question now was if he would be willing to give her another chance.

·

Trystienne's was close enough to completion that Trystan went ahead and took care of selling a large portion of his shares to Grey and Archer. Since he handled their investments, it was a simple procedure. He decided to keep some for himself, since he wasn't foolish enough to let his emotions cheat him out of a good investment. After all the work and planning, all the effort he put into becoming Vienne's partner, it felt oddly sad—wrong somehow—to just give it away. All right, so he sold it and made a bit of a profit, but that wasn't the point. It was as though he had just sold a piece of himself—his soul.

He had fully expected Vienne to offer to buy him out. It was obvious she wanted nothing to do with him. Even though they often worked on site at the same time, he rarely saw her and spoke to her even less. One day she told him that she needed him rested, and his heart had given a painful thump. He almost made a ribald joke, but then he remembered that wouldn't be appreciated. They were nothing to each other now—only associates, and that was it.

It hurt more now than it had years ago, but what had he expected—that Vienne had changed? Or that he would impress her so much, she would have no choice but to fall desperately in love and declare herself his forever? Such things happened in sensational novels, but not in actual life.

So, he would have to accept what was and move on before his brothers beat him senseless for being so maudlin. Archer had already threatened to do just that. "Shite or get off the damn pot," had been his exact words. "Either pull your head out of your arse and go after her, or shut the hell up before I slap you silly."

Archer was a dirty fighter, and certainly not one he wanted to tangle with. He had scars from his childhood to prove it.

Shite or get off the pot. It was quite possibly the best advice his brother had ever given him. However, it didn't matter what he did or said when Vienne's mind was so jumbled. How could she actually blame herself for what had happened? Her family should be heartily ashamed of themselves.

It was the thought of her family that spurned him into action. He knew what he had to do. It was the only way he could convince her of the truth—if it worked. If it backfired, it would ruin everything.

Upon his return to the Barrington late that evening, he poured himself a healthy measure of scotch and went directly to his desk, despite the wariness in his bones and the ache in his side. His physician warned him that he might be sore and stiff for some time given the internal damage done by Gibbs's bullet. *Bloody lunatic.* Attempting to murder someone over a foolish collection of shops. He would never understand people who blamed others for all the misfortune in their lives. Likewise, he could not understand Vienne shouldering unnecessary guilt.

It was his opinion that one learned from one's mistakes and moved on. A grudge could only be carried for so long before you either had to give it up or let the weight smother you. Granted, he should have taken his own advice when it came to Vienne, but he didn't consider her a mistake, not back then and not now.

Trystan took paper from one of the drawers and then reached for his steel pen, which delivered ink from a chamber inside. *Remarkable* little thing. He had seen others like this before, but this one wrote extremely smoothly. He had invested in the inventor and had already seen a tidy profit from the venture. No dipping required. All one had to do was refill the internal chamber when it ran dry. Trystan cleaned it on a regular basis to prevent clogging.

His hand paused over the stationery as he mentally composed what to say. Only when he had it right in his head did he commit to it with ink on paper. When he was finished, he folded it, slipped the two pages into an envelope, and sealed it with glue. He would post it first thing tomorrow morning. If nothing came of it, so be it. But, if he received a favorably response, he would go forward.

And hope Vienne would forgive him.

Trystan did not have to wait long for a reply—it came via telegraph a few days after he sent his letter. It simply read, "Will be in London within the week. Accept your offer."

When the day arrived, he contrived a reason to have Vienne come to the Barrington. It wasn't difficult; he simply told her his schedule was swamped that day and could she please meet with him to discuss a few of their employees? Of course there was nothing to discuss, but he knew the request would bring her quickly as she had hired most of them and liked them all.

Vienne was always quick to defend the underdog.

She breezed into one of the private parlors on the ground floor with the grace and speed of a shark about to strike. She was probably the only woman of his acquaintance who could wear that particular shade of mustard and still look good. The velvet swished around her boots and molded to the curve and contour of her corseted torso. Her hair was up in a fashionable sweep with a jaunty little hat perched upon it, feathers bobbing. She looked more herself these days, and he wasn't too certain it was a good thing. Call him selfish, but he somewhat liked knowing that she was as miserable as he.

"Trystan, I do hope you have not decided to terminate any of our employees. They have been working day and night to have Trystienne's ready to open, and I will not have them cast aside like rubbish now that we are so very close to completion." Her sharp gaze fell upon the table and its array of cold luncheon. "What is this?"

"I thought you might be hungry. I know you have chosen work over food lately."

She shrugged. "I have been very busy. Now, tell me. What is the problem with the employees?"

"There isn't one," he admitted. "They're all wonderful, which I do not have to tell you. I'm afraid I invited you here out of pretense."

Her jewel-bright eyes narrowed, but not before he saw a glimmer of hope in their pretty depths. "What is this?"

How to best approach this? He scratched the back of his neck. "I recently made some inquiries on your behalf."

One sharp ginger brow jumped. "What manner of inquiries?"

She was already on the defensive. Perhaps he should approach from a different angle. "I wrote to one of your sisters. Aline."

All color—not that she had much—leached from her face. "You did what?"

He didn't know if she was going to explode or faint. He pressed on. "It wasn't difficult to find her after you told me about what happened. Do you know she's been looking for you for ten years?"

"What?" She looked shocked. "No."

Trystan watched as she gripped the back of a chair at the table for support. "Apparently they looked all over France for you. They even made trips across the Continent and had inquiries everywhere. She was astounded to learn you were here. They never thought you'd come to London."

"No." Her voice had a hollow sound to it as she stared at the tabletop. "My family is not exactly fond of the English."

"Yes, well, be that as it may, there is someone here I want you to see."

Her head jerked up, and her wild gaze locked with his. "Trystan, what have you done?"

Christ, he had known this might bite him on the arse, but it was too late now. "You can come in," he called out.

A door off the back of the room that adjoined to another parlor opened and three women entered the room. One was older, with graying ginger hair and sparkling eyes Trystan would recognize anywhere. The other two were younger, but older than Vienne. One had rich auburn hair and blue eyes while the other had hair the exact same color as Vienne's, though her eyes were a lighter color. Still, there was no denying who they were.

Vienne reacted as though they were ghosts. She was so very pale, her eyes so huge. Her mouth dropped open on a sharp gasp that she seemed to try to shove back in with her palm. Her body physically reacted to the sight of them—he saw her spine tighten.

The older woman's eyes filled with tears that she did not even attempt to hide. *"Ma petite fille,"* she murmured, holding out her arms.

Trystan held his breath as he watched Vienne's face for a flicker of emotion. Slowly she rose to her feet with hesitant movements as though she feared her legs might not support her.

"What are you doing here?" she asked.

The lighter haired sister responded in French, then looked at Trystan. "Excuse me, please. I do not mean to offend you by leaving you out of the conversation. I told Vienne we came because you were so very kind as to let us know she was here."

He nodded and smiled. "I will leave the four of you alone. I'm sure you have much to discuss."

Just as he was about to leave the room, a strong hand caught his arm. He turned to look into Vienne's unnerving eyes. "Why did you do this?" she demanded. "Did I hurt you so badly, you had to return in kind?"

He shook his head and removed her hand with a gentle grip. "I don't want to hurt you, Vienne. Neither do they. They came because they wanted to see you. Go. Talk to them and see for yourself."

She backed up, spine rigid, mouth tight. "I'm not sure I will ever forgive you for this."

He flashed a sad smile. "That makes two of us."

When the door closed behind Trystan, Vienne didn't know what to do. If she turned around she would have to confront her family. If she didn't turn around she would be a coward. She had felt much braver with Trystan in the room. Much angrier as well. How dare he interfere in her life!

When she gathered the courage to face her family, she found all three of them weeping silently. They looked heartbroken but happy at the same time. Hopeful and anxious.

She supposed she wore a similar expression, though she had yet to burst into tears.

"My little girl . . ." her mother began in French. "Why did you run away?"

Vienne swallowed hard. "I thought you all wanted me gone. I thought I wasn't part of the family anymore."

This caused her mother to cry even harder. Aline had to put her arms around her. They had all aged so very much. Her mother was still handsome, but there was gray in her thick hair.

Marguerite came toward her. She stiffened, uncertain and wary. Those emotions quickly gave way to stunned horror as her eldest sister slowly sank to her knees at her feet. She seized Vienne's hand as tears ran down her face. "Forgive me, Vienne. This is all my fault. If I had only been a better sister, you would not have felt unwanted. If I had taken your word over that lothario I married."

Vienne's entire body—her entire world—went silent for a split second. "Marcel?"

Her sister nodded. "You were not his first young girl and you were certainly not his last." Her tone was as bitter and sharp as a bite of rhubarb.

"I . . . please, stand up. You do not need to kneel before me."

"I want to beg your forgiveness," her sister insisted.

"You have it." And she did. It was that simple. Vienne had never blamed her family, so it was as easy to offer forgiveness. "Please, get up."

Her sister rose, brushing her palms over the skirts of her rust-colored gown to smooth out wrinkles. "You have no idea how much your forgiveness means to me. Or how many times I prayed we would find you so I could ask for it to your face." She wrapped her arms around Vienne in a fierce hug. "It is so very wonderful to see your beautiful face."

Tears burned the back of Vienne's eyes. Since Trystan waltzed back into her life she had cried, or almost cried, a record number of times. The same went for laughing as well. It was as though he took her emotions and magnified them a thousand times.

"Marguerite, you are not the one that has to beg forgiveness. What I did was a horrible thing and I hope that someday you forgive me."

"You!" she and Aline exclaimed at the same time. Marguerite shot their sister a silencing glance. "Sweet girl, you have nothing to be sorry for. You were little more than a child. You had no idea what sort of man my husband was. He took advantage of your innocence and your sweet heart."

Only one word in that entire speech jumped out at Vienne. "Was? What sort of man Marcel *was*?"

Marguerite grimaced and gave a curt nod. "He was shot and killed ten years ago by the father of a fourteen-year-old girl he had seduced and left with child. She was not the only one. Scarcely a girl over thirteen was safe in our village. The monster preferred them to be in the early throes of womanhood. You would not believe the paintings I found in his studio after he was killed. I burned them."

Vienne pressed a hand to her heart as it hammered against her ribs. This was like a dream. A very strange dream. *Marcel was dead?* Shot because he had impregnated a young girl. He liked young girls.

"*Mon Dieu.*" She sank onto a spindly, fashionable chair. "It wasn't my fault."

"I did not want to think so ill of Marcel," her mother said, coming to sit beside her, the dark green of her gown making her eyes all the brighter. "I am ashamed to say that I believed him when he said you came to him. You were such a willful girl. I knew you would never want to hurt your sister, but you all thought the man was wonderful, especially you."

Especially me.

"I should have never have left."

Marguerite took her hand. "In some ways it was good that you did. It spared you the pain of having him toss you aside as he did all the others. I wish you had let us know where you were."

"I didn't think you would welcome contact from me."

The hand on hers tightened. "We are family. No matter what you do, we love you."

"That cockstand cost us almost twenty years without our sister," Aline said, her voice tight with outrage. "I hope the devil is flaying the skin from his bones with a dull knife."

Vienne's mother made a small noise, obviously distressed to hear such vehement language coming from her second youngest daughter.

"How is Papa?" Vienne inquired. She had always enjoyed time with her father, and being the youngest he often indulged her more than he perhaps should have.

Her mother and sisters exchanged anguished glances. It was Marguerite who answered. "Papa passed away six years ago. He left this for you." From her reticule, she pulled a slightly tattered letter sealed with a glob of red wax—her father had been so old-fashioned.

A tear dribbled down Vienne's cheek as she accepted the letter. She wiped the wetness away with the back of her hand. She would cry for him later, when she could be alone with her grief. "I'll read it when I am at home."

Silence embraced them, just for a moment. Then her mother said, "He is proud of you, little one. He tells me so often."

"Papa visits Mama in her dreams," Aline explained with an expression that begged Vienne to simply go along.

Vienne smiled. "Thank you, Mama. I like to think that he would approve of what I've built here. I would have loved for him to see Trystienne's."

"What on earth is that?" Aline asked.

"The emporium Lord Trystan and I have put together. It's a number of fashionable boutiques and a tearoom under one roof. Ladies may shop there for clothing, jewelry, hats—anything they want. We have shops for gentlemen as well."

"All together?" Marguerite's tone was rife with wonder.

She nodded. "Think of it like a pile of building blocks. They fit together to form a whole but each is an individual."

Aline smiled. "So Lord Trystan is your business partner?"

Vienne heard the incredulous note in her sister's statement, but was not offended by it. Aline had always delighted in teasing her. "Yes, he is. And a good one at that."

Marguerite dabbed at her eyes with a dainty handkerchief. "When Lord Trystan contacted us, we knew God had finally answered our prayers. Our other siblings wanted to come, but their lives would not permit it."

"You should come home with us," Aline suggested hopefully.

Vienne didn't need to think about it. "I would love that. I have business to attend to over the next week, but after that I can go. Will you stay until then? I have plenty of room at my club."

Her mother stroked a hand over Vienne's hair, smiling her Madonna smile. "Your Trystan was good enough to give us a suite here, free of charge, though I do feel a little guilty taking advantage of his hospitality."

Why was she not surprised? "He is a good man. One of the best I've ever had the honor to know."

"He certainly thinks very highly of you," Aline remarked. "He paid for our passage here as well."

Vienne missed the sparkle in her sister's eyes because she was too distracted by Trystan's generosity. He had done all of this for her. Why?

The answer came like a blow to the solar plexus. He had done it because he wanted to prove to her that she hadn't been to blame, that she was not the awful person she believed herself to be.

Because he knew it was the only way the two of them might ever have a future. It was worth that much to him that he would take a chance on this being an awful reunion. She was worth that much to him.

Could it be that he loved her? It seemed too good to possibly be true, and yet she allowed herself to indulge in the thought. Wallow in it, even. All was not lost.

"Vienne?" Marguerite's voice brought her out of her thoughts. "What are you thinking?"

Vienne squeezed her sister's hand. "I think that it is so wonderful to have the three of you here with me. I would like it so much if you could stay until after the grand opening. There's going to be a party that I so want you to attend with me. Afterward, we can go to France together."

Her sisters turned to their mother for the decision. How little some things change. Jeanette Moreau was a matriarch in every sense of the word in their family.

"Yes," the older woman replied. "I would like that very much. Aline, see about sending a telegram home to let them know we're extending our stay."

Aline beamed. "Of course, Mama."

Vienne's heart swelled. This was one of the best days of her life. It felt as though angels had come down to take all of her worries and cares away. As though she had been in a cage and now the door was open for her to run free.

This time she wouldn't run away from what she wanted. She would run toward it.

Chapter 16

Trystan sometimes lamented his family—as anyone with family generally did—but on most occasions he thought them the best people he knew. The party to celebrate the completion and opening of Trystienne's was one of those occasions.

Grey and Rose, his mother, and Bronte and Alex returned from the country for the occasion. Archer was there as well, looking tidier and more sober than Trystan had seen him since his return to England. Whatever it was that made Arch feel sorry for himself, it seemed to have passed, and he decided to move on to greener pastures.

Trystan suspected the change might have something to do with Indara Ferrars—he hadn't been able to take his eyes off her all evening. Truthfully, Trystan couldn't tell if the look in Archer's eye was predatory in a good way or bad. Still it was better than drunk.

He was surprised to see Rose there in her delicate

condition, but no one could tell by looking at her that she was with child. He supposed one might notice a very slight thickening around her middle beneath her pale blue gown, but that was probably the sort of thing only another woman might notice as they eyed each other in such a critical fashion.

Bronte and Alex looked well and could scarcely leave each other's side for more than a moment. It was lovely to see his sister so happy in her marriage. Alex was a charmer, which gave Trystan pause as most charming men were not to be trusted—he knew this from growing up with Archer. However, Alex was completely besotted and didn't care if anyone noticed. That drove Trystan's estimation of him up a notch or two.

He surveyed the great hall and one of the ladies' boutiques to the right. There were some displays set up, but most of the shops were low on inventory simply to allow guests to mill about. One of Vienne's ideas had been to keep one of everything on display while extras were kept out of sight or in a back room. This gave the illusion that the customer was buying something extraordinary—and they were—but it was all in the presentation.

A footman appeared before him with a tray. "Champagne, Lord Trystan?"

"Excellent notion," he replied with thanks, and

took a glass from the tray. It was delicious—just tart enough, crisp enough, and cold enough. *Perfection*. He had to give Vienne the credit she deserved. The woman certainly knew how to throw a party.

Speaking of his former partner, she was on the other side of the hall chatting to one of her sisters— Aline, if he hadn't mixed their names up. Vienne wore a beautiful tea-colored velvet gown cut low across her shoulders, baring a lovely expanse of pale ivory skin. The bodice was snug, but not so much that it made a vulgar display of cleavage. The hint there was just enough to whet the appetite. Her copper hair was swept up into an elaborate construction he longed to dismantle just for the pleasure of touching her hair.

She looked beautiful, and it had very little do to with her lovely gown or artful hairstyle. It was happiness that lit her from within, making her skin and eyes glow with a light so pure it took his breath every time he looked at her.

He deliberately avoided being alone with Vienne since her family's arrival. It wasn't difficult, as most of her time was taken up with them and the rest divided between Trystienne's and Saint's Row. Oftentimes he would be attending other business while she was at the shops, or he would be at the shops while she was elsewhere. He thought it for the best;

and now that he saw her with her family, he realized he'd been wrong in that assumption. Obviously everything had been sorted out between them, so it was unlikely that Vienne wanted his head on a platter.

"I've a novel idea," came Archer's voice from behind him. "Why don't you stop staring and go talk to her instead?"

Trystan didn't move. He simply waited for Archer to move to his side. "Why don't you mind your own business?"

His brother made a tsking sound. "You are my business, more's the pity for you."

"Indeed." Trystan took a sip of his drink. "Don't you have a skirt or two to chase? There must be some pretty lady here you haven't bedded before."

"Surprisingly, there are several, but I'm not on the hunt tonight."

Trystan turned his head to present his disbelieving face to his brother. "Are you ill?"

Archer grinned. "No. I'm merely . . . rethinking my priorities. Does that intrigue you?"

It did. "No. I have no interest in your conquests or lack thereof."

His brother's grin remained. "Liar. You're just as concerned and nosy about me as I am of you."

That was true. "What's going on with you, Arch?"

The grin faded. Archer took a drink and then glanced down into the glass. "Took a bit of a stumble a few months ago. Offered my heart to a lady who didn't want it, and my pride took a bit of a pounding for it. However, I believe I have almost entirely removed my head from my arse, so we'll see how things progress from here."

Trystan frowned. "That was perhaps the most telling and the most cryptic answer I've ever heard. You've a talent there."

His brother laughed. "Let's just say I'm trying to make a fresh start. Take my life in a new direction."

He raised his glass. "To fresh starts." They both drank.

"Seriously," Archer began. "Go to her, Trystan. If you love her, you cannot give up."

"She basically told me it was never going to happen, Arch."

Pale blue eyes locked with his. "Then change her mind. Maybe some time with her family has softened her up."

He should be so lucky. But Archer was on to something. If Marguerite absolved Vienne of any blame for the affair with her husband, then just maybe Vienne might have a different opinion of herself.

It was a lot to ask for, but perhaps Archer was right—*shocking!*—and he should toss his pride to the wind and try again to win Vienne's heart. If she rejected him again, he could leave for New York whenever he wanted and literally put her behind him.

The healing wound in his side ached, so he rubbed his hand over it. Archer caught the movement. "Are you in pain?"

"Just a twinge. It's healing quite well. I'm told it's quite normal to have discomfort linger for a while. Getting shot is serious business, did you know that?"

Archer nodded with mock gravity. "So I hear. But that is the price one pays for being a hero."

"Who's a hero?" Grey asked, coming up on Trystan's other side. They formed a small circle now, the three of them.

"Me," Trystan informed him. "Or rather I *was*. Archer says I deserved to get shot."

His brother scowled. "I never said you deserved it, you little snot. I said it was the price you pay for being a hero."

Grey scratched his jaw, calling attention to the scar that ran down the length of his face. "There's a price for being unheroic as well. Seems one just cannot win these days."

"I think Archer is just jealous because we have manly scars and he is as unmarked as a little girl," Trystan suggested.

Grey grinned. "There is that."

"That's not true," Archer retorted with mock offense. "I have a scar on my left arse cheek where Lady Newton bit me in the spring. Perfect set of teeth marks."

Trystan snorted, but it was Grey who responded. "Dear Lord, it's a wonder you survived to tell the tale. Please *do not* tell us the tale."

Archer gave a careless shrug of his shoulders. "Now who is jealous? There he goes again. Grey, tell him to either stop staring at La Rieux or go talk to her. It's embarrassing standing here while he fawns like that."

Trystan hadn't even realized he was staring again. He tore his gaze away. "If I'm so embarrassing, go stand somewhere else."

"No. I wish to stand exactly where I am. You have the best view of the room here. You go stand somewhere else. I see a spot over by Madame La Rieux that would be perfect for you."

"Bugger off." But the retort lost its heat when he laughed his way through it.

"Here, have another glass of champagne." Grey snagged new glasses for each of them from an obliging footman in exchange for their empty ones. "That will give you courage."

"Oh yes, because she'll be so enamored of me if I stagger and breathe fumes all over her."

"I like to pretend I'm drunk sometimes," Archer admitted. "Makes the lady I'm intent on feel as though she's seducing me."

"I did not need to know that," Trystan replied.

Grey grimaced. "I thought it was common knowledge that any woman in London could have you for a smile."

"That's a little of the pot and kettle, don't you think?" Archer shot back. "I'm hard-pressed to find one over five and twenty that you haven't shagged."

Trystan laughed. "The two of you realize that you're arguing over which one of you has been the most debauched? It's hardly the sort of contest a man should strive to win, don't you think?"

The two of them turned their heads toward him in unison. It was unsettling. It was like being a wounded rabbit faced with two vultures.

"How did he turn out so morally high standing?" Archer asked, gaze unwavering.

Grey was just as still. "Watching us, I suppose. Learned from our mistakes."

"So, we were good influences after all."

"It would appear so." Grey winked at Trystan. "And people thought you would turn out to be the worst of the lot with the two of us as your guide. I'm vastly amused that you proved them wrong."

Archer glanced at him. "Tad bit proud too, don't you think?"

Grey nodded. "Wouldn't admit it in public, of course, but I will own a certain amount of pride in his accomplishments, yes. A very small amount, mind you."

"Miniscule, really."

Trystan laughed. "Good God, the two of you belong on a stage somewhere. Will you just stop?"

His brothers joined him in a chuckle, and then Grey clapped him on the arm. "I'm going to embarrass you now." With that he clanged on his champagne class with his pocket watch, and when that didn't silence the crowd, Archer let out a piercing whistle that brought conversation to a standstill. Trystan's cheeks warmed as all gazes turned in their direction. What now?

"Ladies and Gentlemen, please pardon the interruption," Grey began. "I will only keep you for a moment. I would like to propose a toast to Vienne La Rieux and my brother Trystan for this amazing enterprise they've built." A chorus of voices rang out in agreement. "And I want to publicly say just how proud my family and I are of our Trystan and the man he has become. To Trystan and Vienne." He raised his glass and every other glass in the room followed.

"Trystan and Vienne!" the crowd roared. It sounded like they had just gotten married, Trystan thought. And that realization sobered him.

His brother was right. He shouldn't give up on her. Not yet. He had to try one last time.

Across the hall his gaze met hers and he raised his glass in salute. Her color was high and he wondered if she had thought of the toast in the same way he had.

"Go," Archer whispered in his ear.

Trystan was just about to step forward when Vienne turned to her sister, breaking their gaze. "Later," he said.

First, he needed another drink.

"You have been watching him all evening. Why don't you talk to him?"

Vienne glanced at Aline over the rim of her champagne glass. "I'm not exactly certain of what I would say." Her cheeks were still warm from that toast that sounded like something one would say at a wedding. She hadn't missed the way His Grace had looked at her as he said it, with just the most subtle nod of his head. It was a blessing, if she had ever seen one—as though he welcomed her to his family.

Mon Dieu.

"Perhaps . . . 'I love you, please forgive me for being such a cabbage head'?"

She chuckled. "I have not been called a cabbage head for a long time." Almost twenty years. Odd how she had despised the nickname as a child, but it sounded so good to her now.

"I cannot believe you still need to be called so," her sister replied lightly. "Really, Vienne. You should take after me and be a highly intuitive, intelligent woman."

Vienne arched a good-natured brow. "You have been engaged six times and married zero."

Aline conceded with a slight shrug. "I have not found true love as you have."

"Is it," she asked softly, "true?"

Her sister sighed, her expression all exasperation. "He loves you still, after seven years apart. You love him enough that it scared you back then, and now makes you want to throw yourself at him. I say it doesn't get much truer than that. Commence with the throwing."

It had taken her a few days to become comfortable enough with her sisters to confess how she felt about Trystan, but after the initial reacquainting period they had fallen into old behaviors and comforts. It was as though twenty years hadn't happened and they were family again. All forgiven—*almost* all forgotten—Mother and daughters so happy to be together again that nothing else mattered. There had been a lot of tears and many apologies.

It was amazing how much the love of family could cure and repair. Vienne had spent so many years blaming herself. It hadn't mattered when Trystan told her she was wrong—well, it had mattered, but not as much as when Marguerite said it, or as when Marguerite asked for *her* forgiveness.

In a way, she felt like a new woman. And this woman realized how foolish she had been to push Trystan away. He was the brightest part of her life. He made her feel whole, made her feel as though nothing else mattered so long as they were together. Aline was right: it was time she told him that, before she lost him forever—if she hadn't already.

No, she wouldn't think of that. She hadn't lost him. She couldn't have.

Her gaze sought him out and found him easily—as though some secret compass inside her was pulled to him. He was so very attractive in his evening clothes, his hair a little too long so that it fell over his brow into his eyes. There was a boyish quality to his smile that she found devastating, something about his face that made her want to stare at it forever, though not a classically handsome face.

He wore so much of his emotions on his face, in those eyes. Perhaps that was the appeal, or perhaps love made the object of that love perfect in the eye of the beholder. Because to her, Trystan was perfection on legs, even if he did know exactly how to provoke her.

"Hold this," she said, shoving her almost empty glass at her sister. Aline took it with a chuckle.

Vienne touched her hair to make certain it was still perfect, smoothed her gown, squared her shoulders. Then, courage gathered, she moved toward Trystan with purposeful strides. He was talking to his brothers, a detail that threatened to bow her shoulders, but she would not let the disproval of the elder Kane men deter her.

"Lord Trystan, I wonder if we might speak for a moment?" How calm *and* sweet she sounded!

Three pairs of eerily similar yet completely different eyes turned to her. His Grace's gaze was cool, Lord Archer's cool, and Trystan's . . . his was curious with the slightest glint of pleasure. He was happy to see her—happy that she had come to him.

"Of course," he replied. "I'm sure my brothers will excuse me."

They said they would, and bowed their heads to Vienne before turning and walking away. Vienne watched Archer lean into the duke, no doubt speculating as to what Vienne might say or do to their precious younger brother.

She had been reminded what it was to be a younger sibling over these last few days. She knew the love and the thorns of it. There was no escaping it, for older siblings would always treat younger ones as though they were children in some way and try to protect them from the world. It was love, no matter how infuriating it might be.

"You wanted to talk?" His tone was low, a little cool. He wasn't going to make this easy for her, and she didn't blame him.

"Let's go to the office," she suggested.

He followed her through the great hall toward the back and behind the staircase, where a small room had been set aside as an office for both of them. She supposed it was hers alone now, as he had sold much of his ownership to his brothers.

It was a comfortable space, decorated in shades of cream and sage with dark oak furniture upholstered in fabric with touches of gold and crimson. The desk was large, but not pretentious, elegantly carved without being gaudy, as was the taste these days.

"What did you want to talk about?" he asked as soon as they crossed the threshold. Was he eager to be out of her company? No, she wouldn't believe that.

"Two things," she replied, pausing to gather her

courage again. Honestly, this man flustered her to no end sometimes. "First I want to apologize for my behavior when you brought my sisters and my mother to me. I was shocked and afraid, but that is no excuse for the way I spoke to you. I hope you will forgive me?"

"Of course. How are relations between the four of you? Good, I hope."

She couldn't hide her happiness—why should she? "Yes. Talking to them has given me so much . . . perspective. I feel as though a huge burden has been lifted from me. It's very liberating."

"I'm glad to hear it." And he meant it. His sincerity was blatant. "What is the second thing?"

"I'd like to propose a wager."

He scrunched up his eyes. "Vienne, it's late . . ."

"One game." Lord, she sounded desperate.

He nodded wearily. "All right, fine. What stakes?"

"If I win I get your shares of Trystienne's."

He didn't seem terribly surprised by the suggestion, so she could only assume he expected her to try to buy him out. "And if I win?"

She shrugged. "Whatever you want."

His eyebrows slowly rose. "Whatever I want?"

"Have you ever noticed how often you and I repeat what the other has said? I feel as though we arc a pair of those birds that talk. Yes, whatever you want."

"You don't want me to decide before we play?"

She waved a hand. "Why bother? You're not going to win, so there's no need." She almost believed her bravado. "Come, let's sit."

They sat across from one another at the low table. Trystan shuffled and dealt out cards. They played as they had that night at Angelwood's. Was he thinking of that as well? Of how they'd groped and strained at each other in a room where anyone might have seen them, but they were too swept away by passion for a moment to care? Yes, she'd bet he was.

"Do you still think about me?" she asked in a low voice as they played. She was already ahead. She didn't look up, but she felt his sharp glance.

"Yes," he replied. "Though I know I shouldn't admit to it."

"What if I were to confess that I think of you as well? Would that make it easier for you, do you think?"

"It does indeed." There was a faint hoarseness to his voice. "You shouldn't ask me such questions or tell me such things, not when you've made it clear that there is nothing between us."

"I don't recall ever saying there was nothing between us. I believe I said I was too much of a mess for there to be anything, and you agreed and called me broken."

He winced. "I apologize for that."

"You were right. What if I told you I am starting to feel as though all my broken pieces are slowly gluing themselves back together?"

He didn't look up from his cards, but she could see a faint flush in his cheeks. "If that were the case, then I would be very happy for you indeed. *Damn*, woman. Do you have a horseshoe in your bodice?"

She chuckled. "I have always been extremely lucky." That was true to an extent, after all she had been given another chance not only with her family but with Trystan. He was her good-luck charm. But now it was time for her to stop being so lucky and to let Trystan's "luck" take over. For the first time in her life, Vienne was playing not to win, but to lose.

And lose she did—rather splendidly at that. She lost so well, that Trystan sat there for a moment, staring at the tally as though he couldn't quite believe it. Oh dear, had she taken it too far? It didn't matter, he had won and now she needed to set her plan in motion.

"Before you tell me what you want, there's something you must hear." She took a breath. "I need you to run Trystienne's with me."

He gathered up the cards and put them away. "I'm no longer a partner, Vienne. I don't own fifty percent."

She reached over and placed her hand on top of one of his larger, darker ones. "You will always be my partner, Trystan. It does not matter how much you own—I will share my half with you."

He went completely still. "Why would you do that?"

She tilted her head. "Don't you know?"

"No, I'm afraid I don't."

"Because I love you, you foolish man."

Trystan froze. It would have been comical if she wasn't so afraid that the expression on his face was one of horror and not happiness. "You love me?"

She nodded. "Now that you know, does that at all influence what you want as your prize for winning our game?"

He blinked. Honestly, she had never seen him before in such an unsettled state. And then, it was like someone pulled all of the confusion out of his head and out of his expression. The fog lifted, and he turned to her with a bright, determined gaze. She held her breath.

"It does," he replied. "I was going to be completely shameless and ask for one more night with you." Her heart skipped a beat. "But now I want something entirely different."

Was that a good answer or a bad one? "What?"

He folded his arms over his chest. "I would like for you to propose to me."

Elation and confusion smashed together in Vienne's head. Was this a joke or was he serious? "As in marriage?"

He nodded. "Exactly that."

"Isn't that normally the man's responsibility? He asks the woman he loves to marry him." Was this a twisted way of saying he didn't feel the same way for her?

Trystan took a step closer, narrowing the gap between them to just a few inches. "Yes, but I'm not certain what the woman I love will say if I ask her. This way if she asks me, I know the answer will be yes."

As the implication of his words sank in, joy trilled through her veins. She had to be grinning like a simpleton. Arranging her skirts, she sank down to one knee before him, strangely aware in her happiness that it was a very sexually suggestive pose.

They'd get to that later.

"Lord Trystan Kane, would you do me the great honor of consenting to be my wedded husband?"

The infuriating man actually took a moment—as though he had to consider it! A lopsided grin tilted his lips. "Why, Madame La Rieux, how unexpected and exciting. I would be delighted to marry you."

She would have rolled her eyes at his silliness if she weren't just so very, very happy. "Really?" With his help, she rose to her feet. "You want to marry me even though there will be times when I'm competitive, ill tempered, and bull-headed?"

"Yes, I do."

She smiled, still not quite believing her good luck. "Even though I'm a pessimist oftentimes, and can behave irrationally?"

He put his arms around her. "Oddly enough, yes."

Vienne raised her face to look at him. His gorgeous eyes sparkled like sapphires in the low light. "Trystan, reuniting with my family has helped me put the past where it belongs, but it's difficult for me to suddenly change twenty years of habits."

"I wouldn't expect it to be easy, my sweetness."

"There are going to be times when I'm a madwoman, when I doubt your feelings and my own. When I think I'm not good enough for you."

Gentle fingers came up to caress her cheek. "There will be times when I am mad and doubtful as well. Part of marriage is helping each other through those times. No one is perfect, and love doesn't mean we won't ever fight or despair. It means wanting one person by your side for the rest of your days—good and bad. A bad day with you is still better than a good day with anyone else. So yes, I will marry you and I don't want to hear another word about it."

He kissed her then, before she could say anything else. There really wasn't anything to say. He accepted her for who she was. He always had—she had just been afraid back then. She wasn't afraid anymore, and while it would be difficult to change how she thought and felt about her past, having her family with her again made it easier. She felt worthy of happiness she never would have dreamed of before this.

She felt worthy of Trystan. It didn't matter that he was younger or that he came from a noble family. The class difference between them had only ever been a superficial obstacle because, while she might doubt that she was good enough for Trystan, she knew for a fact that she was just as good as any lady.

"Vienne?"

"*Oui?*" She missed his lips already.

"Did you let me win?"

She only smiled, and pulled his head down to hers once more—this time so she could kiss him. His arms tightened around her, lifting her off her feet as they smiled against each other's mouths. Laughter didn't ruin the kiss, it only made it better. Vienne reveled in the joy, knowing that she and Trystan were partners in every sense of the word, and that they always would be.

Next month, don't miss these exciting new love stories only from Avon Books

The Sins of Viscount Sutherland by Samantha James
Claire Ashcroft has good reason to despise Viscount Grayson Sutherland. A reckless man with a frightening reputation, he is responsible for a death that deeply pains her. She'd kill him if she could, but instead she plans seduction that will result in a shattered heart: his. Her scheme works perfectly...too perfectly.

Devil Without a Cause by Terri Garey
Faith McFarland is so desperate to save her sick child that she's willing to make a deal with the Devil: steal a ring worn by bad-boy rock star Finn Payne and receive a miracle. Temptation and seduction become necessary evils, yet Faith's salvation means Finn's damnation... he sold his soul years ago and the ring is all that stands between him and Hell.

Guarding a Notorious Lady by Olivia Parker
She may be the sister of a duke, but Lady Rosalind Devine can't seem to stay out of trouble—which is why the duke asks his friend Nicholas Kincaid to keep an eye on her while he is away. But Rosalind will not make things easy for an unwanted guardian, and Nicholas finds himself desiring an entirely different role....one of passion and unavoidable scandal.

Too Wicked to Love by Debra Mullins
Genevieve Wallington-Willis knows better than to trust *any* man—which is why her attraction to John Ready is so disturbing. He's devilishly handsome, but far too mysterious— and a coachman, no less! John dares not reveal his true identity until he can clear his name, but being this close to the exquisite Genevieve could be the greatest risk of all.